Praise for the first book in
the Booktown Mysteries

MURDER IS BINDING

"[A] smart, fast-paced novel with likeable characters and enough plot twists and turns to keep things interesting."
—Suite101.com

"Charming . . . The mix of books, cooking, and an engaging whodunit will leave cozy fans eager for the new installment." —*Publishers Weekly*

"Move over, Cabot Cove. Lorna Barrett's new cozy creation, *Murder Is Binding*, has it all: wonderful old books, quirky characters, a clever mystery, and a cat named Miss Marple!" —Roberta Isleib, author of *Asking for Murder*

"A mystery bookstore in a sleepy New England town, a cat named Miss Marple, a nasty murder, and a determined heroine make Barrett's delightful debut mystery everything a cozy lover could want and more. Bravo!"
—Leann Sweeney, author of the Yellow Rose Mysteries

D0950622

Berkley Prime Crime titles by Lorna Barrett

MURDER IS BINDING
BOOKMARKED FOR DEATH
BOOKPLATE SPECIAL

BOOKPLATE
SPECIAL

Lorna Barrett

BERKLEY PRIME CRIME, NEW YORK

THE BERKLEY PUBLISHING GROUP
Published by the Penguin Group
Penguin Group (USA) Inc.
375 Hudson Street, New York, New York 10014, USA
Penguin Group (Canada), 90 Eglinton Avenue East, Suite 700, Toronto, Ontario M4P 2Y3, Canada
(a division of Pearson Penguin Canada Inc.)
Penguin Books Ltd., 80 Strand, London WC2R 0RL, England
Penguin Group Ireland, 25 St. Stephen's Green, Dublin 2, Ireland (a division of Penguin Books Ltd.)
Penguin Group (Australia), 250 Camberwell Road, Camberwell, Victoria 3124, Australia
(a division of Pearson Australia Group Pty. Ltd.)
Penguin Books India Pvt. Ltd., 11 Community Centre, Panchsheel Park, New Delhi—110 017, India
Penguin Group (NZ), 67 Apollo Drive, Rosedale, North Shore 0632, New Zealand
(a division of Pearson New Zealand Ltd.)
Penguin Books (South Africa) (Pty.) Ltd., 24 Sturdee Avenue, Rosebank, Johannesburg 2196,
South Africa

Penguin Books Ltd., Registered Offices: 80 Strand, London WC2R 0RL, England

This is a work of fiction. Names, characters, places, and incidents either are the product of the author's
imagination or are used fictitiously, and any resemblance to actual persons, living or dead, business
establishments, events, or locales is entirely coincidental. The publisher does not have any control over
and does not assume any responsibility for author or third-party websites or their content.

PUBLISHER'S NOTE: The recipes contained in this book are to be followed exactly as written. The
publisher is not responsible for your specific health or allergy needs that may require medical supervision.
The publisher is not responsible for any adverse reactions to the recipes contained in this book.

BOOKPLATE SPECIAL

A Berkley Prime Crime Book / published by arrangement with the author

PRINTING HISTORY
Berkley Prime Crime mass-market edition / November 2009

Copyright © 2009 by Penguin Group (USA) Inc.
Excerpt from *Chapter and Hearse* by Lorna Barrett.
Cover illustration by Teresa Fasolino.
Cover design by Diana Kolsky.
Interior text design by Laura K. Corless.

ISBN: 978-0-425-23119-7

BERKLEY® PRIME CRIME
Berkley Prime Crime Books are published by The Berkley Publishing Group,
a division of Penguin Group (USA) Inc.,
375 Hudson Street, New York, New York 10014.
BERKLEY® PRIME CRIME and the PRIME CRIME logo are trademarks of Penguin Group (USA) Inc.

PRINTED IN THE UNITED STATES OF AMERICA

10 9 8 7 6 5 4 3 2 1

For
Gwen Nelson and Liz Eng,
my staunchest cheerleaders

ACKNOWLEDGMENTS

Writing a book is always an adventure—and often I have no idea where the journey will take me until I reach the end.

I could not have written this book without Mona Durgin of the Greece Ecumenical Food Shelf. She gave me an extensive guided tour and shared her experiences, as well as other information concerning the operation and maintenance of a food pantry.

Gail Bunn of Grammy G's Café kindly let me pick her brain on more than one occasion, and even let me "play" behind the counter for a shift to get the feel of the workings of a small café.

Michele Sampson, director of the Wadleigh Memorial Public Library in Milford, New Hampshire, took me on a guided tour of Milford, and encouraged me to write about the Milford Pumpkin Festival. (And she knows all the best places to eat in Milford, too!) My Guppy Sister in Crime, Pat Remick, has been extremely generous answering my questions and offering me more "local color" to enrich my stories.

My blog buddies at Writers Plot were there to encourage me when I painted myself into corners, especially Sheila Connolly and Leann Sweeney, who were always ready for an impromptu brainstorming session. And I can't forget my wonderful first readers, Sheila Connolly, Nan Higginson, and Gwen Nelson, who pointed out the places where I tripped up.

Thanks, too, to my editor, Tom Colgan, and his wonderful assistant, Niti Bagchi, and to my agent, Jacky Sach.

Please visit my website, www.LornaBarrett.com, for news and information on the Booktown Mysteries. And if you can, please support your local food pantry—and your favorite bookstores!

ONE

 "**Get out** of my house!"

"Get *out* of my house!"

"Get out of my house *right now*!"

Tricia Miles had always considered annoying fixtures to be expendable. Like the stainless steel sink in her last home. The key to a clean kitchen was a clean sink. Water spots became the bane of her existence. So without a hint of remorse, she'd had the sink replaced with a white porcelain one that came clean with a little bleach and very little effort.

Other fixtures in her life weren't quite so easily taken care of. For instance, Pammy Fredericks, her college roommate. Pammy had arrived two weeks before to "stay the weekend," and had since taken over Tricia's living room— and her life.

That was about to end. In fact, while Pammy was taking the first of her twice-daily, forty-minute showers, Tricia had packed one of her suitcases and placed it in the dumbwaiter at the end of her loft apartment over her mystery book-store, Haven't Got a Clue, in the picturesque little village of Stoneham, New Hampshire—also known as Booktown.

By the time the water stopped running, Tricia had gulped down two cups of black coffee and rehearsed her speech at least a dozen times, with as many inflections.

The bathroom door opened and Pammy appeared, wear-ing Tricia's robe—which was at least three sizes too small for her—underwear, and a grubby, once-white T-shirt. A wet towel hung around her neck, and her damp, shoulder-length, bleached-blond hair fell in stringy clumps around her face. "Any coffee in the pot?" she called.

"No," Tricia answered, and forced herself to unclench her fists. Her nails had dug into her palms.

"Why don't you make some more while I go grab some clothes?" Pammy said, evidently missing Tricia's clipped tone, and headed for the living room.

"Pammy, we need to talk," Tricia said.

Pammy halted, though not because of Tricia's words. She took in the now tidy living room, which had been clut-tered with her possessions before she'd hit the shower. "Hey, where's all my stuff?"

"I packed it. Pammy, it's time for you to go," Tricia said succinctly.

Pammy turned, her mouth hanging open in shock. "But why? I thought we were having fun."

"We had fun the night you arrived. Since then . . . you've had fun. You have lain around my home, annoyed my cat, and interfered with my employees and my customers. It's time for you to go."

"I cooked you several delicious gourmet meals—supplied the food and everything. You said you enjoyed them."

"Yes, I did. Thank you."

"What about that box of books I gave you for your store? Haven't I always looked for books for you?"

"It was very generous of you . . . but they're not really what I carry."

Pammy's expression darkened. "If this is about what happened yesterday, I told you I was sorry," she said defensively.

Saying "I'm sorry" wouldn't have helped if the coffee she'd spilled on a customer's foot had been hot—which would have netted Tricia one nice, fat lawsuit. As it was, it had cost her one hundred dollars to pacify the woman and replace her coffee-stained leather shoes. Next up: getting the carpet shampooed.

But that wasn't the worst.

Tricia crossed her arms over her chest. She was through giving hints. "Pammy, I know about the check."

Pammy blinked. "Check?"

"Yes, the one you stole out of my checkbook and wrote to yourself for one hundred dollars."

Pammy laughed nervously. "Oh, that check. Well, you weren't around, and you've been such a generous hostess that I figured—"

"You figured wrong."

Pammy didn't apologize. In fact, she just stood there, her expression blank.

"Besides, two weeks is too long for a drop-in visit. It's time for you to move on."

"But I don't have anywhere to go!" Pammy protested.

"You have family in the next county."

"But I hate them—and they all hate me. You know that," she accused.

After sharing digs with Pammy once again, Tricia could

well understand why the woman's family might not want her around. Pammy hadn't changed a bit since college. Lazy. Noisy. Freeloading. Irresponsible. And now a thief. How had Tricia tolerated living with her in that tiny dorm room for eight semesters?

This time, Tricia didn't back down. "I'm sorry, Pammy. You can't stay with me any longer."

A tense silence hung between them for interminably long seconds. Tricia waited for an explosion—or at least tears. Instead, Pammy's face lost all animation, and she shrugged. "Okay." She turned away to poke through the open suitcase Tricia had left on the couch. She picked up a blouse, sniffed under the arms, and set it back in the suitcase. She repeated the process until she found a shirt she deemed acceptable, grabbed a pair of jeans, and headed for the bathroom once again. "I'll be out of your hair in ten minutes," she said over her shoulder, with no hint of malice.

Tricia stood rooted to the floor. Her little gray cat, Miss Marple, jumped down from the bedroom windowsill, then trotted up to Tricia in the living room, giving her owner a "what gives?" look.

"You've got me," Tricia said. "But she *is* leaving."

"*Yow!*" Miss Marple said, in what sounded like kitty triumph.

True to her word, Pammy emerged from the bathroom less than five minutes later, her still-damp hair now gathered in a ponytail at her neck. "You didn't have to wait for me," she said. "Or did you think I'd steal your stainless cutlery?" Then she laughed.

"I thought I'd help you with your things."

"No need," Pammy said quite affably. She rearranged some of the clothes in the suitcase, latched it, and hauled it off the couch. She slipped her bare feet into her scuffed-up Day-Glo pink Crocs and eyed a carton on the floor. It was filled with books she'd acquired during her stay. "Can I leave this here for a couple of days—just until I get settled? I don't have room for it in my car right now."

"Sure," Tricia said, eager to do whatever it took to get Pammy out of her hair and out of her home. But then, even though her kindness had been abused, everything about this seemed so wrong, so . . . nasty . . . so unlike Tricia. "Where will you go, what will you do?"

"Today?" Pammy asked, and smiled. "I might just go to the opening of the village's new food pantry."

"The what?"

Pammy glowered at Tricia. "Don't you even know what's going on here in Stoneham? Stuart Paige is in town to dedicate the Stoneham Food Shelf."

"Who?"

Pammy gave her a withering look. "Do a Google search on the man—see what good he's done here in New Hampshire. You might want to follow in his footsteps." Pammy grabbed her purse, slinging the strap over her shoulder before wrestling the heavy suitcase toward the door.

Stuart Paige? The name did sound familiar.

"Do you need some money?" Tricia asked, the guilt already beginning to seep in.

Pammy managed a wry smile. "You already took care of that, thank you. Look, I'm sorry I told you I had nowhere to go. That wasn't exactly true. I've hooked up with some people here in Stoneham. I'm pretty sure I have a place to stay for the night—or maybe a few. You don't have to worry about me, Tricia. I've survived on my own for a long time now, although I may have to actually get a job."

For a moment, Tricia was speechless. Was it possible she

could have tossed Pammy out days—even weeks—earlier, instead of fuming in silence? And what about the threat of actually looking for work? From what she'd said, Pammy had never held a job for more than a couple of months before some catastrophe would occur and she'd be asked to leave. Still, Tricia couldn't shake feeling like a heel. As Pammy brushed past her, Tricia reached out to stop her. "I'm sorry, Pammy. It just wasn't working out."

"Don't worry, Tricia. I always have a contingency plan." She dug into her jeans pocket and came up with Tricia's extra set of keys, handing them over. "Thanks." And with that, she went out the door.

"Miss Marple," Tricia called, and the cat dutifully hurried to the door. It was time for work. Tricia closed the dumbwaiter and sent it down, then shut and locked the apartment door as Miss Marple scampered down the stairs ahead of her. By the time Tricia got to the shop, Pammy was waiting for her to unlock the door that faced Main Street. Tricia retrieved Pammy's second suitcase from the dumbwaiter and carried it to the exit. Pammy's cheeks were pink, and for a moment Tricia was afraid she might be on the verge of tears. But when she spoke, her voice was steady.

"Good-bye, Tricia."

"I'm sorr—"

"No, you're not." Pammy shrugged. "I'll be back for those books in a couple of days. Bye."

Tricia unlocked the deadbolt and waited for Pammy to exit, but her departing guest stayed rooted.

"Did you piss anyone else off?" she asked.

Tricia frowned. "What do you mean?"

Pammy stepped over what had once been a carved pumpkin. Now it lay shattered on the sidewalk just beyond the welcome mat outside the shop's door.

"It didn't belong to me."

"No, carving a pumpkin is fun, and that's something I'll bet you haven't had in a long, long time," Pammy said, stepping over the orange mess. She continued north down the street, without another word or a backward glance.

Tricia studied the shattered pumpkin; its crushed, lopsided, toothy grin looked menacing. She closed the door and went in search of a broom and a trash bag.

"Today is the first day of the rest of your life."

Never had an old saw held so much promise—and guilt—for Tricia. Though preoccupied with the whole Pammy situation, she managed to get through the store's opening rituals. Pammy's comment, that she might learn something from the likes of Stuart Paige—whoever he was—and the crack about having fun, had stung. She was a productive member of her community, pitched in at community events, and liked to think she treated her employees and customers well. And she had fun . . . sometimes.

Okay, not so much lately. She worked seven days a week, had no time for friends or hobbies, and her love life . . . .

Lost in thought, she barely noticed when her assistant, Ginny Wilson, showed up for work a full fifteen minutes late.

"Sorry," she apologized, already shrugging off her jacket. "The car wouldn't start. Brian had already left for work, and I thought the guys from the garage would get to my place quicker than they did. And when I went to call you, the battery in my cell phone was dead."

Tricia waved a hand in dismissal. "The day started out crappy, so nothing could upset me this morning."

"Oh, good. Maybe I should ask for an extra day off—with pay," Ginny said, and giggled.

"You're not improving my mood," Tricia said, but didn't bother to stifle the beginnings of a smile that threatened to creep onto her lips.

"Isn't Russ back today? That should cheer you up. Have you got a date with him tonight?" Ginny asked, rolling her Windbreaker into a ball and shoving it under the sales counter, along with her purse.

Tricia's statement that nothing could upset her had obviously been a lie. Things hadn't been going so well on the romance front. Pammy's presence these past few weeks hadn't helped. "I'm not sure if he's back yet." Russ had been traveling on business a lot lately, although he hadn't exactly been candid about what that business entailed. As the owner/editor of the *Stoneham Weekly News*, why did he even need to *go* out of town, when nearly all his revenue came from local ads?

Ginny looked around the store, which was devoid of customers. "Goodness. Are we to have a Pammy-free day, or is she still in bed?"

"She's gone for good—I hope," Tricia affirmed. "After what happened yesterday, I felt I had to ask her to leave. I can't risk a repeat of her carelessness—not when it comes to my customers." She wasn't about to mention the forged check.

"Hallelujah! Now the cookies and coffee we put out will actually go to our customers, instead of being hogged by that—that—" Ginny seemed at a loss for words. She scrutinized Tricia's face. "What's wrong?"

Tricia sighed. "I feel bad about the way I—"

"Tossed her out?" Ginny suggested.

"I did not toss her out. I merely suggested that two weeks was a tad long for a short visit. Pammy wasn't the least bit fazed. In fact, she said she'd 'hooked up' with some local people."

Ginny pursed her lips and raised an eyebrow, but said nothing.

"Do you think she could've found a boyfriend here in Stoneham?" Tricia asked.

"Stranger things have happened." Ginny cleared her throat.

"Pammy mentioned the opening of a new food pantry here in Stoneham. What do you know about it?"

"Oh, yeah, I heard Stuart Paige is in town to dedicate it," Ginny said.

"Stuart Paige . . ." Tricia repeated. "I've heard the name. I just can't remember who he is."

"Some rich mucky-muck. He gives away money. That's got to be good karma, right?"

"I guess," Tricia said. The circa-1930s black phone on the sales desk rang, and she grabbed the heavy receiver. "Haven't Got a Clue, Tricia speaking."

"Tricia, it's Deborah Black." Tricia's fellow shopkeeper; owner of the Happy Domestic book and gift shop. "I just had a visit from your friend, Pam Fredericks. She wanted to know if I had a job opening. As it happens, I do. Did you know she's listing Haven't Got a Clue as her last place of employment?"

"What?"

"I thought that would be your reaction." Tricia could hear the smile in Deborah's voice.

"She never worked here. She only annoyed, and perhaps even alienated, a portion of my customer base by her presence."

"I thought so. I told her I would let her know, but with

T-shirts and jeans, she doesn't dress appropriately for the image I want to convey."

And that was another reason Tricia had objected to Pammy hanging around Haven't Got a Clue. "Did Pammy list an address on her application?"

"Yes—yours; two twenty-one Main Street, Stoneham, New Hampshire."

"She is no longer staying with me," Tricia said emphatically.

"About time you finally got fed up with her."

"That happened two weeks ago. I asked her to leave only about an hour ago."

"You know what they say about fish and house guests: after three days they stink. I'd have asked her to leave eleven days sooner than you did."

"But I—"

"Felt sorry for her?" Deborah asked, sarcastically.

"I always considered compassion an admirable trait," Tricia replied.

"It is, sweetie. If you don't let people take advantage of your goodwill."

Tricia's entire body tensed at the dig. Oh, yes, she'd been a real sucker. "I'll try to remember that," she said coolly.

"Oh, Trish, don't get mad. Angelica feels the same way I do—as all your friends do. You do too much for everyone. You're just too nice. Think of yourself first, for once. You deserve it."

Talk about a backhanded compliment. At least Deborah thought Tricia was a good person. Pammy had just been upset when she'd tossed off her parting slurs. "I'd better get going," Tricia said, and glanced at the clock as though it would give her permission to end the call.

"Talk to you later," Deborah said, and the line went silent.

Tricia hung up the phone. She had better things to think about than Pammy Fredericks. And if Pammy used her name again as a reference . . . Well, she'd deal with it when and if it happened.

And it happened about half an hour later when Russ Smith walked through the door, carrying two take-out cups of the Coffee Bean's best brew. "Good morning," he called cheerfully, and paused in front of the sales counter. He leaned forward, brushed a kiss on Tricia's cheek, and handed her one of the cups.

"You're a sight for sore eyes," she said, giving him a pleased smile.

"So are you." He removed the cap from his cup, blowing on the coffee to cool it. "I had a visit a little while ago from—"

Tricia felt her blood pressure skyrocket and held up a hand to stop him. "Don't tell me; Pammy Fredericks. And I'll bet she was not only looking for a job, but listed me as her last employer, and my address as her residence."

"You've developed psychic abilities," he declared, and laughed.

"No. You're not the first person to give me this news," she said crossly.

Russ sipped his coffee.

"Are you likely to hire her?" Tricia asked.

"I asked her if she could type. She admitted to using only two fingers."

"Did you let her down gently?" she asked, hoping he hadn't.

"I didn't need to. I'm not looking for help. In fact . . . things haven't been going real well on the advertising front. I may have to let one of my girls go."

Tricia removed the cap to her coffee and frowned. "Yes,

I've noticed the last couple of issues have had more filler than usual."

"Tough economic times mean tough measures." Russ took another sip and stared into the depths of his cup, his expression dour.

Time to lighten the mood. "Why are you wandering around town during working hours?" Tricia asked.

"I'm heading out for the opening of the new food pantry. You going?"

"No. I have a business to run."

"Stuart Paige will be there," he said with a lilt to his voice. Was that supposed to be some kind of inducement?

"Why does everyone think I'd care? I've met lots of famous people, especially authors. I'm not the least bit impressed by celebrity."

Russ held his hands up in submission. "Okay, don't shoot the messenger." He glanced up at the clock on the wall. "I'd better get going. Maybe I can get a couple of quotes for the next issue." He leaned forward, again brushing a soft kiss on her cheek. That made twice he'd missed her lips.

He started for the door. "Do you have plans for tomorrow night?"

"No."

"Good. How about dinner? We could go to that nice little French bistro you like in Milford."

Tricia shook her head; they'd been apart too much lately, and she didn't want to share Russ with a room full of other people. "Let's stay in. My place or yours?"

"Mine." He recapped his coffee. "Come on over as soon as you close the store. I'll have dinner waiting."

"Sounds great."

"There's something I want to talk to you about." He

threw a glance at Ginny across the way. She was with a customer, but her gaze kept darting in their direction.

"I'm intrigued," Tricia said, hoping her inquisitive look would get him to give her more information.

Instead, Russ opened the shop door. "See you tomorrow, then." And out he went.

The vintage black phone on the sales counter rang once again. Tricia picked it up. "Haven't Got a Clue, this is Tricia. How can I help you?"

"Oh, good, it's you. I need a favor," said the disembodied voice of Bob Kelly, head of the Stoneham Chamber of Commerce, president of Kelly Realty, and her sister Angelica's significant other.

Tricia had learned to tolerate him for her sister's sake, and even managed to sound cheerful when she replied, "What?"

"The Stoneham Food Shelf reopens today in their new location. The Chamber needs warm bodies to show up at the dedication."

"I'd love to go, Bob," she lied, "but I'm so tied up with the store."

Her customer had gone back to perusing the bookshelves, and Ginny joined Tricia. "I can take care of things here while you're gone. And Mr. Everett will be in here at two this afternoon. Go. Have a good time."

"That's great," Bob said, since he'd obviously heard Ginny. "It's a quarter mile north of Stoneham. That new pole-barn structure they've been building. Just head out Main Street, you can't miss it. I'll see you there in twenty minutes."

"But, Bob—!"

He hung up.

Tricia put the phone down and turned her gaze on her assistant. "Why did you say that?"

Ginny bounced on her feet, looking pleased with herself. "I thought you might like to go. Maybe Russ will take your picture and you can give the store some free publicity. Besides," she said, delivering the coup de grace, "it's for charity."

Stoneham was ready for the leaf peepers—tourists who came to New Hampshire to enjoy the beauty of autumn. It seemed like every store and home was decorated with red and orange wreaths, pumpkins, and corn shocks, while big plastic spiders in imitation webs covered bushes and inflatable ghosties and goblins swayed in the gentle breeze. Kelly Realty had a stack of small pumpkins in its drive with a sign declaring FREE PUMPKIN WHEN YOU LIST WITH US.

Parking for the dedication was more difficult than Tricia had imagined. Of course, the Food Shelf's lot was meant to hold only a dozen cars, and so both sides of the road were lined with another twenty or so. Flattened in the center of the street was the remnant of another smashed pumpkin. She shook her head. Kids!

Tricia watched traffic zooming past, waiting for a break before making her way across the road to the newly constructed building. As Bob had described, it was corrugated metal with a green metal roof. According to the sign atop the long, low building, the Food Shelf would be sharing space with the Stoneham Clothing Closet. She hadn't heard about that, either. Maybe she didn't get out enough.

The heavy glass front door had been wedged open, and Tricia entered the building with trepidation. She soon relaxed when she recognized a number of other Chamber members—no doubt they, too, had been bullied by Bob to attend. She took in the space. The room was painted a flat white, and lined with chrome-wire shelving. Some of the shelves were already filled with sealed cardboard cartons. Cryptic notes in heavy black marker adorned the sides of the boxes. Colorful posters that encouraged donations helped make the interior a bit more cheerful.

Beside one of the shelves was a Lucite brochure stand filled with folded leaflets that looked like they'd been made on a home inkjet printer. Tricia picked up one of the brochures, stuffing it into her purse to read through at a later time.

A hum of voices filled the space, and Tricia inched past several people. In the center of the room stood a sturdy, wooden workbench. It held a glass punch bowl filled with what looked like pink lemonade and several plates piled with an assortment of cookies. A little tent card announced that the baked goods had been donated by the Stoneham Patisserie. Tricia saw no sign of its owner, Nikki Brimfield. She was probably back at her bakery serving her customers—something Tricia felt she ought to be doing as well.

Bypassing the food and drink, Tricia saw Russ, his Nikon camera slung around his neck, working the room, encouraging people to stand together as he took their photographs, and then penciling their names in his ever-present steno pad.

Tricia's elderly employee, Mr. Everett, and his lady friend, Grace Harris, stood to one side, conversing with other attendees. Mr. Everett caught sight of Tricia, and gave her a cheery wave. She waved back.

Bob Kelly stood near the podium, chatting with a man Tricia didn't know. The guest of honor, perhaps? The silver-haired gentleman in the charcoal gray suit looked thin and wan, but as he nodded, taking in whatever Bob was saying, his dark brown eyes seemed kind. A group of bystanders hung on their every word, looking ready to pounce on the poor man the minute Bob let him loose.

"Excuse me," a middle-aged woman said, and sidled past Tricia. Dressed casually in navy slacks and a navy sweatshirt embroidered with red roses on white hearts, the fifty-something woman with gray-tinged brown hair stepped up to Bob, politely interrupted, and indicated it was time to get the show on the road. Bob stepped right in line. Tricia might have to make friends with the woman—anyone who could get Bob to stop talking had to be some kind of miracle worker.

The woman stepped in front of the podium and tapped the microphone. "May I have your attention, please?"

The buzz of voices quieted as all heads turned to the front of the room.

"Hello, I'm Libby Hirt, Chairperson of the Stoneham Food Shelf's Executive Committee. I'd like to introduce the rest of our board—" Tricia tuned out of the next portion of her speech as her gaze drifted to the shelving units. Canned and nonperishable boxed goods lined the shelves to her left, and were separated by type: dry cereal, pasta, canned sauces, fruits and vegetables. Pretty basic food items. Another shelf held nonfood items like shampoo, soap, dishwashing liquid, and paper goods.

Tricia studied the canned goods, her thoughts drifting to the sodium content of each unit. What about fresh food: fruits, vegetables, bread, milk, and meat? Did the Food Shelf supply those to its clients? She had a lot to learn— and suddenly she found she *wanted* to learn more about it, and was glad she'd taken a brochure.

Libby Hirt had moved on to thanking the Chamber of

Commerce. "We're grateful for all their support—in terms of dollars *and* collection points." Bob positively beamed at the praise, as a smattering of applause broke out.

Collection points?

"I cannot thank Mrs. Grace Harris enough for her years of tireless work on our behalf. She has been a driving force for soliciting funds from the private sector. Thank you, Grace."

More applause. Mr. Everett patted Grace's hand, and she smiled shyly.

"But most of all, we'd like to thank our most generous benefactor, Mr. Stuart Paige. As most of you know, we've planned this expansion for a number of years. The Paige Foundation offered a matching grant, and I'm proud to say that we have met our financial match through the generous contributions of our supporters, allowing us to build this new home for the Food Shelf." A burst of vigorous applause interrupted her speech, and Russ stepped forward, raising his Nikon to snap a few photos.

"In the past twenty years," Libby continued, "we've been located in a number of churches, always outgrowing the space we've been allocated. This new building will allow us to house not only the Food Shelf, but the Stoneham Clothing Closet, which has been located in the basement of St. Rita's Church for the past two years. Having both resources available in a single location will save us time and expense, and will better serve our clientele."

Another round of applause greeted that announcement.

"Without further ado, let me introduce Mr. Stuart Paige."

The applause grew more robust, but Paige raised a hand to stave off the attention. It was only after Libby cajoled him that he stepped up to the podium. "Thank you. I'm pleased the Paige Foundation was able to help out. We're very proud of—"

A scuffling noise and sudden shouting behind them all interrupted his words. Tricia looked over her shoulder to see what was happening, and caught sight of Pammy Fredericks outside. One of the male bystanders had grabbed her arm and was pulling her away from the open doorway. The more he pulled, the more shrill her voice became.

"No, I've got to see him," she shouted.

"Miss, you'll have to leave!"

"Not until I've seen Stuart Paige," Pammy hollered.

Another suited man threaded his way through the crowd. He kicked aside the wedge in the door and it closed, shutting out the noise.

"Er . . . as I was saying," a disconcerted Paige continued, but few faces turned back to listen. "It's been a pleasure to be here today. My continued hope is that hungry people will always find the help they need here at the Stoneham Food Shelf. Thank you."

Pammy and the two men disappeared from view, but it took Libby Hirt's voice to bring everyone's attention back to the podium. "Thank you, Stuart. I'd like to remind everyone that we're always looking for new collection points, either for nonperishable food or for putting out a can to collect cash donations. If you're interested in helping out, please feel free to speak to me or any of the other Executive Committee members. And thank you all so much for coming."

Again, everyone applauded politely as Paige and Libby left the podium. Paige paused to greet Grace like an old friend, giving her a brief kiss on the cheek.

Tricia glanced back to see the two men reenter the building, trying but failing to look inconspicuous as they melted back into the crowd.

Immediately the whispers began. Who was that woman? What did she want?

Libby had steered Paige toward the food, with Bob and a group of others shuffling along behind, like groupies at a rock show.

Tricia sidled past a crowd of the other guests and exited the building. She looked left and right, and saw Pammy's retreating figure heading back for town.

What was so important that she'd try to interrupt the dedication ceremony? What could she have possibly wanted to tell Stuart Paige?

TWO

 By the time Tricia left the reception some ten minutes later, there was no sign of Pammy on the road. She arrived back at Haven't Got a Clue just in time for Ginny to take her lunch break. The next hour practically evaporated as Tricia served a flurry of customers who were in a hurry to get back to their Granite State tour bus. A glance across the street told her that the new café's lunchtime crowd had rivaled her own. Booked for Lunch would be in the black in no time.

Ginny was ten minutes late getting back from lunch. By then Mr. Everett had arrived for his afternoon stint. He'd asked to work fewer hours for the past few weeks, and Tricia was concerned. He'd seemed tired. Was his health declining? She didn't like to ask, yet she'd come to depend on him, and she enjoyed working with someone who took pleasure in serving Haven't Got a Clue's customers as much as she did.

Mr. Everett was happily dusting the back shelves, and

Ginny took Tricia's place behind the register. "Sorry I'm late," she said, but offered no explanation. Late to arrive, late from lunch. A pattern seemed to be developing. If it continued, Tricia would have to bring up the subject. She decided to wait another few days before mentioning it.

It was well after three, and Tricia's stomach growled furiously. "I'm going to slip over to Booked for Lunch to grab a bite. That is, if they have anything left," Tricia said, and donned the jacket she'd taken from the peg some twenty minutes before.

"Don't worry. We'll be fine," Ginny assured her, as a woman carrying a stack of books by Josephine Tey arrived at the register.

Though the sun had reappeared from behind a bank of clouds, the crisp October air was a bit of a jolt after the drowsy warmth inside Haven't Got a Clue, but it also felt invigorating. Any sunny fall day was worth celebrating. All too soon the winter chill would be upon Stoneham. A long, cold, gray—dull—season of ice and snow. Of course, the months before the holidays were the bright spot for retailers, but after New Year's, Tricia knew she'd find herself counting the days until spring—and the influx of tourists—would return to her adopted hometown.

Tricia waited for a lull in traffic before jaywalking across Main Street, heading for Booked for Lunch. Once again, she passed a flattened carved pumpkin. Was there a crime wave in Stoneham, or just a vendetta against small, round squashes?

Tricia's older sister, Angelica, had opened Booked for Lunch with great fanfare only two weeks before. But she hadn't given up owning Stoneham's charming little cookbook store, the Cookery. After hiring an exceptional manager six months before, she figured she could extend her entrepreneurial empire. It was her love of cooking and the long-held ambition to open a restaurant that had encouraged her to open the little bistro. "Little" was right—the storefront she'd rented was the smallest on Main Street. It had previously been used as office space. The village depended on the tourist trade and boasted only a small diner, so adding another venue to the lunchtime crunch had been encouraged by the head of the local Chamber of Commerce—Bob Kelly, who also had been dating Angelica for just over a year.

The tourists were happy. The booksellers were happy. Everyone was happy.

Except Angelica.

"This is a lot harder work than I thought," she'd confided to Tricia after her first week in business. Now, seven days later, she looked even more haggard.

Ignoring the CLOSED sign that hung on the plate-glass door, Tricia entered the charming 1950s retro café with its chrome-edged, white Formica tables, the red-and-silver-sparkled Naugahyde booths, and the counter with six matching stools to her right. It wasn't what she'd expected in the way of decor when Angelica had first told her of her plans to open an eatery. But then Angelica was always a bundle of surprises.

Angelica stood behind the counter. Her blond hair was pinned in a chignon; crimson lipstick gave her face color, along with a matching scarf tied around her neck. A black-and-white polka dot blouse and tight black slacks completed the outfit. She looked like she'd stolen her costume from an *I Love Lucy* rerun.

"About time you showed up," Angelica said. She wiped her hands on a towel, reached for the undercounter fridge, brought out a plastic-wrapped plate, and set it on the counter. "I saved you a tuna salad plate."

Tricia settled on one of the red, round-cushioned stools. "How do you always know what I want?" she asked, delighted.

"I've known you your whole life." Angelica laughed. "I can read you like a book—you're not a mystery to me."

Tricia wasn't sure if that was good or bad.

Angelica supplied a napkin, fork, and knife. "Coffee or something else?" she asked.

"The chill in the air these past couple of days has put me on a hot chocolate kick."

"Hot chocolate it is," Angelica said, reaching under the counter and coming up with a paper packet. She grabbed a Booked for Lunch mug, which sported a stack of old-fashioned books along with Day-Glo pink lettering that matched the sign out front. After shaking the packet, she tore off the top, spilled the contents into the mug, and added hot water from the urn on the shelf behind her. "You can take off your jacket and stay awhile, you know."

"Oh. I hadn't even noticed." Tricia shrugged out of the sleeves, parking the garment on the empty stool beside her.

Angelica poured herself a cup of coffee and leaned against the rear-end-high shelf behind her. "I had to pull waitress duty again today—me, an about-to-be famous author," she said, and blew a loose strand of hair away from her cheek.

Since Angelica's literary agent had sold her cookbook, *Easy-Does-It Cooking*, last spring, Angelica somehow managed to remind everyone—in nearly every conversation—that she was about to be published. "About" being relative, since the book wasn't slated to appear for another eight months. Tricia ignored the reminder. "What happened to Ana?"

"Immigration came after both her and José. It's too bad—he was really good at food prep, and she was wonderful with the customers. I don't know what I would've done if it wasn't for my new hire."

Tricia speared a piece of lettuce, more concerned with her lunch than the immediate conversation.

"Jake"—the cook—"was in a tizzy," Angelica continued rather theatrically. "Luckily my *new hire*"—she stressed the words—"had done salad prep before. Breaking in a new person during the lunch hour would've been too much to take. Thank goodness I didn't have to train her *and* handle the customers."

The tuna salad had chunks of celery mixed in, just the way Tricia liked it. She swallowed a mouthful. Angelica had seen herself in more of a hostess-cum-manager role, a raconteur more than a hands-on member of her kitchen or waitstaff. But honestly, did a café the size of Booked for Lunch need a manager and three employees? Still, Tricia didn't want to get involved in *that* conversation.

"Did you know there was a food pantry in Stoneham?" Tricia asked, thinking about her earlier conversation with Pammy.

"But of course. They dedicated it earlier this morning."

"Yes, I know. I was there. Bob bullied me into going."

Angelica ignored the assault on her boyfriend's character. "Libby Hirt is a wonder. And she can write a mean grant request, too."

Grant? "How do you know about all this?"

"I've talked with her dozens of times at the Cookery.

She's one of the few locals who actually patronize my store. Like many of my customers, she's a frustrated amateur chef. Besides, your boyfriend just ran a big story about her and the Food Shelf in the last issue of the *Stoneham Weekly News*. Don't you ever read it?"

Though she usually glanced at it, the local weekly rag wasn't on the top of Tricia's to-be-read pile. Not when there were hundreds of new mysteries published every year, and thousands of her old favorites to be read and reread again.

"Stuart Paige himself was in town for the dedication," Angelica went on, sounding just a little catty.

"Everybody seems to know about this guy except me. Who is he?"

"You don't remember the scandal?"

"Scandal?" Tricia echoed.

"Yes. Senator Paige's playboy son. The guy who crashed his Alfa Romeo into Portsmouth Harbor. He saved himself and let his father's secretary drown."

Something about that did sound familiar. "When was that?"

Angelica exhaled a long breath. "Oh, must be twenty or so years ago now. Rod and I were living in Boston at the time. You were still in college."

Rod had been Angelica's husband number one.

"Paige was so consumed with guilt, he practically became a monk," Angelica continued. "And he's spent the rest of his life doing good deeds."

"Good deeds?" Tricia asked skeptically, poking at the lettuce on her plate.

"Oh, you know what I mean. He's made giving away his family's fortune into a lifestyle."

Tricia vaguely remembered the story, which hadn't

fazed her at the time and had obviously had no lasting impact on her, either. Although it was refreshing to know the former bad boy had had a personality turnaround.

Thinking about Paige reminded Tricia about Pammy. "I may as well tell you; I asked Pammy to leave this morning. I mean, two weeks was way too long for a drop-in visit."

"And?" Angelica drew out the word.

"She seemed okay with it. She also put in applications around the village listing me as her last employer."

"Really." It wasn't a question.

"Pammy also showed up at the Food Shelf's dedication."

"No!"

"Yes. She was hauled off and asked to leave."

"Why?"

Tricia shrugged. "I don't know. The last I saw her, she was walking back to the village. She'd apparently been trying to talk to Mr. Paige."

"Is that so?" Angelica said thoughtfully. She glanced at the clock above her work space, then stretched her neck to look back through the swinging half-doors that separated the kitchen from the dining area. She sighed. "My goodness, my new hire's been on her break a long time."

Tricia pushed aside the orange-slice garnish on her plate.

Angelica sighed and again glanced at the clock. "It may have been a mistake to take on my new hire. It's . . . it's . . ." She stammered. "Oh, I may as well just tell you. I hired Pammy."

Tricia nearly choked on her tuna. "You what?" she spluttered, and started choking.

Angelica clumped around the counter in her black high-heeled shoes to slap Tricia on the back. "Do you need me to do the Heimlich maneuver? I learned how to do it properly at my county-sponsored safety course, you know."

Tricia pounded on her chest, and then took a sip of her cooling cocoa to help control the urge to cough. "Why on earth did you hire Pammy?"

"I felt sorry for her, what with you throwing her out and all."

"I did not throw her out!" Tricia took another sip of her cocoa. "I simply asked her to leave, and she agreed it was past time."

"Really." Again, it wasn't a question.

Tricia took in her sister's guilty expression. "What did she tell you?"

"Not much. But when she spoke about it, she sounded quite wounded." And Angelica sounded quite judgmental. Trust Angelica to take someone's—anyone's—side against her.

Tricia glared at her sister for a long moment before returning to her lunch.

"Why don't you go out back and apologize to Pammy? I'm sure she'd forgive you. And it wouldn't hurt to let her come back and stay with you for a few more days—just until she gets settled."

"I don't have anything to apologize for," Tricia said, viciously stabbing a chunk of tuna. "And I do *not* want her staying with me for even one more night. You've got just as much room in your apartment—she can stay with you, if you're that worried about her."

Angelica ignored the suggestion. "Well, then, just go talk to her. You two have been friends for way too many years to just throw it all away."

Would she feel that way if Tricia told her about the stolen check?

"I'd seen her maybe three times in the last eighteen years, before she camped out in my living room for two weeks, so it's not like we've been close."

"Yes, but it's important to maintain old friendships—especially as we age."

Tricia eyed her sister's getup; she looked like she was more than two weeks early for Halloween—hardly an example of aging gracefully. Angelica had added on years, but her outlook hadn't caught up with the inevitable march of time.

Angelica nudged Tricia's arm. "Go on. And while you're out there, you can see if they've delivered my one-and-a-half-yard Dumpster. It was supposed to arrive by this afternoon—two weeks late."

"I don't want to go out there at all."

"Tricia," Angelica said, using the same tone of voice their mother had employed when she'd tried to shame the girls into doing something she wanted.

"What?"

"Go out there and make nice with Pammy while I call my soda distributor. I think they shorted me by a case. I'm going to need it for tomorrow's crowd. Now, where did I put the business card with their phone number?" she said, and crouched down to search the shelf under the counter.

"Okay, I'm going. But when I get back, I'm going to finish my lunch and then I'm going back to work."

"Of course, of course," Angelica muttered, her voice muffled as she leaned further under the counter.

Tricia sidled past the lunch counter and pushed through the swinging half-doors into the narrow kitchen. For a short-order cook, Jake was fairly temperamental. Angelica had complained that he'd often leave without fully cleaning his work space. As expected, he was already gone for the day and had left the place a mess of unwashed pots and pans. Angelica, or more likely Pammy, had her work cut out for her.

The door to the back alley was closed. Tricia opened it and stepped onto the concrete pad. It was obvious no Dumpster had yet been delivered. Nestled close to the building were two large gray, bulging ninety-five-gallon trash carts. Sticking out of one of them was a pair of jeans-clad legs, with a worn pair of pink Crocs on the feet.

THREE

 Yet another white-and-gold Hillsborough County Sheriff's Department car pulled up outside Booked for Lunch. A tall, sandy-haired man got out of the driver's side, then stooped down to grab his flat-brimmed Mounties hat, settled it on his head, and marched purposefully toward the café. Distracted, Tricia watched him as he paused outside the entrance and then spoke to one of the other deputies for several minutes. By the number of bars on his uniform sleeve, he outranked all the other officials on the scene. Finally, the deputy pointed at the café.

The newcomer nodded his thanks, opened the café's door, and stepped inside. He bypassed everyone else, making a beeline for Tricia. "I'm Captain Grant Baker, and I'll be handling this investigation. I'm sorry we have to meet under these circumstances, Ms. Miles."

"Where's Sheriff Adams?" Tricia asked.

"Busy, I'm afraid. I hope you won't mind dealing with me."

Tricia found herself drawn to Baker's green eyes. Her ex-husband, Christopher, had green eyes. That relationship hadn't worked out, and—

Tricia shook her head to rid herself of the flood of memories that threatened to engulf her.

"No. Not at all," she found herself saying. Any time she didn't have to deal with Sheriff Wendy Adams was worth celebrating. They'd had run-ins before, and those experiences were not ranked among those Tricia cherished.

Baker glanced around Booked for Lunch, his gaze settling on Angelica, who perched on the end of one of the booths' bench seats; a high-heeled shoe discarded on the floor, she was massaging her left foot as she conversed with another deputy. "I understand this isn't your first encounter with the law here in Stoneham," Baker said to Tricia.

She frowned. "Uh, no."

He leaned forward, lowering his voice. "Are you okay, ma'am? You look a little pale. Would you like to sit down?"

"No, thank you." Tricia studied his kind face, and her frown deepened. "Why are you being so nice to me?"

His eyes narrowed in confusion. "I don't understand."

"Sheriff Adams—"

"Ah." He nodded. "The sheriff explained there'd been some conflict between the two of you. That's why she suggested I handle this investigation."

"Maybe I *should* sit down," Tricia breathed. She'd never expected Sheriff Adams to cut her any slack. Then again, Baker could be trying to lull her into a false sense of security. He might be playing good cop in contrast to Sheriff Adams's bad cop routine.

Captain Baker ushered Tricia to one of the stools at the counter. "I know you've already told your story several times to the other deputies, but would you indulge me as well?"

Polite, too.

Tricia nodded and sobered. "Pammy Fredericks—"

"The deceased," Deputy Placer supplied.

"—was my friend. Sort of." Tricia shivered as she glanced over her shoulder to the café's back door, which had been wedged open, letting in drafts of cold air. Thankfully, the garbage cart was no longer visible. The image of Pammy's legs sticking out of it . . . Tricia shuddered involuntarily.

"Can you explain that 'sort of' comment?" Baker asked, not unkindly.

"We were roommates at Dartmouth and sort of kept in touch over the years."

"I take it you were no longer friends as of this afternoon."

Tricia's insides squirmed. "Until this morning, Pammy had been my houseguest for the past two weeks."

"And what changed that?" Baker asked patiently.

"I . . . asked her to leave," she said, her voice growing softer. "I didn't really throw her out. I swear! She'd simply overstayed her welcome. If you know what I mean."

"Go on," he encouraged.

Tricia sighed. "Pammy took it well. She said she had made friends here in Stoneham and assured me she'd be all right."

"When was that?"

"About nine forty-five this morning."

"And you didn't see her again?"

"Yes, I did see her. But I didn't speak to her."

"Where was this?"

"At the new food pantry just out of town. They held the dedication this morning."

Baker waited for her to continue.

"A lot of people were there. Apparently Pammy wanted to speak to the guest of honor. She made a rather loud fuss, and was asked to leave."

Baker looked very interested. "Who asked her to leave?"

"Someone in a suit. I think he was part of Mr. Paige's entourage."

"Mr. Paige?"

"Stuart Paige. Have you ever heard of him?"

"It would be hard to live in New Hampshire and *not* hear about his good works."

"Yes, well, apparently he gave the Food Shelf half the money they needed to open their new facility."

"And did you speak to the deceased following the event?"

Tricia shook her head. "I didn't see her again until I found her out back."

"And what time was that?"

"About an hour or so ago."

Baker checked his watch. "Approximately three fifty?"

Tricia nodded.

"And other than seeing her at the dedication, you hadn't heard from her since this morning?"

"I heard *of* her—but I didn't talk to her."

Baker frowned. "What does that mean?"

"She apparently spent the morning going around town putting in job applications and listing me as her last employer."

"And were you?"

"No! She hung around my store during the last couple of weeks, disrupting things—but she didn't work for me."

"Did her 'hanging around' anger you?"

Tricia chewed the inside of her lip, knowing where this line of questioning was going to lead. And what would he think when she told him about the forged check?

"I wasn't happy about it. In fact, yesterday she spilled coffee on a customer's foot. That was kind of the last straw."

"But you waited until this morning to throw her out?"

"I did *not* throw her out," Tricia said, and realized her voice had risen higher than she would've liked. She took a breath to calm down. "I asked her to leave. We had a civil conversation, and Pammy agreed it was time to go."

Baker nodded, but said nothing.

"There was one other thing . . ." She hesitated. Did she really have to tell him about the check? He—or his boss— was sure to think it was a motive for murder. No one but she knew about it—unless Pammy had gone around blabbing about it, which she doubted. Angelica hadn't mentioned it.

"You were saying?" he prompted.

"Her carelessness in spilling coffee on one of my customers really annoyed me," Tricia blurted. "I could've been sued."

Baker eyed her, waiting for more.

She could still say something about the check. She ought to say something about the check.

Why didn't she say something about the damn check?

Maybe because she knew she hadn't killed Pammy. It wasn't pertinent to her death. Baker might follow in his boss's footsteps and waste a lot of time trying to pin the crime on her—letting Pammy's killer get away with murder.

"Look, I was in my store, with witnesses, all day. That

is, until I came across the street to eat my lunch and talk to my sister."

"Sister?" Baker asked.

Tricia glanced in Angelica's direction. "Yes, she owns this café. She hired Pammy today."

"Why?"

Tricia sighed. *Probably to bug me.* "You'll have to ask her."

Baker looked over at Angelica, then shifted his gaze back to Tricia—assessing them? "Tell me what you saw when you found the body."

"Pammy. Headfirst in the garbage cart. I suspected she might be dead because she wasn't moving. I had to force myself to touch her. I found her wrist, but I couldn't find a pulse." The stench of rotting food and the revulsion she'd felt at touching the dead had worked together until— "And then I threw up."

Baker nodded, his expression bland. "Yes, the deputy told me."

"I didn't mean to contaminate the crime scene. It just . . . happened."

"How do you know about contaminating crime scenes?" Baker asked.

"I own Haven't Got a Clue, the mystery bookstore across the street. I read a lot of crime stories."

"How many is 'a lot'?"

"Not as many as I used to. Only two or three a week."

Baker didn't roll his eyes, but he looked like he might want to. Something captured his attention, and Tricia looked to her left. Someone had entered through the open back door—a man Tricia recognized from her last brush with murder. A member of the county's Medical Examiner's office greeted Baker with a curt nod.

"Have we got a probable cause of death yet?" Baker asked.

The man had a laminated ID card on a lanyard around his neck. The name on it was Ernesto Rivera. "Suffocation, most likely. Her face was covered by a plastic bag full of trash. Looks like she panicked when she couldn't get out of the garbage cart. She couldn't reach the edge of the can. Looks like she tore the trash bags apart while struggling. Her fingernails have all kinds of debris under them. We bagged 'em, and will know more once we get her on the table."

Tricia cringed at that piece of information. Pammy—her chest and abdominal cavities emptied like a gutted deer. Her scalp peeled forward until—

Tricia shuddered again. Why had she read so many Kay Scarpetta mysteries? The knowledge she'd picked up about autopsies made for an interesting read—if not applied to someone you'd actually known.

"Did she fall into the garbage can?" Baker asked.

"No way—the thing's about four foot tall. She was on her back. Someone had to put her in there."

Tricia's thoughts, exactly.

"Thanks, Ernie." Baker turned to question Angelica. "You're the owner?"

Angelica sighed theatrically. "Yes. Angelica Miles. Soon to be published, I might add. Penguin Books, *Easy-Does-It Cooking*, twenty-four ninety-nine—available on June first."

It was Tricia's turn to roll her eyes. Much more information than *anyone* needed to know.

She leaned against the counter stool and listened as Captain Baker took Angelica through the same set of questions. His demeanor was just so different from that of his boss. If the circumstances were different, she decided, she might even like him.

"And why was it you hired Ms. Fredericks?" Baker asked.

Finally, the question Tricia had been waiting to hear answered.

Angelica sighed, looked over to Tricia for a moment, and then turned back to the captain. "I figured it would keep her out of my garbage."

Baker blinked in disbelief. So did Tricia.

"Of course," Angelica continued, "I had no idea someone would actually kill her and put her *in* my garbage cart."

"Wait a minute," Tricia said, leaning forward. "What do you mean, 'keep her out of my garbage'?"

Angelica shrugged. "She came by every day—after closing, of course—and poked through my cans to see what she could salvage."

"I don't understand," Captain Baker said.

Angelica sighed impatiently. "To take."

"But it's not like you throw out anything valuable—something Pammy could actually use or sell," Tricia protested.

"Apparently she thought I did."

Baker held up a hand to interrupt. "What am I missing here?"

"It's no secret Pammy was a scavenger. I believe she was employed as an antiques picker at different periods of her life," Angelica said.

"What's that got to do with the café's garbage?" Tricia asked.

"Pammy was a freegan," Angelica said matter-of-factly.

"A what?" Baker asked, confused.

"A what?" Tricia echoed.

Angelica frowned. "She Dumpster dived for food." Taking in the incredulous faces before her, she continued. "Of course, lots of freegans give you some lofty explanation about alternative lifestyles, bucking convention, and minimizing waste in a materialistic world. I think they're just a bunch of cheapskates looking for free food."

"Pammy salvaged food out of Dumpsters?" Tricia asked, feeling the blood drain from her face. Pammy had cooked for her—had provided the food she'd used to prepare those meals. Had she found it by—?

The thought was too terrible to contemplate.

"How do you know all this?" Baker asked Angelica.

"Pammy told me—last week when we talked, and today, in between customers."

"How long was she here today?" Tricia asked.

"About two hours. A regular little chatterbox, that one."

Baker eyed Tricia. "Ms. Fredericks told you she was a freegan—but in two weeks she didn't tell your sister?"

"Apparently not."

He looked back to Angelica. "And you didn't tell her, either?"

Angelica laughed. "Of course not. Well, just look at her. She's already a lovely shade of chartreuse."

A lump rose in Tricia's throat. "How long have you known?"

"For a week or so. I knew someone was going through my garbage the day we opened. I caught Pammy at it one day last week."

"You should have told me."

"Why? You'd have been freaked out—like you are now. Believe it or not, I don't live to just irritate you, baby sister."

It was Tricia's turn to frown. So now Angelica decided to spare her feelings. Hadn't she informed her that Pammy had cooked for her?

Right now, Tricia couldn't remember.

A wave of guilt passed through her. Here she was worrying about eating food past its prime—food that obviously hadn't sickened her—and Pammy had been killed. Where were her priorities?

"Did the deceased tell you where she planned to stay tonight?" Baker asked Angelica.

Angelica shook her head. "And I didn't have her fill out a job application, either. I needed someone right away—she walked in the door. I figured we could catch up on the paperwork after the lunch crowd had gone."

Baker turned to Tricia. "Did Ms. Fredericks tell you where she planned on staying?"

"No. But she said she'd 'hooked up' with some local people."

"Probably more freegans," Angelica said.

"Do you know any local freegans?" Baker asked the women.

Angelica shook her head once again.

"I didn't even know they existed until just a few minutes ago," Tricia said.

"Can you think of anybody we can ask?" Baker asked.

"You might try talking to the other food vendors in the area. There's the Brookside Inn, the Bookshelf Diner, the Stoneham Patisserie, and the convenience store up near the highway. That's about it. But it wouldn't surprise me if the local freegans went to Milford, or even Nashua or Portsmouth. They're much bigger than Stoneham. They'd scavenge—or, as I'm sure they'd say, 'salvage'—much more food from grocery and convenience stores than restaurants and bakeries."

"Do freegans try to hustle food from charities like the Food Shelf?" Baker asked.

Angelica shook her head. "I shouldn't think so. But it's something you could ask Libby Hirt about."

"Who?"

"Libby Hirt." She spelled the last name. "She runs the Stoneham Food Shelf."

"The one your friend crashed this morning?" he asked Tricia.

She nodded.

Baker made a note. "Did the deceased have a car?"

Tricia nodded. "She'd been parking it in the municipal lot."

"Make and model?" he asked.

"I have no idea. I don't think I ever saw her drive it the whole time she was here. In fact, when she left the dedication, she walked back into Stoneham."

"She probably couldn't afford the gas for it," Angelica added.

At least not until she'd cashed Tricia's forged check. *You should say something*, a little voice within her nagged.

"Can we narrow it down? Did she have an out-of-state license plate?" Baker asked.

"Maybe. She was originally from Portsmouth, but had lived in Connecticut for the past couple of years. I think," Tricia added lamely.

"I thought you said she stayed with you for two weeks?" Baker asked.

"She did, but we didn't spend a lot of quality time together." At his puzzled look, she clarified. "My store doesn't close until seven most nights. On Tuesdays, I host a book club. That doesn't usually break up until after nine. A couple of times Pammy didn't come in until after I'd already gone to bed."

"Didn't you ask where she'd been, what she'd been doing?" Baker asked.

Answering truthfully was going to sound awfully darned cold. Still . . . "No."

Baker turned away. "Placer." The deputy stepped forward. "Grab Henderson and scout out the municipal lot down the street. See if you can find a car with Connecticut plates. Ask around. See if anyone has noticed a car parked in the lot for the past two weeks."

"Sure thing, Cap'n."

"Captain?" Rivera waved to Baker from the back entrance.

"If you'll excuse me, ladies." He left them and rejoined the technician.

Angelica watched him go. "Nice set of buns."

"Ange," Tricia admonished.

"And wasn't he just the nicest thing? Quite a change from Wendy Adams."

"Yes," Tricia agreed. She gazed at the captain, who filled the back doorway. He did have a nice set of buns at that.

"She's dead. She's really dead," Ginny murmured for at least the hundredth time. "I admit I didn't like her, but I never wanted her dead."

"Ginny, please," Tricia implored, not bothering to lift her gaze from the order blanks before her. As it was, her last sight of her . . . kind of, sort of . . . friend had not been a pleasant one. Was that how she'd always remember Pammy, as a pair of stiff legs?

"But I feel guilty," Ginny said, then grabbed a tissue from the box under the counter and blew her nose. "I didn't want her around, and I got my wish. But I never thought—"

Tricia sighed. She removed her reading glasses, setting them on the counter. Captain Baker had dismissed her some twenty minutes before—and it would be another hour before she closed shop for the day. It seemed like weeks since her day had begun, and she was looking forward to a nice, quiet evening, although she wasn't sure she was up to reading a murder mystery. Not just yet, anyway.

"I think I'll take out the trash," Tricia said, and then she thought of Pammy in the garbage cart and winced. Still, the wastebasket under the counter was full.

She picked up the basket and headed for the back of the store, disarming the security alarm before opening the door. The alley that ran behind this side of Main Street was a good five feet lower than the front of the store, and she trotted down the steps to the waiting Dumpsters. Haven't Got a Clue didn't really create enough refuse to warrant such large receptacles—one for cardboard boxes only, the other for other trash—and she wondered if she could trade one of hers for Angelica's two trash carts.

She emptied the basket and turned to head back into the building just as the door to the Cookery slammed shut, giving Tricia a start. With Angelica tied up at her new café, her newly promoted manager, Frannie Mae Armstrong, was in charge of the village's cookbook store. As far as Tricia knew, Frannie was still working alone at the store. Why would she have slammed the door upon seeing Tricia? And then she saw two matching bowls on the landing near the Cookery's stairs. Angelica would not be pleased.

For the past couple of weeks Frannie had been feeding a little stray orange cat that had been hanging around the alley. Tricia had seen it only once, but Miss Marple, her own cat, seemed to have stray-kitty radar. Miss Marple did not appreciate other cats invading what she considered to be her territory—even if her territory didn't go beyond the confines of Haven't Got a Clue and the storeroom and loft apartment above it. Angelica wasn't a cat lover, and had warned Frannie not to encourage the cat to come around . . . something Frannie obviously hadn't taken to heart.

Tricia climbed the steps and reentered her store. Ginny was still at the register, sniffling as she waited on a customer. "I'm going next door for a few minutes. Be right back," Tricia said, and headed out without grabbing her jacket.

The Cookery was quiet, with only one or two customers browsing the bookshelves. Now that Angelica had dismantled the cooking demonstration area, she'd gained more retail space. The store was doing well—too well for just one employee. That was just Tricia's opinion, of course. Frannie insisted she could handle the additional work, but she did look a bit frazzled, something Tricia hadn't ever seen in the year since she'd met her.

Frannie stood by the register, waiting for her next customer to check out. Her expression darkened when she saw it was Tricia who'd just entered the store. She plastered on a fake grin and called out in her infamous Texas twang, "Howdy, Tricia. What can I do for you?"

Tricia gave her friend a genuine smile. "Hey, Frannie, I just dropped in to see how things are going."

"I'm sure surprised to see you . . . after what happened and all." Frannie nodded toward Booked for Lunch across the street, which was visible through the large display window. A sheriff's patrol car—probably Captain Baker's—was still parked outside. It might be hours before the forensic squad finished gathering evidence.

Tricia had momentarily forgotten about Pammy. Frannie's words brought the memory of her in the garbage cart back with the force of a hurricane. "Oh. Yes. It was awful. I hope you don't mind if I don't want to talk about it."

"Of course," Frannie said, and shook her head sadly.

"I was out behind my store a few minutes ago, and I couldn't help but notice—"

"Please don't tell Angelica," Frannie pleaded, her face drawn with concern. "I know she doesn't want me to encourage Penny—"

"Penny?" Tricia asked.

"That darling little kitty. She's the color of a bright copper penny, so I've taken to calling her that. But, Tricia, she's got no collar and she's as thin as a rail. I'm only setting out a little water and some dry cat food during the day. And I make sure the dishes are put away before Angelica gets back from her café."

On the one hand, Tricia wanted to commend Frannie for her compassion. But as a business owner, she wasn't sure she should encourage deceit or out-and-out insurrection— especially as the store's proprietor was her own sister. And yet . . . she'd seen that hungry little cat and her heart had ached for it, too.

"I won't tell," she promised. "But now that you've been putting out food, she'll expect to be fed. If Angelica finds out—"

"I've got it all planned," Frannie said, but a customer approached the register with a stack of cookbooks before she could tell Tricia exactly what that plan was. The shop's door opened, and another three potential customers trooped in. Rats! Tricia had wanted to ask what Frannie knew about Stuart Paige. There was always tomorrow, she supposed.

This time it was Tricia who forced a smile as she waggled her fingers in a wave and headed out the door for Haven't

Got a Clue. And true to her word, she had no intention of telling Angelica about Frannie's feline indiscretion.

Before she could make it back to the store, Tricia heard her name being called. She looked around and saw Captain Baker hailing her from across the street. He waited for a car to pass before crossing to meet her on the sidewalk.

"Sir, you are guilty of a crime," Tricia said, straight-faced. Of course, she'd been crossing Main Street at its center for weeks, ever since Angelica had rented her new property.

"I beg your pardon?" Baker said.

"You jaywalked across Main Street," she explained, huddling to keep warm in the stiff breeze.

"Ms. Miles," he said, his voice growing somber, "my men found a car several blocks from here, apparently abandoned. It has Connecticut plates and was registered to Ms. Fredericks. The trunk was open and it contents ransacked. If you could look at what's left, perhaps you can tell me what, if anything, was taken."

A wave of fresh grief coursed through Tricia. "I suppose I could look, but I really don't know what she had, other than the suitcases she kept at my apartment for the past two weeks."

"Would you be willing to try?"

She stared into his green eyes, and her willpower dissolved. What was the hold men with green eyes had on her?

"Of course. But I need to let my assistant know I'll be gone for a few minutes."

Baker accompanied her to Haven't Got a Clue, where she grabbed her coat and told Ginny she'd be back as soon as she could.

Outside, Baker bowed like a gallant knight, and made a

sweeping gesture toward the cruiser parked on the opposite side of the street. Then he walked her across the pavement, opened the passenger-side door, and held it open until she'd seated herself, grasping the seat belt and buckling herself in.

As he walked around the car, Tricia took in the police scanner, the little printer that sat in the middle of the bench seat, and the cup of cold coffee in the beverage restraint device. She'd never sat inside a cop car before. How many police procedurals had she read over the years? How many scenes had taken place in such a car? But the reality was far different from fiction. There was an atmosphere of . . . tension—mixed with stale coffee and sweat and a touch of angst?—that seemed to hang inside the vehicle, and she doubted that even a prolonged airing could remove the lingering scents of stale urine and vomit from within that small space.

Baker climbed into the driver's seat and started the engine. He glanced in the rearview mirror before easing the gearshift into Drive and pressing the accelerator.

"You should buckle your seat belt," Tricia admonished.

"The law here in New Hampshire requires seat belt use only by those eighteen years and younger," he said with confidence.

"Just because the law doesn't require you to use your seat belt doesn't mean it's not the smart thing to do."

He tossed a glance in her direction for the merest part of a second, then focused his attention back on the road. "I think I can take care of myself."

She sighed. "Just like a man."

Again his gaze darted in her direction. "What's that supposed to mean?"

"It's just that men can be just so . . . stupid. What's

wrong with being safe? Haven't you read the federal highway statistics reporting the percentage of deaths due to *not* wearing seat belts?"

"Officers of the law need to be able to react—to get out of their vehicles at a moment's notice."

"Not if they're smushed into paste in an accident."

"Smushed?" Baker repeated.

"Yes. It's a variation of smashed. Smushed is when what used to be a solid becomes almost a liquid. Human flesh can be smushed when it's contained in crumpled steel and glass."

"Smushed," Baker said once again. "I don't think I've ever considered that."

"Well, you ought to. I'm sure the State of New Hampshire has invested thousands of dollars in your training. If you were killed or maimed in an accident, you'd be costing taxpayers like me a lot of money."

"Smushed," he murmured again, turning left onto Hanson Lane.

Tricia kept her gaze riveted out the windshield. "I'm sure your family wouldn't appreciate the call telling them their husband and dad was now the consistency of tomato puree."

"As it happens, I am no one's husband or dad, so you don't have to worry on that account."

Tricia glanced at her companion. "Your loss." Or someone else's.

The scanner crackled, reporting an accident on Route 101. Tricia frowned. She couldn't stand the sound of a dispatcher dispassionately reporting trouble. Too often Russ insisted on allowing his scanner to act as the background noise on their so-called dates. It wasn't the most romantic backdrop.

Baker pulled up behind a parked car with Connecticut plates. Another Hillsborough County deputy stood alongside the vehicle, apparently guarding it. His thumbs were hooked onto his Sam Browne belt.

Baker opened the car door.

"Wait," Tricia blurted, reaching out to touch his arm. Should she trust him? So far he hadn't given her a reason not to. "There's something I didn't tell you."

He settled back in his seat, waiting for her to go on.

"There's another reason I asked Pammy to leave this morning."

Why didn't he look surprised, she wondered.

"She . . . stole from me. She took one of my checks, made it out to herself for one hundred dollars, and cashed it."

"When was this?"

"Several days ago. I was online going over my account this morning and found out. It was the last straw, and I asked her to leave."

"And her reaction was?"

"She left."

"You didn't argue about it?"

"Pammy freely admitted it."

"Why didn't you tell me this sooner?"

Tricia sighed. "Because it's been my experience that Sheriff Adams likes to blow insignificant events out of proportion, trying to make them look like motives for murder. With that in mind, I figured you'd probably think I killed Pammy. Believe me, Captain, it wasn't the money, it was the breach of trust that made me ask her to leave. And as you continue your questioning, you'll find I didn't have the opportunity to kill her. As I said, I've been with people the entire day."

His green eyes bored into her. Was that disappointment reflected in them?

Without a word, Baker got out of the car. Tricia unbuckled her seat belt and did likewise.

"The tech team should be here when they're finished at the café," Deputy Bracken said.

Baker nodded. "Ms. Miles, would you care to take a look?"

Tricia moved to stand over the opened trunk, taking in its contents. "Those are Pammy's suitcases all right." They'd both been forced open, their contents dumped. Pammy's scrunched-up, dirty clothes mingled with old magazines, copies of their college yearbook, an old, colorful granny-square afghan, cassette tapes, photo albums, and a lot of wrinkled papers. A ripped-open envelope was addressed to Pamela Fredericks, General Delivery, Stoneham, New Hampshire.

Remorse flushed through Tricia once again. Could Pammy have been living in her car before she came to Stoneham?

The guilt intensified. Perhaps if she hadn't asked her to leave, Pammy might still be alive.

Might: a word that held a lot of power.

Tricia sighed, her eyes filling with tears. Maybe Pammy had left on an extended trip and intended to eventually return to whatever she considered her home base. But she hadn't mentioned that. In fact, whenever the subject came up, Pammy had been evasive.

"Are you okay, Ms. Miles?" Baker asked.

Tricia nodded, trying to blink away the unshed tears. "Pammy's dead. I guess it didn't hit me until right now. The stuff in her trunk may be all she had. She's really dead, and then someone tried to rob her. Is there anything more despicable than stealing from the dead?"

"Yes," Baker said. "Killing them in the first place."

Tricia had to agree with that.

More letters lay scattered among the junk, as well as a sagging, empty shoebox that sat on a pile of old clothes. Their former home? Baker poked at the letters and clippings with a pen. The yellowing envelopes bore twenty-two-cent stamps, indicating their age. "Mrs. Geraldine Fredericks. Who was that?"

"Pammy's mother."

"What would Ms. Fredericks be doing with a bunch of old letters?"

Tricia shrugged.

Baker waved a hand to take in the trunk. "Does there appear to be anything missing?"

Tricia's gaze wandered over the contents. "I don't know. Pammy didn't seem to have much with her. From what I could see, she had clothes and maybe a few toiletries." Very few toiletries. She'd used nearly an entire bottle of Tricia's favorite salon shampoo. "I'm sorry I can't be of more help, Captain Baker."

He frowned. "So am I."

FOUR

 Tricia's loft apartment seemed especially empty that night. Miss Marple's happy purring, scented candles burning, and even soft music playing in the background couldn't fill the void that Pammy's absence had left.

Under other circumstances, Tricia would have felt elated to have her living space all to herself again. But now . . . her once warm living room seemed chilled by a death pall.

Curled on the couch, her wineglass within reach, Tricia had read the same opening page of Frances Hodgson Burnett's *A Little Princess*, her favorite childhood book—a story without a murder—for the eleventh time when Miss Marple's ears perked up. In seconds, the cat jumped from the couch and trotted toward the kitchen.

"Tricia? You there?" came Angelica's voice.

Angelica's drop-in visits had diminished over the past few months, as her relationship with Bob Kelly had become more serious. Thanks to Pammy's untimely death, this was one night Tricia welcomed her sister's presence.

"I'm coming," she called, and set her book aside, grabbed her wineglass, and headed for the kitchen.

Angelica had already hung up her coat and was unpacking a picnic basket of comfort food. Good French bread; sweet butter; a thermos no doubt filled with what was left of Booked for Lunch's soup of the day; a quart of vanilla ice cream; and a jar of chocolate sauce.

"You didn't have to bring me dinner," Tricia said, although she was supremely grateful Angelica had done just that. Homemade soup and buttered bread always seem to hit the emotional spot at times like this.

"We both need to eat, and you need the company." Angelica put the ice cream in the freezer, and paused. "If I'm honest, I need the company, too." She shuddered. "I'm so glad it wasn't me who found Pammy."

"And I suppose you think I jumped for joy at the prospect," Tricia snapped, and instantly regretted it.

"Don't be silly," Angelica said, taking no offense. She opened one of the cupboards and took out a saucepan. "Of course it's upsetting to me that you had to find her. But don't you see, I don't have an alibi for killing her."

"Why do you need one? Although you may have been the last known person to see Pammy alive, you certainly didn't have a motive to kill her."

Angelica emptied the thermos of soup into the pan. "That's true. But the Sheriff's Department hasn't always let facts like that stand in the way of naming someone a 'person of interest.' Once they do that, you might as well have a tattoo on your forehead that says 'I killed fill-in-the-blank.' And today that would be Pammy Fredericks."

"Captain Baker can't seriously think you killed her. He seems a lot more reasonable than Sheriff Adams."

"Yes, and wasn't it a stroke of luck the sheriff decided to delegate this investigation instead of taking it on herself? We might just see justice served." Angelica removed the paper sleeve from around the bread. "Do you want plain bread, or would you rather have garlic bread?"

"Definitely garlic bread."

Angelica knew where everything was located in Tricia's kitchen—better than Tricia herself, if the truth be told—and she went straight for the correct cupboard, removed a baking sheet, and began to assemble everything else she'd need: garlic powder, dried parsley, and grated Parmesan cheese.

"This would really taste better with real garlic and fresh parsley, but I know better than to look for it. You never buy the good stuff," she said judgmentally.

"Garlic would sprout before I could use it. If I had any plants, they'd die a lingering death, which would be cruel."

Angelica gave her sister a withering stare. "For someone as careful about her diet as you are, you'd think you'd have learned that the fresher the ingredients, the healthier the food."

"I don't eat a lot of fat or red meat, or drink hard liquor, and I intend to live forever."

"That'll be a lonely life," Angelica said as she unwrapped a stick of butter. "Seeing as everybody you love or care a whit about will be long gone."

Everybody long gone. Like Pammy Fredericks was gone . . . Tricia glanced at the kitchen clock. Pammy had been dead for less than five hours. Already it seemed a lifetime.

"You're probably right," Tricia admitted. She settled on one of the stools at the kitchen island. "I guess at our age, we're still lucky to have Mother and Daddy. Not that we see them all that often. Where are they now?"

"Rio. I expect they'll stay until summer. They didn't want to come back for Christmas to be with us last year. I'm not holding my breath for this year, either," Angelica said, creaming the butter and the dry ingredients together in a little bowl with unnecessary force.

"I thought we had a lovely Christmas together."

Angelica paused in her assault on the contents of the bowl. "Yes, we did. I'm surprised at how many people came for Christmas dinner last year. How many of us were there around my dining room table?"

Tricia thought back. Ginny and her boyfriend, Brian Comstock, had come, as had Grace Harris and Mr. Everett, and Russ and Bob. "Eight of us."

"Well, we'll have to invite Frannie this year. And maybe Nikki—if she doesn't go to visit her new family in Canada. And—"

"Let's not get ahead of ourselves. It's only October."

Angelica sighed, and set the bowl aside. "I guess I just don't want to think about what happened today."

Tricia frowned. Neither did she, and now Angelica had brought it up again.

"Here we are thinking about our little family of friends in Stoneham, and today you lost a friend of many years, even if Pammy was a pain in the butt—almost just like family."

Tricia was sure Angelica didn't count herself as being a pain, but she kept her silence.

"That didn't mean in your heart of hearts you didn't love her in some capacity," Angelica continued. "You've got to give yourself time to mourn her, just like everyone else you've ever lost."

"I suppose right now *I'm* Captain Baker's chief suspect." Tricia told Angelica about the forged check. Somehow, she didn't seem surprised. "Why did I have to choose this morning to ask Pammy to leave? Why couldn't it have been yesterday—or why didn't I put it off until tomorrow?"

"Just one of those unanswerable questions," Angelica said. "But don't think you've got the market cornered on being chief suspect. If Captain Baker takes after Sheriff Adams, I'm probably his chief suspect. I don't even know if I can reopen tomorrow."

"Why shouldn't you? The murder happened outside the café. Did they seal the premises? Put up crime scene tape?"

"Not out front."

"Then I don't think you have a problem." Tricia sighed. "Damn Pammy anyway. Why did she have to be so secretive about her life?"

"Obviously she was in some kind of trouble," Angelica said.

"She could've confided in me."

"Would you have listened?"

Tricia didn't meet her sister's gaze. "I listened to what she had to say."

"How hard?" Angelica pressed.

Maybe not as hard as she could have, Tricia admitted to herself. "It's difficult to be a loving, caring friend when you feel put upon and your generosity is abused."

"Did you ever ask her why she stayed so long?"

"I assumed it was because she'd run out of money. You know she could never balance a checkbook. And she never worked much. She depended on the generosity of friends and relatives."

"Which was about to end," Angelica said.

"How do you know?"

"Pammy told me. She was expecting a windfall that would set her free for life."

"Did you tell Captain Baker that?"

Angelica thought about it. "I don't think so. I mean, cops aren't always interested in witnesses volunteering information."

"I agree, but that could be the reason Pammy was killed."

"What are you thinking? That she was blackmailing someone?"

"It's a classic motive for murder."

Angelica waved a hand in dismissal. "You think about murder too much."

"Well, I would, wouldn't I? My job *is* selling mystery books."

Angelica retrieved a bread knife from the wooden block on the counter, commandeered the cutting board, and sliced the baguette into half-inch pieces, but not cutting all the way through the loaf. Then she spread the butter-garlic mixture on both sides of each slice of bread. "Turn the oven on to three fifty, will you?"

Tricia got up, turned on the oven, and grabbed another wineglass from the cupboard. She made another stop by the refrigerator to grab the already opened bottle of chardonnay. "I hope that soup goes with white, because I'm flat out of merlot."

"It's chicken pastina, so it'll go fine." Angelica set the bread on the baking sheet, wrapped the loaf in foil, and popped it into the oven, before grabbing her glass. "What could Pammy possibly know about anybody that would warrant blackmail?"

"You said she was a Dumpster diver. I suppose she could've found financial statements or something of that order."

"She was a freegan. Looking for financial papers is just not on their scavenging agenda."

Tricia sipped her wine, and frowned. "I just don't understand how anybody could eat food that's been in a Dumpster. I mean—think about all the germs. Wouldn't that kill you, or at least make you deathly ill?"

"What kills people these days is not *enough* germs in their systems. We're all antibioticed to death, if you'll pardon the pun. Between hand sanitizers and antibiotics in the food chain and water, we're at the mercy of super staph germs and the like."

"Let's get back to Pammy." Tricia bit her lip. "Do you think we ought to tell Captain Baker about our suspicions?"

"What suspicions? I don't have any."

"Well, I do."

Angelica shook her head. "Look what trouble sharing your suspicions with the law has gotten you before."

"Yes, but that was when I was dealing with Sheriff Adams. I think Captain Baker is a lot more"—she paused, trying to come up with an appropriate term—"sympathetic."

"It's those green eyes of his. You're a sucker for them."

"So are you," Tricia countered. Bob Kelly had green eyes, too.

Angelica swirled the wine in her glass. "Maybe so. But it's immaterial. I'm sure we haven't seen the last of Captain Baker—but unless he asks, keep your ideas to yourself. We'll both be better off if you do."

"Okay. But I still think I must know something that could be helpful to the investigation. I just wish I knew what it was."

FIVE

Tricia found it hard to sleep that night. Maybe it was the quiet. Pammy's snores had awakened her more than once during her lengthy stay. Staring at the ceiling for hours on end gave Tricia plenty of time to think about Pammy's visit and her untimely death.

Why had she shown up at the Food Shelf just hours before she died? Why had she wanted to speak to Stuart Paige? Maybe if she could talk to Paige, she could find out what his connection to Pammy was. That is, if she could find someone to introduce her to him.

Bob Kelly probably knew the philanthropist.

Tricia winced at the thought. Because of Pammy's death—and her link with Pammy—Bob wasn't likely to introduce her to the man. Not if it meant the possibility of straining relations with the Chamber of Commerce. Could she entice the Food Shelf's chairperson, Libby Hirt, to do so? It might be worth trying.

With that decided, Tricia was finally able to drift off to sleep.

She never heard the alarm clock ring the next morning, and awoke only half an hour before Haven't Got a Clue was to open its doors. After a fast shower, she dressed, fed Miss Marple, and dashed down the stairs to the shop. Mr. Everett was already waiting at the store's entrance.

"My, we're late today," he commented after Tricia had unlocked the door and let him in.

"I had a rather sleepless night," she admitted.

Mr. Everett headed straight for the coffeemaker. "After what happened yesterday, I can well understand that. I'll get this started if you want to get the register up and running."

"Thank you," Tricia said gratefully.

By the time she'd taken money from the safe and counted it out for the till, the aroma of fresh-brewed coffee filled the front of the store. Mr. Everett brought her a cup, fixed just the way she liked it.

"I'm afraid the wastebasket behind the coffee station wasn't emptied last night," he said. Something else Ginny was supposed to have done, but hadn't. "Shall I do it now?"

"Oh, no," Tricia said. "I know how those back stairs bother your knees. I'll do it. Would you watch the register for a few minutes?"

"I'd be delighted," the elderly gent said, and gave her a smile. Come to think of it, he'd been smiling a lot lately. He took his place behind the register, and Tricia found a cap for her cup and set it on the counter at the coffee station. She grabbed the wastebasket.

"I'll be right back."

The wind was brisk on this sunny October morning as she trundled down the steps that led to the Dumpster. On her way back she again noticed two bowls on the concrete steps leading to the Cookery's back door. She moseyed over to have a look. Sure enough, one contained the remains of dry cat food; the other contained water that had already attracted a few stray locust leaves. She picked them out and tossed them on the ground. The poor kitty shouldn't have to drink dirty water.

Poor Frannie if Angelica found out she was still feeding the neighborhood stray.

Tricia glanced at her watch. By now Angelica would be at her café, getting ready for the lunch crowd that would start filing in within the hour. Frannie was safe from detection—for another few hours, at least.

Tricia reentered her store and found that they already had a customer—or at least a guest. Grace Harris, Mr. Everett's special friend, had arrived before the onslaught of tourists. Tricia had met her just a year before, under not very pleasant conditions—at least for Grace, who'd been forced into a nursing home under suspicious circumstances. Tricia had helped extricate her from the home, and since that time, Grace and Mr. Everett had renewed their decades-old friendship.

As usual, Grace was dressed to the nines. Beautiful name-brand clothes, exquisite jewelry, and expertly coiffed hair, too. With her lovely skin and natural poise, she could have easily made a fortune as a senior citizen model, but her late husband had left her very well off. She liked to read, and she liked Mr. Everett. A lot.

"Good morning, Grace. You're here early."

"I have so much to do today, and I decided I'd best start early."

"Don't overdo, dear," Mr. Everett said kindly.

Grace reached across the counter to clasp his hand. "I won't." She gazed back at Tricia, her expression luminous.

She looked back at Mr. Everett. "I don't suppose you've told Tricia our good news."

Mr. Everett shook his head, a blush coloring his cheeks as his gaze dipped to the counter.

"Shame on you," Grace scolded. "Shall I?"

Again he shook his head. "It's my duty."

Duty? That sounded serious.

Mr. Everett cleared his throat and focused on Tricia's face. "Ms. Miles, you and Ginny are like family to me. That's why we want you to be one of the first to know—"

"We're engaged," Grace announced, and pulled the leather glove from her left hand, revealing a modest solitaire diamond. "And Tricia, I want you to be my maid of honor."

Tricia held Grace's outstretched hand, admiring the stone. "I don't know what to say."

"That you'd love to, would be an acceptable answer," Mr. Everett prompted with a hopeful smile.

Tricia beamed. "I'd be delighted! When's the happy day?"

"We haven't set a firm date, but at our age we don't see much point in waiting," Grace said. "Either this Sunday or next."

"What are your plans for the ceremony?"

"Something small and dignified. We have an appointment later this afternoon to talk to the head of catering at the Brookview Inn. That is, if you can spare dear William."

"Of course you can have the afternoon off," Tricia told Mr. Everett. "And you must let me know what I can do for the wedding day. Can I provide the cake? The music? The flowers?"

"That is so kind of you," Grace said, "but I think we'll have everything in hand."

"I'd really like to do *something* for you on your day."

"Just be there. That will be more than enough," Mr. Everett said, and his eyes shone with unshed tears.

Tricia smiled and threw her arms—gently—around the old man. "You better believe I'll be there. I'll close the store if I have to."

"We chose a Sunday morning so that none of our bookshop friends would have to miss the ceremony. We thought we'd have a brunch reception, and that way we'd also have plenty of time to take an afternoon flight to our wedding-night destination." Grace actually blushed at this last announcement.

Tricia felt a lump rise in her throat. Here these two dear people—who deserved decades of happiness together, and weren't likely to receive it—were thinking more of accommodating their guests than of their own circumstances on their most joyous day. Surely no two finer people deserved an abundance of marital bliss.

Tricia clasped Grace's hand. "Do you have your dress? What are your colors? Where are you going on your honeymoon?"

Grace actually giggled. "I haven't given a thought to most of the details. I imagined we'd figure it all out this afternoon. After we get the wedding license, of course." Another titter of laughter escaped her throat. "This is so much fun. I don't remember when I've been this entertained."

Again, a wave of strong emotion passed through Tricia, threatening to engulf her as the memories of planning her own wedding—what she had always considered the happiest day of her life—gushed forth. "I wish you two many years of happiness."

"I'll take what God gives me and hope I live it in relatively good health," Mr. Everett said sensibly.

"Don't be such a pessimist," Grace scolded. "I think we've both got many years left—especially if we take care of each other." The fond look she gave her husband-to-be nearly brought Tricia to tears. Weddings—and all they entailed—had that effect on her.

"Now, Tricia," Grace said, "again, I hope it won't inconvenience you too much if William has an hour or two off this afternoon."

"Take as much time as you need. You have my blessing," Tricia said, and smiled.

"I'm sorry I can't give you more than a few days' notice, but I will need a week off work for our honeymoon," Mr. Everett added in all seriousness.

"I think Ginny and I will be able to manage for a mere seven days," Tricia said, and smiled. Then again, Ginny was already five minutes late.

A customer came in, and Mr. Everett, who took his job very seriously, excused himself to help the man.

"I was surprised to see you at the Food Shelf dedication yesterday," Tricia told Grace.

"It's long been one of my favorite local charities. And who could say no to dear Libby Hirt? Over the years she's been a guardian angel to so many here in Stoneham. She and her husband are the nicest people. They took in that sick child and raised her. Others would've been put off by the prospect of all that surgery, but not Libby. She's got the biggest heart in the world."

A sick child? "I'm sorry I didn't get an opportunity to meet and talk with her."

"She's a real asset to this community." Grace glanced at her diamond-studded watch. "Oh, my, I must dash. I want to speak to the florist. Oh, I have so many things penciled in on my to-do list—I just hope I can accomplish them all before the end of the day." The excitement in her voice was contagious.

"Well, do let me know if I can be of any help. It would be an honor and a privilege," Tricia said.

"Don't worry, dear. I will." Grace crossed the store to join her fiancé and, scandalously, gave Mr. Everett a quick peck on the lips.

"My dear!" he scolded.

Grace grinned. "I don't think your employer minds one bit."

"Minds what?" Tricia asked, and looked up at the decorative tin ceiling, pretending she hadn't noticed a breach in store decorum.

"Good-bye, dear," Mr. Everett said, and Grace waved as she exited the shop.

Tricia risked a glance at her employee. Mr. Everett's cheeks were quite pink. He cleared his throat.

"I think I shall go back to work," he said, and, with head held high, went in search of his lamb's wool duster.

The shop door opened with the soft jingle of the bell that hung over the door. A couple of women bundled in heavy sweaters bustled in, adhesive name tags identifying them as being part of an Apollo Tour.

"Good morning, and welcome to Haven't Got a Clue, Stoneham's—"

"Mystery bookstore," one of them finished. "We read all about you on the Internet." She reached into her purse. "I've got a long list of books I need to find. Could someone help me?"

"I'd be glad to." Before Tricia could even inspect the list, a breathless Ginny burst through the shop door. "Sorry I'm late," she said, already struggling out of the sleeves of her jacket. She raced to the back of the store and hung up the jacket, then hurried to join Tricia with the customers.

"Tricia, I'm sorry, I—"

"We'll talk about it later. Perhaps you could help this lady here." She pointed to the other customer.

"Sure, I'd be glad to. What author were you looking for?"

"Rex Stout. I'd like a copy of *The Golden Spiders*."

"I'm pretty sure we have that in stock. Follow me, please."

Twenty minutes and three hundred and forty dollars later, the ladies departed the store, their shopping bags bulging with books. Despite the good start to the retail day, Ginny's anxious expression kept Tricia from mentioning her tardy entrance—at least for the time being.

"That was an excellent couple of sales," Mr. Everett said, approaching the register with a tray of the store's cardboard coffee cups. "We should celebrate."

"I agree," Tricia said, grateful for the opportunity to cheer her other employee.

Mr. Everett passed around the cups. "Here's to a wonderful day."

They raised their cups and took a sip. "Mr. Everett, wouldn't you like to tell Ginny your good news?" Tricia suggested.

Mr. Everett blushed, and he ducked his head in embarrassment. "Grace and I, we're—well, we've become engaged."

Ginny's mouth drooped. "Engaged?"

"Yes, isn't it wonderful? They're going to get married in the next week or so," Tricia said.

"Married?" Ginny repeated, her voice cracking, and then she burst into tears.

Tricia grabbed Ginny's coffee before she spilled it onto the carpet, while Mr. Everett stood rooted, stricken.

"Ginny, what's wrong?"

"We can't afford to get married," she wailed. "Brian's working two jobs, I've been trying to find a second job, and somehow we have to find the time to work on the house. And . . . oh, everything is all messed up."

"If I thought the news would upset you, I never would have mentioned it," Mr. Everett apologized, obviously distressed by Ginny's reaction. His words only made her cry harder.

"I'm so sorry, Mr. Everett. I'm very happy for you and Grace," Ginny managed. "And I hate myself for being so terribly jealous, but I can't help it."

Tricia pulled Ginny into an awkward embrace. "You and Brian will get married someday, and I'm sure it'll be a lovely ceremony."

Ginny's sobs increased, and she waved her ringless hand in the air. "We're not even officially en-en-gaged."

"Oh, dear—oh, dear," Mr. Everett said.

The shop door opened, the little bell above it jangling cheerfully. Two women stepped into the store, took in the scene, and quickly retreated.

"Oh, dear—oh, dear," Mr. Everett repeated, his heavily veined hands clenched, no doubt to keep from wringing them.

"Come on, Ginny, let's go upstairs," Tricia said, and guided her employee toward the back of the shop and the stairs leading to her loft apartment.

"I'll take care of things here," Mr. Everett called with relief.

Tricia opened the door marked PRIVATE and led the way up the stairs. She unlocked the apartment door and Ginny followed her in. Her sobs had wound down to sniffling, and Tricia led her to one of the stools in front of the kitchen island. "Would you like some cocoa?"

Ginny wiped a hand over her eyes. "Yes, please." She sounded about twelve years old.

Tricia filled her electric kettle with water and plugged it in. She watched as Ginny snatched a paper napkin from the holder and blew her nose. She blinked a few times and took in the kitchen with its sparking white, painted cabinets, granite counters, and thirteen-foot ceiling. "Wow, this is a great space," she managed, and hiccuped. "And there's no drywall dust or exposed wiring. I'd almost forgotten how real people live."

"When you've finished all your renovations, you'll have a lovely home, too."

Ginny sniffed and shrugged.

Tricia took a couple of mugs from the cabinet and found the cylinder of Ghirardelli Chocolate Mocha Hot Cocoa mix. She measured out the powder. The kettle was starting to sound like an engine—a prelude to boiling. "It won't be long now," Tricia said.

"I wish I led a charmed life like you," Ginny said, and sighed.

"Me? I'm divorced, my sister lives next door, and I keep discovering dead bodies. How charmed is that?"

"At least you *have* your sister nearby. Since Mom and Dad moved south, I sometimes feel like I'm all alone here in Stoneham."

"What about Brian?"

"He works so much we hardly ever see each other." She let out another shuddering sigh.

"Seems like you need to make plans for the future. Give yourself a goal. How big a wedding do you want?"

"Not big at all," Ginny said. "I'd like to have our friends, our parents, and some of the people here in the village—like you and Mr. Everett and Grace, and Frannie and Nikki, and our friends Pete and Lisa. Nothing really big."

"Have you ever heard of a potluck wedding?"

Ginny shook her head. "No."

"You could rent a picnic shelter, invite your friends to bring a dish to pass—just like an old-fashioned wedding."

"Is that what you did when you got married?"

Tricia thought about the cathedral, the eight attendants, the five-tiered wedding cake with masses of colorful fondant flowers, and the princess gown and veil. "Not exactly," she said. "But if I had it to do over again, I'd have a much simpler affair." Easy to say, now that the marriage had failed. And, the truth was, she'd loved every minute of the preparations, the ceremony, and the reception. Ending the marriage hadn't been Tricia's idea.

"If simple is what you want, I'm sure it can be arranged. Just pick a date—preferably in warm weather—and start making plans. I'm sure all your friends would love to pitch in. I could get Angelica to help with the food. She's spoken often about starting a catering service as part of the café—once she gets established."

"Angelica would not be happy about you volunteering her services for me."

"Why not?"

"For one thing, she's angry with me because I don't patronize her café. But it costs money to do that and, besides, it's always crowded with tourists. I pack my lunch and eat it in my car."

"You can't do that much longer—it's getting cold."

"Where else am I supposed to go?"

Tricia thought for a second. "You could use the storeroom downstairs. We could put a table in there. And I'll get one of those dorm fridges and a microwave. It would give you and Mr. Everett somewhere to go on your breaks and save you money at the same time."

"You'd be going to an awful lot of trouble."

"It's no trouble. You're both valuable employees. I want to keep you."

Ginny dabbed at her nose with the napkin. "Thank you."

The kettle began to whistle. Tricia unplugged it and poured the hot water into the mugs. "I can't make it happen today, but I'll see what I can do about getting it pulled together in the next couple of days."

"You're the best boss I've ever had."

"If I was, I would've thought of this a long time ago."

"You always have a lot on your mind. Especially since yesterday."

"Yesterday?"

"Pammy dying and all."

For just a few minutes, Tricia *had* actually forgotten about it. She handed Ginny her cup.

"I'm sorry I got all weepy over this whole marriage thing. I should go down and apologize to Mr. Everett. He's the sweetest person on the earth. I feel terrible about hurting his feelings. I think it's wonderful they're getting married, and I really am happy for them." Ginny blew on her cocoa to cool it before taking a tentative sip. "Do you mind if I go down now and apologize? Can I take the cup with me?"

"Yes, of course."

Ginny slid from her stool. "Thanks, Tricia. You really are the best boss in the world." Treading carefully, she made her way to the door without spilling a drop.

Best boss in the world? Tricia didn't know about that. And where would she get one of those dorm fridges? She'd probably have to drive to Nashua or Manchester to find one. Or maybe she could find one in the ad section of the *Stoneham Weekly News*. Too bad she'd tossed out the last one. On the other hand, she was having dinner with Russ later that evening. He probably had one hanging around his house.

Tricia leaned against the counter, sipping her cocoa, and caught sight of the box of books Pammy had left behind. Setting down her mug, she circled the kitchen island and crossed into the living room. She sat down on the couch, leaned over, and ran her fingers across the book spines. Nothing here that interested her. A couple of old cookbooks, something Angelica might stock at the Cookery, a few mainstream titles circa 1970, and a few battered children's books.

Poor Pammy was dead. At least Captain Baker seemed interested in finding her killer, unlike his boss during previous murder investigations in Stoneham. But what if Sheriff Adams interfered with his investigation? What if she decided for him that he should concentrate on pinning the murder on her or Angelica?

Tricia couldn't allow that to happen. What she needed were facts. What she needed to do was to find out why Pammy had wanted to speak to Stuart Paige.

Tricia stood and glanced around her apartment, looking for and finding her purse. In seconds she'd retrieved the crumpled brochure for the Stoneham Food Shelf she'd stashed away the day before. A glance at the hours of operation made her heart sink. It was open Monday·mornings from nine to eleven *only*. However, the Clothing Closet was open weekdays from nine to noon. Tricia frowned.

Food would seem to be more essential than clothing . . . unless, of course, you were buck naked. Why the difference in hours?

She'd just have to ask.

The problem was that Libby Hirt was the head of the Food Shelf, not the Clothing Closet. Still, perhaps someone at the Closet could give her Libby's number. Perhaps. She might need a reason other than pure curiosity to get that number. She could volunteer Haven't Got a Clue as a food drop-off site. But that still didn't guarantee she'd get the number.

Of course, she could just look Libby up in the local phone book.

There were four Hirts listed, but no Libby; no L. Hirt. She was probably married, or had an unlisted number. Or didn't have a landline at all. A lot of people had given them up, using just their cell phones. But that seemed to be younger people, more Ginny's age. She could try all four . . . and say what? *"I'm just being nosy, asking what happened at the dedication the other day . . ."* And Libby Hirt might not have a clue, thinking Pammy was just one more pushy broad who wanted to get her money-sucking paws on a philanthropist like Stuart Paige.

Tricia scrutinized the brochure, figured what the heck, and dialed the Food Shelf's number. If nothing else, voice mail might give her an emergency number to call. Instead of voice mail, a real person answered. "Stoneham Food Shelf, this is Libby. Can I help you?"

"Oh, it's you," Tricia blurted.

"Y-e-s." The word was drawn out.

Tricia laughed. "Sorry. I was expecting voice mail. My name is Tricia Miles. I was at the dedication yesterday. I run Haven't Got a Clue, the mystery bookshop in Stoneham."

"Oh. How nice. And thank you for coming to our party. You must be a Chamber member."

"Yes. I wanted to talk about the possibility of having my store be a drop-off point for the Food Shelf. I'd also love a tour of your facility."

"We gave tours at the dedication."

"Unfortunately, I got there a bit late. I would love a personal tour—if it's not too much trouble."

"Not at all. When would you like to visit?"

"How about now?"

"Now would be fine."

"Great. I can be there"—Tricia glanced at the kitchen clock—"in ten minutes."

"Fine. I'll be waiting for you. Good-bye."

SIX

Tricia was a little out of breath when she arrived at the Stoneham Food Shelf. Five cars were parked in front of the Clothing Closet's door, and a blue Toyota Prius was in the slot farthest from the Food Shelf's entrance, which sported a CLOSED sign.

Tricia pressed the doorbell at the side of the plate-glass door. Libby Hirt soon appeared and greeted Tricia with a smile. After exchanging pleasantries, she gave Tricia a complete tour of the facility, including opening the connecting door to the well-stocked Clothing Closet. Several women sorted through the racks of clothes. They didn't look poverty stricken to Tricia, and she voiced that opinion.

The twinkle in Libby's eyes, as well as her quick smile, vanished. She closed the door. "Appearances can be deceiving, Tricia. Right here in Stoneham there are families living paycheck to paycheck—living near the brink. House foreclosures, the tight economy—it all takes a toll on the working poor."

"I guess I never gave it much thought, and I feel ashamed. I've been living in Stoneham for about eighteen months, and I'd never even heard of the Stoneham Food Shelf until yesterday."

Libby managed a smile. "There are several hundred people who've lived in Stoneham all their lives and have never heard of our food pantry, so you're not alone." The smile faded from her lips. "Since the booksellers came to town, everyone seems to think that the prosperity has been shared among all Stoneham's citizens. It hasn't. And this is New England. People don't like to admit they have to accept charity."

People like Ginny.

"I'm beginning to realize that," Tricia confessed. "I'd like to do all I can to help."

Libby's smile returned. "I was hoping you'd say that. We've found a collection jar near your cash register is best for a business like yours. Often tourists feel generous with their change, and readily dump it into one of our jars."

"I'm afraid a great many of my customers pay for their purchases with credit cards."

"We realize that, but anything you collect will help local families deal with hunger. That's a big plus, in my book."

Now to pull out the big guns. "What do you know about the local freegans?" Tricia asked.

Libby's mouth went slack, the color draining from her face. "I know of them."

"Have they ever contributed to the Food Shelf?"

Libby hesitated before answering. "There's a stigma attached to such donations. Even hungry people don't want to eat food that may have been salvaged from garbage bins."

"Is the food unsafe?"

"Not necessarily. But if we were to accept such donations—and I'm not saying we knowingly do—we wouldn't know how clean the trash receptacle was. Was the food in plastic bags before it was, er, liberated? It's a question of bacterial contamination. We wouldn't want to expose our clients to any kind of risk."

"So such donations are not something you readily welcome."

"Unfortunately, we don't always know where the donations come from. If we do, we naturally screen it, as we screen everything that comes in."

"Screen it? How?"

"First of all, we accept only nonperishable items," Libby said, and seemed grateful for the opportunity to veer away from the initial question. "Next, we examine every container. Cans that are dented near the seams are not distributed, nor are rusty cans. If the product comes in glass, we make sure there are no cracks. Nothing with bulging lids is accepted, either. And we check the expiration dates on everything that's donated. We'll accept food up to two years after the expiration date."

Tricia wrinkled her nose. "But isn't it spoiled by then?"

"Not at all. Admittedly, it may not be at its best, but when you're hungry, you're not as fussy."

Tricia took in the boxes, cans, and jars of donated food that lined the shelves along the walls. "Surely a steady diet of all this processed food isn't healthy."

"We're an emergency service," Libby explained. "The Food Shelf was never intended to supply individuals for an extended length of time. I'll admit processed food isn't always the healthiest food on the planet. It's full of sodium and high-fructose corn syrup, but when the alternative is to go hungry, donated food is literally a lifesaver. We do look out for a number of our chronically ill and elderly clients who depend upon us for food when their Social Security money runs out—usually the third week of every month. We take their dietary limitations into account and supply them with as much low-sodium and fresh food as possible."

"How many of those clients do you have?"

"Right now, ten—that number varies throughout the year."

"You mentioned fresh food?" Tricia prompted.

"Yes. Money donations buy bread, milk, cheese, fresh vegetables, and meat to last our clients several days."

"Has the Food Shelf ever run a soup kitchen?"

"No, but one of the local churches did. That was before Everett's Food Market went out of business. The owner, William Everett, donated all his less-than-perfect produce. It was a big blow when he went out of business."

"Did you know he now works for me?"

"Yes, I think Grace Harris did mention that to me. I've been told to save the date for their upcoming wedding. Isn't it sweet that two such nice people found each other?"

"Yes. Now, you were saying—?" Tricia prompted.

"Oh, the soup kitchen. Yes, they tried to solicit donations from other sources outside of Stoneham, but they were already donating to programs in their own towns. It would be nice if we could get another such service going again—but it doesn't seem likely."

Tricia nodded and looked around the gleaming new facility. "It was very generous of Mr. Paige to make a matching donation to the funds your organization has collected."

"Yes. He's been a good friend to the Food Shelf over the years. We're grateful for people like Grace Harris, and for all the Chamber of Commerce has done, too. We never could have come up with the funds if it hadn't been for the Chamber. Bob Kelly is a saint."

Tricia had never thought of him in that regard. "Can just anybody use your services?"

Libby shook her head. "We're here for individuals and families who need emergency assistance. I'm sure you can understand that some people might want to take advantage of such a program, and that's why our volunteers verify the need before our drivers make their weekly deliveries to those who've requested help."

"You make deliveries?"

"Every Monday. That's also when our volunteers make pickups from food drop-off points. At the end of the month, they collect the money from the change jars."

Which explained the limited hours the Food Shelf was open.

"It's important that we let the people who need assistance maintain their dignity," Libby continued. "And with the price of gas these days, they often don't have the wherewithal to get to us."

Tricia nodded in understanding. She couldn't think of anyone she knew who would want to advertise the fact that they needed charity.

She thought about the real reason she'd come to the Food Shelf. Time to get down to business. "It was a wonderful dedication. Too bad it was marred by that woman's temper tantrum," Tricia said, not admitting her acquaintance with Pammy.

"Yes," Libby agreed. "I never did find out what she wanted. Someone told me later she wanted to talk to our guest of honor. Harangue, more like. I was grateful that Mr. Paige's security people dealt with her. It would have

been extremely embarrassing for him had she made a fuss
during the ceremony. Especially since the press was in
attendance."

The press? Oh, she meant Russ. Funny, Tricia never
really thought of the *Stoneham Weekly News* as a serious
news organ. Wouldn't Russ be furious if he knew what her
real opinion was?

Too bad Libby hadn't known why Pammy had tried to
crash the dedication . . . but then again, if she did, she had
no reason to divulge that information to Tricia. And why
should Libby speak frankly? Until today, she hadn't met
Tricia, and had no reason to share anything she knew.

Too bad.

"Goodness, look at the time," Tricia said, with a show
of looking at her watch. "I'm sorry to have kept you so
long."

"Not at all," Libby assured her. "Let me get one of
our change jars for you. One of our volunteers will visit
your store to collect what's been contributed at the end of
every month. We're very grateful to the Chamber members
who've elected to help us out in this way."

Tricia took another look around the tidy room as Libby
rummaged in a locker for a collection jar. She thought
about the Clothing Closet next door, and the boxes of food
ready to be delivered to the people of Stoneham who were
too ashamed to let others know their circumstances . . . and
felt grateful for what she had and the life she lived.

After missing breakfast and talking food for so long with
Libby Hirt, Tricia was hungry enough to eat her own foot.
As it was almost noon, she parked her car in the munici-
pal lot, grabbed her new collection can, and hoofed it to

Angelica's café, figuring on grabbing a quick bite before returning to Haven't Got a Clue.

Ginny was right. Booked for Lunch was booked solid. There wasn't a seat to be had, and people stood in the entryway, waiting for an opening. Tricia did an about-face and headed north down the sidewalk for the Bookshelf Diner.

Another destroyed carved pumpkin lay in the gutter outside the restaurant. How many of the village's children were heartbroken over such vandalism? Tricia bypassed the mess and entered the diner.

Though Angelica's café had put a dent in the Bookshelf's lunchtime trade, it hadn't killed it. All but one booth was taken, and the one Tricia was given was only a two-seater. She shrugged out of her jacket, set it over her purse and the collection can, and sat down. Not thirty seconds later the waitress arrived, pouring fresh water from a frosted glass jug into Tricia's waiting glass.

"What can I get you?" Eugenia, the perky, blond, college-aged waitress asked. "The usual?"

Tricia shook her head. "Today I think I'll be daring. How about a bowl of vegetarian chili—with extra crackers?"

Eugenia winked.

"Hey, I thought you only worked evenings," Tricia said.

Eugenia smiled. "I do. But Hildy called in sick today, and since I only have a couple of morning classes, I agreed to fill in. I'm a starving college student. I can always use the extra money. Be right back with your chili," she promised, and headed toward the kitchen.

Was it Tricia's imagination, or had Eugenia lost some of the hardware she usually wore? Gone were the eyebrow rings and nose studs—although the young woman still had at least three sets of gemstone-like post earrings, in a multitude of colors, decorating each ear. Should she mention the young woman's new look, or had Eugenia taken enough teasing about her former look from the more staid villagers that acknowledging the change wouldn't be appreciated?

Eugenia reappeared in record time with Tricia's order. She settled the bowl, with the requested extra crackers, on the paper placemat in front of Tricia. "Hey, I heard you met my mom."

Tricia looked into the intense blue eyes above her. "I did?"

"Yeah, Libby Hirt. She runs the Food Shelf. I talked to her on the phone a few minutes ago. She said you'd been by to scope out the place and that you'd volunteered to be a drop-off point. That was really nice of you. Thanks."

News traveled fast. She'd left Libby only some fifteen minutes before. Hadn't Grace mentioned that Eugenia had been ill as a child? She certainly didn't look the worse for wear now. "Oh, well. Just my civic duty."

"No, it's more than that. Thanks to Mom, I grew up knowing that there were hungry people all around here. Not everyone is as enthusiastic about helping the Food Shelf. They think it encourages people to be bums or something." She rolled her eyes disapprovingly.

"Since most of my customers are tourists, I don't know that they'll feel generous toward the cause, but I figured it wouldn't hurt to try." And she intended to salt the jar to get things going.

"You're right," Eugenia agreed, "but you'd be surprised how fast loose change mounts up." She nodded toward the collection can that sat by the diner's register. It was at least a third full with quarters, nickels, dimes, pennies, and a few folded-up dollar bills. "Add up all the collection cans in town, and it makes a big difference to the Food Shelf's bottom line," she continued. "I mean, we can't depend on bigwigs like Stuart Paige to pick up the tab all the time. The people of Stoneham have to take some responsibility for the villagers who need help making ends meet."

The words didn't sound rehearsed, but they weren't the jargon of a twenty-year-old, either. Eugenia must have grown up hearing the same speeches over and over again. That she'd taken them to heart said a lot about her character.

"I'm glad I can help."

"I do what I can, too," Eugenia said, her gaze traveling back toward the kitchen.

"Hey, what's it take to get some service around here?" called a male voice from behind Tricia. The accent sounded like he was a Long Islander.

"'Scuse me," Eugenia said, and took off to take care of her customer.

Tricia turned her attention to her lunch, plunging her spoon into the chili. She had always enjoyed talking with Eugenia. She was a nice kid. Like her mom . . . although with that brilliantly blond hair, and her little pug nose, she looked nothing like her mother. Then Tricia remembered again that Grace had mentioned the girl had been adopted.

She unwrapped the first of her cracker packets, crumbling them on top of the chili.

A minute later Eugenia returned, this time with a carafe of coffee. "Sorry, I never asked if you wanted anything other than water."

Tricia shook her head. "I'm fine, thanks."

"All set?"

Tricia nodded.

Eugenia dipped into the pocket of her apron, withdrew a piece of paper—the check—and set it on the table. "Thanks for coming by today—and for helping my mom."

Tricia nodded, and the young woman headed back up the booth-flanked aisle, checking with the rest of the patrons, making offers of refills as needed.

As Tricia finished her lunch, she wondered what Eugenia had meant when she said she'd done all she could to support her mother's cause. Did she contribute some of her tips, or was she one of the volunteers who packed canned goods into cartons at the Food Shelf?

Today wasn't the day to ask.

Tricia finished the last of her chili, picked up the check, her jacket, purse, and the collection jar, and paid at the register. Minutes later she was back at Haven't Got a Clue with time to spare before it was time for Ginny's lunch break.

Tricia hung up her jacket, stashed her purse, and settled the collection jar beside the register.

"Another one of Libby Hirt's soldiers against hunger, I see," Ginny said, crossing her arms across her chest.

"Yes. I hope we can help make a difference," Tricia said. She opened the register and took out a couple of dollars in quarters, dimes, and nickels, adding it to the jar. The money made a rather shallow layer. It would take an awful lot of change to fill it.

A woman approached the cash desk and set four books down by the register. Tricia rang up the sale while Ginny bagged the books. The woman handed her thirty dollars, and Tricia returned her twenty cents change, which the woman promptly dropped into the collection can.

"Thank you," Tricia said as Ginny stifled a grin.

The woman sketched a wave good-bye and headed out the door.

"See, we're making a difference already," Tricia said. She looked around the store. "Did Mr. Everett leave?"

"Grace stopped by and picked him up. Something about

talking to the caterer at the Brookview Inn," Ginny said, and sighed. "While you were gone, we had a lull. By the way, it looks like the book club is off for tonight. Grace and Mr. Everett are busy; Nikki and Julia both called to say they can't make it, either. I figured what the heck, and made an executive decision to cancel the meeting."

"It's just as well," Tricia said, and sighed. "I forgot I have a date with Russ for tonight. Does everyone know?"

"Yes, I called them all. We should be good to go next week—although Grace and Mr. Everett will be on their honeymoon. We may want to postpone the meetings until they return."

Tricia nodded.

"I also called the Board of Selectmen to see about renting the gazebo in the park for our wedding. No go."

"Have you tried Milford?"

"They've got a big gazebo in the Oval, but I'm not sure they'd rent that."

"What about that ball field next to the hospital?"

"I could try that next," Ginny said uncertainly.

"What about your own yard? It's pretty big. And you could rent a tent just in case it rains."

"I hadn't even thought of that. I'll put it on the back burner. I mean, I haven't even talked to Brian about any of this. He might not want to get married at home or under a tent."

"I think an at-home wedding would be lovely."

"I'm warming up to the idea," Ginny said. "Oh, the music's stopped. I'll go change the CD." She headed for the coffee station, which also housed the store's stereo system.

"Anything else happen while I was gone?" Tricia asked.

Ginny flipped through the jewel boxes. "Captain Baker called. He said he'd call back some other time."

"What did he want?"

"He didn't say." Ginny chose *A New Journey* by Celtic Woman, setting it on low volume. "It probably had something to do with Pammy's death, though—don't you think?"

"Undoubtedly. But I don't know what else I can tell him. She didn't confide in me all that much. And sometimes she'd disappear in the evenings and didn't tell me where she'd been. If only I could find one of the local freegans, I might find out more about what Pammy was up to."

Ginny returned to the sales counter. "What do you mean?"

"Pammy told Angelica she was a freegan. They Dumpster dive for food."

"I know what they are," Ginny said.

"I asked Libby Hirt about them, but she didn't want to talk about it. Obviously there are people in the village who know about them, but I don't know who else to ask."

"I might be able to help," Ginny said. Her voice had dropped.

"You know someone?"

Ginny nodded. "In fact, I know several freegans."

"Could you introduce me to them?" Tricia asked eagerly.

"You already know them."

Tricia blinked. She couldn't imagine anyone she knew in Stoneham who would be reduced to digging through garbage for food. "Who?"

Ginny shrugged. "Well, for one—me."

SEVEN

 Tricia's mouth dropped. It felt like someone had just kicked her in the stomach. It took a long moment before she could speak again. "Ginny, I can't believe you dig through garbage for food."

"I never intended for you to know," Ginny said, her head lowered so she did not meet Tricia's gaze.

"Why would you do such a thing, especially after Brian ended up in the hospital last spring with food poisoning?"

"Ah, but he wasn't poisoned by anything we got Dumpster diving."

That was true. Brian had eaten tainted food meant for Tricia.

"Just answer one question. Why? And don't tell me you're making a political statement."

Ginny sighed. "I was a freegan back in college. I thought I didn't have any money back then, but now it's a matter of economic survival. Buying our house has been a lot more expensive than either of us thought it would be—that's why we can never afford a nice wedding."

"Are you sorry you bought the house?"

"When I pay the bills, yes. When I drive home from work at night and see the lights on in our little cottage, no, I'm not sorry. We both love the house. It just needed a lot more work than we anticipated, and we have to cut corners where we can."

"Have you thought about using the Stoneham Food Shelf?"

Ginny shook her head. "That's for desperate people."

"And you don't think digging through trash to get your food is a desperate measure?"

Ginny held her head high. "No, I don't. Although I don't like to advertise it," she added sheepishly.

The shop door opened, and a man and woman entered the store.

Tricia stood straighter and forced a smile. "Hello. Welcome to Haven't Got a Clue. Can I help you find anything?"

"No, just browsing," said the woman, who gave her a return smile.

"Our authors are shelved in alphabetical order. Nonfiction titles are on the left. Please, help yourself to some coffee, and let us know if you need help or a recommendation."

"Will do," said the man, and he and the woman split up, each heading for a different part of the store.

Tricia turned her attention back to Ginny. "I don't know that we should continue this conversation."

"Agreed. At least this part of it. But you wanted to know about Pammy," Ginny reminded her.

"Yes. What was she doing in Stoneham? Did she confide in you or any of your . . . freegan friends?"

"She didn't talk to me—she didn't *like* me. The feeling

was mutual. But she was friendly with some of the others. One of them told me she'd mentioned she was hanging around Stoneham to meet someone."

"Did she find this person?"

Ginny shook her head. "I don't think so."

"Who are these people? Can I talk to them?"

"Stoneham is a small town. We don't like to advertise who we are to just anyone. We don't do much scavenging here in the village. We don't want to catch the flack."

"Where do you go to . . . find . . . what you're looking for?"

"Sometimes Milford—but Nashua, mostly. But Brian and I have also been to Manchester and Portsmouth, too. We've got friends all over."

"You said I'd know some of these people," Tricia reminded her.

"I don't feel comfortable telling you who—at least not without talking to them first."

Good grief! Who could she be talking about? Fellow booksellers? Respected members of the Chamber of Commerce?

"Would you ask them if they'd mind speaking to me?"

"I'll try," Ginny said, "but I can't promise that anyone will."

Libby had mentioned the stigma attached to being a freegan. "Fair enough. But I'm not out to expose anyone. I just want to find out who killed Pammy, and why. You can understand that—right?"

"Yes. But I'm certain that none of my friends had anything to do with Pammy's death. I'd stake my life on it."

Tricia wasn't sure that was a wise bet.

*   *   *

It was after five when the phone rang. Since Ginny was at the counter, she picked up the telephone. Tricia looked up from her position at the coffee station. She was proud of that phone, a relic from another age. She liked to imagine that Harriet Vane used the same kind of instrument to talk to Lord Peter Wimsey. The look of distaste on Ginny's face, however, gave Tricia pause. Ginny laid the receiver on her chest to muffle the mouthpiece. "It's Angelica. Does she have to remind everyone she talks to that she's"—she dropped her voice to a whine—"*about to be published*, and then give the daily countdown?"

Tricia flipped off the switch on the coffeemaker, removed the filter and grounds, and dumped them in the wastebasket before heading for the register and the phone. She took the receiver, which Ginny held out as if it had cooties. "Hey, Ange, what's up?"

"I need your help," Angelica said, her voice filled with drama. "Jake has taken off again, and I've got no one to help me, and—"

"Ange, I have a store to run—"

"Then can you loan me Ginny or Mr. Everett?"

"Mr. Everett has the afternoon off."

"Again?" Angelica wailed.

"What do you need?" Tricia asked.

"I've got the kitchen back in shape for tomorrow's lunch crowd, but I need help bringing my garbage over to the Cookery. Captain Baker took one of my garbage carts, and the other one is overflowing. I've got bags of trash I have to dump somewhere. I may even need to put some in your Dumpster. Will you help me, please?"

The last thing Tricia wanted to do was soil her pretty peach sweater set, but she couldn't very well ask Ginny to ruin her clothes, either.

"I can give you ten minutes. No more."

"That's all I need. Now get over here, will you? I've got paperwork to finish over at the Cookery. Why I ever thought I could run two businesses at the same time . . ."

Tricia hung up the phone and shifted her gaze to her employee. Ginny didn't look pleased.

"I've got to help Angelica with her trash problem," she said, and forced a smile. "I'll be back in about ten minutes."

Ginny folded her arms across her chest, but made no comment.

Tricia headed for the door without a backward glance. Why should she feel guilty? After all, they weren't exactly inundated with customers, and Angelica was her sister. She was short-staffed and—

Why was she making excuses—if only to herself?

She crossed the street and found Angelica had piled several black plastic trash bags outside the door to Booked for Lunch, and was already locking the door for the day.

Tricia came to a halt at the edge of the pavement. "You needed help for four bags? Couldn't you just make a couple of trips across the street by yourself?"

Angelica turned hard eyes on her sister. "Don't start with me. I've had a rough day. You should wait on eighty-seven customers while wearing heels and no one to do food prep."

"For heaven's sake, buy some sensible shoes."

"I don't have time to buy new shoes. I don't have time to scratch my—"

Tricia held up a hand to stave off the rest of that statement. "Never mind. I'll grab two of these bags. You get the others."

"Be careful, they're heavy," Angelica warned.

Tricia grabbed the first bag and nearly staggered under its weight. "What have you got in here? Lead?"

"I told you they were heavy. It's paper, mostly. Napkins, milk shake cups, et cetera. And food waste."

Tricia picked up the other bag, holding it at arm's length, her muscles straining under the load. "Let's hurry up. I've got my own end-of-day chores to do at Haven't Got a Clue."

The sisters hefted their bags, waited for a minivan to pass, and staggered across the street.

"Do we have to walk around the block to get to your Dumpster?" Tricia asked.

"It's too far," Angelica said. "We'll walk straight through the Cookery. But for heaven's sake, don't drop those bags. If one of them splits on my carpet—"

The cheerful bell rang overhead as Angelica opened the Cookery's door and led the way. "Coming through," she told a surprised Frannie, who stood at the register with a woman customer.

Tricia plastered on a smile as she nodded a hello to Frannie and the well-dressed tourist who clutched a Cookery shopping bag in one hand. "Hi," she said, and shuffled after her sister.

Angelica had just punched in the code to disarm the security system when Tricia caught up with her. She opened the door. "If my Dumpster's full, we can put the overflow into—" Her words ended abruptly as she gazed at the top step outside the Cookery's back exit.

Tricia remembered the two bowls that had sat on the step earlier that day. "Let's get this stuff into the trash before a bag splits. Remember your carpets," she admonished.

Angelica turned, leveled an icy glare at Tricia, and then hefted her own bags of trash before trundling down the concrete steps to the metal trash receptacle. She grunted as she slam-dunked her two bags of trash into the Dumpster, then took Tricia's from her. Tricia refrained from speaking and followed her sister back up the steps to the store. Angelica paused on the top step, retrieving the empty food bowl and tossing aside what was left in the water bowl.

The store was devoid of customers as she stalked through the aisles of books, halted at the cash desk, and slammed the bowls onto the counter. "Frannie, I've asked you not to encourage that cat to come around, and you've gone and done it again."

Frannie managed a strangled laugh. "Done what?"

"You're feeding that stray cat when I've asked you not to."

"But it's hungry. And the nights are getting colder. I wouldn't want that poor kitty to be hungry, let alone cold."

"It's wearing a fur coat," Angelica stated.

"It's got bare feet," Frannie countered.

Angelica turned to Tricia. "Are you going to help me out here?"

Tricia shook her head and shrugged. "I think it's wonderful that Frannie wants to help this little cat."

"Well, I don't. I don't want a store cat like you've got. Can the two of you understand that?"

"I wasn't trying to catch her so she'd be the official Cookery mascot, although I think it would be a wonderful idea," Frannie said. "I want to take her home—make her my pet."

Angelica blinked. "Oh. Well. I'm sorry. I didn't realize—"

"Jumping to conclusions, eh, Angelica?" Tricia asked.

Angelica leveled a withering glare at her sister. "You stay out of this." She turned back to Frannie. "And how are you going to catch this cat? I didn't see a trap."

"I've got to gain her trust first. I've already talked to Animal Control. They're going to loan me a Havahart trap."

"When?"

"I thought I might try to trap her in the next couple of days."

"Well, make it sooner rather than later, will you? I don't want it hanging around my store. It might have fleas, or some cat disease that could infect my customers."

"Cats don't have—" Tricia started.

Angelica whirled on her. "What about allergies? I could get sued if one of my customers has allergies, enters my store, and has a seizure or something."

"Don't be ridiculous. None of my customers has ever so much as sneezed because of Miss Marple."

Angelica leveled a glare at her sister. "I believe I asked you to stay out of this."

"Fine. I'm leaving. Good luck catching Penny," Tricia said to Frannie.

"Penny?" Angelica asked.

"My cat," Frannie said, and smiled.

Tricia shut the door. The wind had picked up as the sun sank toward the horizon. She wrapped her arms around her chest and stalked back to Haven't Got a Clue. The leaves on the trees were ablaze with color, and already the leaf peepers were descending on the village. That was good for business but bad if she was going to be shorthanded, with Mr. Everett going on his honeymoon.

She was preoccupied with thoughts of the busy week ahead when she caught sight of a Hillsborough Sheriff's Department patrol car moving toward her. She paused, squinting to see who was at the wheel; it was Deputy Placer. She realized that she had hoped it would be Captain Baker.

A gust of wind made her shiver.

Now why would she want to see *him*? Because he'd called and hadn't left a message? Or was it those maddening green eyes that reminded her of her ex-husband, Christopher?

And why think about him at all when she had a date with Russ in just over two hours?

The cruiser rounded the corner as she opened the door to Haven't Got a Clue.

Don't even think about that man, Tricia chided herself as she resumed her position behind the sales counter. But for the next hour, she kept finding herself looking out the big glass display window, on the lookout for another Sheriff's Department cruiser.

EIGHT

Tricia showed up at Russ's house at precisely seven thirty. He met her at the door, looking relaxed in a beige sweater with suede elbow patches. Light from the sconces that flanked the door glinted off his glasses, and his hair curled around his ears. At that moment, he reminded her of an absentminded professor. He leaned forward to give her a kiss. This time his lips actually landed on hers, and she found herself returning the kiss with enthusiasm.

"Whoa, come on in," Russ urged, holding the door open for her, a bit overwhelmed by her greeting.

After a year of what her grandmother would've called "courting," Tricia felt at home at Russ's house. She shrugged out of her jacket and he took it from her, hanging it in the closet. As usual, there was a platter of cheese and crackers on the coffee table in his living room. She usually had to ask him to turn off his police scanner when she dropped by, but this night the scanner was silent. Instead, soft jazz played on the stereo. Perhaps things were looking up on the romance front.

As usual, a cut-glass carafe of sherry and glasses sat on the coffee table as well. Tricia took her accustomed seat on the couch, and Russ soon joined her.

"You look tired. What have you been up to all day?" Russ asked, pouring sherry for them both.

Tricia leaned back against the soft leather. "Besides selling books and annoying Angelica? Thinking a lot about Pammy Fredericks. I even went to see Libby Hirt at the Food Shelf, to ask her if she knew why Pammy would want to talk to Stuart Paige."

He handed Tricia her drink. "And did she?"

"No. Did you know Pammy was a freegan?"

"One of those weirdos that eats garbage?"

"I don't think freegans think of it as garbage. More as salvaged food. It turns out Ginny is a freegan, too, although she doesn't want it getting around."

"I can see why."

Tricia thought about what she'd seen at the Food Shelf's dedication. "Russ, you took a lot of pictures at the ceremony yesterday. Was Pammy in any of them? Maybe—"

He shook his head. "She never made it inside the building. And honestly, why would she think Stuart Page would want to talk to her?"

"She asked everyone in town for a job. Maybe it was that simple."

He shrugged. "Let's not talk about your ex-friend."

That was unusual. The last time there'd been a murder in Stoneham, it was all Russ wanted to talk about—and he'd especially wanted to grill Tricia on what she knew about the victim, who'd been a stranger. Come to think of it, he hadn't even called her after the news of Pammy's death broke.

Russ leaned forward, spread some Brie on a cracker, and offered it to Tricia. She shook her head. "I've been thinking about the future. How I might like to try something different," he said.

"Different?" Tricia asked, and took a sip of her sherry.

He leaned back against the cushions. "I've been thinking about writing a novel."

Tricia nearly choked on her drink. "You, write a novel?"

He looked hurt. "Why's that so hard to believe? I'm a journalist. How hard can it be? Plenty of print reporters have turned to fiction. And when I worked at the paper in Boston, I covered a lot of stories that were ripe for a 'ripped-from-the-news' kind of book."

Tricia could think of more than a few journalists right off the top of her head who'd switched gears to become novelists: Laura Lippman, Carl Hiaasen, Edna Buchanan, Michael Connelly . . . But Russ a novelist? Ha! He was so grounded in facts, she wondered if he would be able to spin a tale and keep up the pace for eighty or one hundred thousand words. Of course, she wasn't about to voice that opinion.

"I wish you luck," she said, and raised her glass. "To your new career."

Russ laughed and raised his glass, touching hers so they clinked. Then he settled back on the couch. "I've been thinking a lot about the future and what it means for us, too."

Tricia's stomach tightened involuntarily. "Oh?"

"Yeah. We've been going out for . . . oh, just about a year now, right?"

Something inside Tricia squirmed. Was she about to be dumped? "Yes."

"We've had some rough times," he admitted.

"I wouldn't say rough," she interrupted, studying his face. "Just not exactly smooth."

"But overall, would you say you've been happy?"

Happy was a relative thing. Still . . . "Yes, I'd say so." Oh, God. Was he about to propose?

Russ leaned in closer. Could he have a velvet-covered ring box tucked inside his sweater pocket? What was she going to say when he pulled it out? She hadn't even considered marrying again. It had only been two years since her divorce. And—

"It's time we had a serious conversation about the future," Russ went on.

Tricia's spine stiffened, and she drew back. "Are you sure this is the right time?"

He nodded and gave her an affectionate smile. "I am."

Tricia leaned forward, grabbed her drink, and took a large mouthful, gulping it down.

Russ laughed. "Am I that intimidating?"

"No, but you sound so serious, which makes me think bad news is coming."

"Not bad news. Good news."

Oh, no. Here it came. And how would she reply to his proposal? *No? Yes? I'm not prepared to answer such a serious question on such short notice?*

The sherry made her flush. "Russ, don't you think you might be rushing things?"

"I've been thinking about this for the past couple of months. Seriously thinking about it. I think it might be time."

Tricia looked away, exhaled. She was not ready for this. She was not ready for this at all.

Russ captured her hands in his, looked deeply into her eyes. "Tricia, I've put the *Stoneham Weekly News* up for sale."

"What?" she asked, and yanked back her hands.

"I know this will come as a bit of a shock, but I might have a job in Philadelphia. There's an opening for a crime beat reporter. I've interviewed for it, and so far I'm their lead candidate."

"What?" she repeated, still unsure of what she'd just heard.

"It's a terrific opportunity. The pay isn't great, but I'm certainly not making a fortune here in Stoneham, either."

"But, but—" She took a breath to steady her suddenly shattered nerves. "I thought you liked being your own boss. I thought you left the rat race in Boston to have a little peace and quiet—and that you'd found it here in Stoneham."

"It's a little *too* peaceful around here."

"Are you kidding? Pammy Fredericks was murdered yesterday."

He waved a hand in dismissal. "It would be more exciting if I could write about it in tomorrow's edition—not next week's. For all I know, the Sheriff's Department will solve it before I can even report her death. I'm tired of running—and writing—stories about lost dogs, stolen laundry, and the occasional DUI, not to mention vandalism—like the mystery of the smashed pumpkins all over town."

No diamond ring. The heck with that—no Russ!

"And you say you've been thinking about this for a while?" Tricia asked, her throat tightening.

"Uh-huh."

"What about me? Did you even consider me while you were making this decision?"

He shrugged. "To tell you the truth, I was surprised to hear you say you'd been happy with our relationship. I always thought you wanted more."

She had. But he never seemed to be listening.

"When will you know about the job?"

"Friday."

That gave her only a few more days to . . . what? Hope? Mourn?

Think about Grant Baker's green eyes?

"Is there someone else?" she asked, dreading the answer.

He laughed. "Hardly. Unless you call running a dying business a mistress of sorts. The truth is, I'm bored here in Stoneham. I need something more stimulating—something this hick village can't offer."

Tricia swallowed. Apparently she couldn't offer that kind of excitement, either.

She hardened her heart. "What if the job falls through? Will you keep on looking?"

"I think so."

"It's too bad you spent time making dinner. I don't believe I want to stay."

"I figured you'd say that, so I didn't bother to make anything."

Tricia's shock at his previous announcement now gave way to anger. "You invited me here, and then you didn't even make dinner?"

He laughed. "What was the point? You're leaving, just as I thought you would."

So now she was predictable!

Tricia rose to her feet and with a supreme effort offered him her hand.

He took it, albeit reluctantly.

"It's been nice knowing you, Russ. Have a good life."

She yanked back her hand and stormed off for his front door.

"Tricia, wait!"

Tricia paused, turned. "What for? You've made your life's plans, and I'm not a part of them. I don't think there's anything more to talk about."

"You're taking this much too seriously."

"If you're talking about our relationship, I did, but I won't from now on."

She grabbed her coat, opened the door, and then yanked it shut behind her, enjoying the sound of its slam. As she stalked off for her car, she noted the door did not open. Russ did not appear, and he did not call for her to return.

Damn him!

"You broke up?" Angelica cried, dismayed. She placed a huge slice of meatloaf on Tricia's plate, plopped down a gigantic helping of garlic mashed potatoes and a sprinkling of peas, about three times more food than Tricia was ever likely to eat. She didn't protest. Food had always been Angelica's way of coping with disappointment.

"I didn't break up. Russ did." Tricia looked down at her plate. "Meatloaf? You never make meatloaf."

"Of course I do. It's Bob's favorite meal." Bob sat across the table from Tricia, and both watched as Angelica dished up her own dinner. "I know you told me Russ was a little slow in the romance department, but dumping you and leaving Stoneham all in one go? Wow!" She picked up her fork and turned a sympathetic frown on Tricia. "You've had a rough week."

"Tell me about it."

"Can I have some mashed potatoes, too?" Bob asked, offering Angelica his plate.

"Sorry, sweetie." She heaped his plate and handed him the gravy boat. He drowned his entire meal in the stuff, making Tricia cringe.

Angelica poured wine for everyone before seating herself next to Bob.

Bob shoveled up a forkful of peas. "I meant to thank you for showing up at the Food Shelf dedication yesterday, Tricia. We had a great showing. I'm sure Russ will give it good play in next week's issue."

"Don't mention Russ," Angelica snapped at him. "Can't you see Tricia's heart is breaking?"

It was anger more than heartbreak that Tricia felt. She cut a tiny piece of meatloaf with her fork, but said nothing.

"Anyway, thanks for showing up," Bob concluded lamely.

Tricia decided to change the subject. "I went to see Libby Hirt today. I've put one of her collection jars on my sales counter."

"Good for you," Bob said, and attacked his mound of potatoes. "You ought to get one, too, Angelica, for the Cookery *and* the café."

"If you say so," she said, and took a sip of her wine.

Tricia swallowed and looked over at her sister. "Boy, there's a lot of onion in this meatloaf."

"Bob likes a lot of onions, don't you, honey? And they're good for you, too," Angelica said.

Tricia took a sip of her wine, turning her attention back to Bob. "Libby Hirt more or less told me that if it wasn't for you, Bob, the Food Shelf wouldn't have its new home."

Bob shook his head, his gaze still riveted on his food. "That's not true. It was a Chamber effort."

"Led by you," Angelica piped up.

"I think it's a wonderful cause. I had no idea there were hungry people right here in Stoneham," Tricia added.

"Yes, well, not everyone who lives here has benefited from the rebirth of the village."

Before Libby's revelation, Tricia could've sworn there wasn't an altruistic bone in Bob's body—especially because he was the one who had made out like a bandit from the village's rebirth, since he owned half the buildings on Main Street. She decided to push harder. "How did you find out about it? What first got you interested in feeding the hungry?"

"There's a need," he said simply. "Angelica, could I please have another slice of that wonderful meatloaf?"

"Of course." She cut him a big slice, sliding it onto the pool of gravy on his plate.

"Yes, but what was *your* interest?" Tricia persisted.

Bob's gaze hardened as he swung to glare at Tricia. "I grew up in a home where you never knew where your next meal would come from—or even if there would *be* a next meal. I know what it feels like to be hungry—not just for a day, but for days on end. Now, are you happy with that explanation, or do I need to elaborate further?"

Tricia was immediately sorry for her pressure tactics. "I'm sorry, Bob. I shouldn't have pressed you. I just wanted to know more about you—understand you. I took the collection jar because I want to help my fellow citizens of Stoneham—and hope I never have to know who needs that help." She said the words, but she thought about Ginny and Brian, wondering what they were eating for dinner that night.

Bob looked away, his lips pursing. Angelica put a hand on his arm, and he turned to her. She gave him a reassuring smile before he turned back to face Tricia. "Thank you."

Tricia found herself smiling back at him, wondering what it had cost him to say those two very powerful words.

NINE

 Miss Marple greeted Tricia at the door, scolding her for leaving her alone for the evening. To placate the cat, Tricia gave her a bowl of cat cookies, and Miss Marple happily tucked in, purring as she ate.

The light on the phone flashed, indicating a message. Tricia pressed the Play button. The call had come in at seven forty-three; caller ID indicated it was a blocked number. A deep, draggy, electronically altered voice said the same four words, over and over again: "Give back the diary."

Diary? What diary?

Was this someone's sick idea of a joke?

Tricia's finger hovered over the Delete button. Should she erase the call? It was probably just a prank. But what if it wasn't? The words "give back" indicated someone thought she had a diary. She didn't. But Pammy had been murdered. Her car had been ransacked after her death. Did she keep a diary? And if she did, why would someone think Tricia had it?

And then she remembered the box of books Pammy had left behind.

The carton was still at the side of the couch, where Pammy had left it just the day before. Tricia picked up the box, setting it on the cocktail table. She shuffled through the titles again. Most of them were old paperback volumes with faded, cracked spines, fiction from one-hit wonders, writers who'd sold one book and nothing else. Today those kinds of authors could be found published (if that was the term) by the likes of Lulu.com. The competition wasn't as fierce back in the early twentieth century.

The only title of note was a first-edition copy of Edith Hull's *The Sheik*, which might draw a bit of notice from the proprietor of Stoneham's Have a Heart romance book-store, but not much. A novel from the Roaring Twenties was bound to read pretty tame in this day and age.

No diary.

Miss Marple entered the living room, sat down on the rug, and proceeded to wash her face.

The books could do Pammy no good now. Tricia folded the carton's flaps back in on each other. The Friends of the Stoneham Library were having a sale at the end of the month. She could donate the books, and perhaps add a few from her own stock that were used or too shopworn to offer for sale in Haven't Got a Clue. She'd box them all up and take them to the library.

The telephone rang. Miss Marple looked at the offending noise, as though daring Tricia to answer it to stop its bleating.

Tricia picked up the extension. "Hello?"

The same draggy voice. "Give back the diary; give back the diary."

"Who is this?" Tricia demanded.

Undaunted, the voice continued reciting the diary mantra. Was it a recording? She slammed the receiver back into its cradle.

Within seconds, the phone rang again. Tricia picked it up. "Give back the diary."

She slammed it back down. Again, it rang within seconds. Tricia let it ring and went back to the kitchen. Again the caller ID registered BLOCKED CALL. She turned off the ringer, but the phone in the living room continued to trill. She stalked across the apartment and unplugged it from the wall. Now only the phone in her bedroom rang. Thirty seconds later, she'd unplugged that, too, and peace reigned.

"Now, who do you suppose thinks I've got Pammy's diary, and why do they want it?" Tricia asked her cat.

Miss Marple jumped up on the cocktail table, settled herself, and began to lick her left back leg.

"Well, I'm glad you're not traumatized by those calls," Tricia said.

Miss Marple ignored her and started on her other back leg.

Tricia's gaze returned to the carton of old books. If Pammy had a diary, she hadn't left it here. Did someone assume Tricia had it just because it hadn't been on Pammy's person or in her car at the time of her death? Good assumption—only it didn't happen to be true. Unless Pammy had hidden the book somewhere in Tricia's apartment. But why would she do that?

Tricia turned on the stereo. One of Russ's favorite mellow jazz CDs was still in the player. She hit the Eject button, and the tray slid out. Back into the jewel case the CD went. She selected one of her favorites instead, hit the Play button, and Irish Woman began a cheery tune.

Her gaze wandered around the room. Well, she had nothing better to do, and decided she'd search the place. Pammy had had unsupervised access to the premises for hours on end while Tricia was working, as evidenced by her lifting one of Tricia's checks.

She looked through the books on her shelves, on top of the bookcases, in all the cupboards, under the bed and other furniture, even checking to see if Pammy might have attached the diary to the undersides with duct tape. Miss Marple followed her from room to room, eager to see what this new game would produce. Tricia found a few of the cat's missing catnip toys and tossed them aside. A delighted Miss Marple flew after them. But there was no sign of a diary.

Finally, having looked through the entire apartment, Tricia returned to the living room, sat cross-legged on the carpet, and scanned the titles on the lower shelves of one of her bookcases. She selected a rather beat-up copy of Agatha Christie's *The Mirror Crack'd*, and opened it to the flyleaf.

I know you've been lonely without all your books. Maybe this one will be an old friend. And maybe I'll be an old friend one day, too. Your new friend, Pammy.

Pammy had given it to her in October of their freshman year at Dartmouth. She'd never said where she found the book, but Tricia had treasured it simply because she *was* lonely, and their tiny dorm room had no room to house even a fraction of her mystery collection.

Old friend.

Pammy had never fit in at Dartmouth. She wasn't Ivy League material. But a family member had pulled strings with some bigwig alumni and had somehow gotten her in. But Pammy had never distinguished herself in or out of college. After graduation, she'd led a dreary, apparently un-eventful life—mostly mooching off of family and friends. What could be in her diary that would cause someone to kill her?

Unless it wasn't Pammy's diary.

She'd wanted to speak to Stuart Paige. Had it been his diary? Tricia frowned. Men kept journals, not diaries. The word "diary" indicated that it was probably written by a woman.

What woman? And if it wasn't Pammy's, where would she have gotten it?

"In a Dumpster?" Tricia asked aloud.

Miss Marple trotted up to her and said, "*Brrrrurp!*"

"I think you're right," Tricia said, and patted the cat on the head.

The question was where had Pammy found the diary? Surely not here in Stoneham. It was possible she'd Dump-ster dived all over New England.

Miss Marple rubbed her little warm body against Tri-cia's knee, head butting her for attention. Tricia reached out and absently scratched the cat's ears. "If there's a diary hidden somewhere in this apartment, I'll eat your kitty treats." Miss Marple raised her head sharply. "I was only kidding."

The CD had stopped playing ages ago. A glance at the clock told Tricia she had better wind things down and get some rest. She had a lot to do come morning. Including taking Pammy's box of books to the library.

"Bedtime," she told Miss Marple, who jumped up on Tricia's queen-sized bed.

As Tricia got ready for sleep, she found herself won-dering about the diary, wondering who it belonged to, and what it could contain that had cost Pammy her life.

TEN

Despite the late night, Tricia was up early the next morning, determined to find a new home for Pammy's box of books—and do it before Haven't Got a Clue opened for business. Since the library opened at nine, that gave her an hour to drop them off before she'd have to open the doors of her own shop.

As she opened the store's blinds, she saw a white-and-gold Sheriff's Department patrol car parked outside of Booked for Lunch. "Uh-oh," she said to Miss Marple, who had jumped up to see if she could catch and bite the blind cord. "I wonder if Captain Baker is visiting Angelica."

Miss Marple batted the plastic weight on the cord.

"I'm going across the road to see what's happening," Tricia told the cat. "Now don't you bite the cord while I'm gone, or you won't get any kitty snacks tonight."

Miss Marple sat back on her haunches, duly chastised.

Tricia didn't bother getting her coat from the peg out back, but grabbed her keys, locked the store, and headed across the street, dodging the remains of another flattened pumpkin.

Inside the shop, Angelica, dressed in full fifties regalia once again, faced Captain Baker, her arms folded defiantly across her chest, her expression determined.

Tricia opened the door and entered, but Angelica paid her no mind.

"Why would I hire Pammy and then kill her? How stupid do you think I am, Captain?"

Baker didn't blink an eye. "Ma'am, I don't know you at all."

"Just for the record, my sister doesn't go around killing people, and neither do I," Tricia blurted.

Baker turned to face her. "Good morning. I'm not accusing either of you of any wrongdoing. I'm trying to find out who killed your friend, and why."

"This town has a veritable vandalism crime wave going on, and all you can do is badger honest citizens trying to make a living," Angelica accused.

"Vandalism? Crime wave?" Baker repeated.

"Haven't you noticed all the smashed pumpkins around the village? The little kids around here must be heartbroken to see their creations reduced to pulp," Tricia said.

"Smashing Pumpkins? Isn't that a rock band or something?" Baker asked, straight-faced.

"It's also mangled squash. And they're everywhere here in Stoneham!"

Baker frowned. "If this apparent crime wave bothers you ladies so much, I'll have one of my deputies look into it."

"Thank you," Angelica said.

Did she miss his condescending tone?

"In the meantime," Baker continued, "if you two think

of anything that might help in this *serious* investigation, I hope you'll share it with me."

Despite his tone, Tricia considered mentioning the phone calls she'd received the night before. But what if someone was just toying with her? She had no proof the diary the person on the phone had mentioned even belonged to Pammy.

And how sincere was Baker? His superior officer, Sheriff Adams, had openly scoffed at Tricia's theories on more than one occasion. And since Baker reported to her, would his opinion be colored by his boss's?

"Is everything all right, Ms. Miles?" he inquired.

Tricia started at the sound of her name. She looked up at the captain. "Excuse me?"

"You look deep in thought. Is there something you want to tell me?"

Tricia shook her head. "No."

Not yet, at any rate.

Baker looked skeptically at her before turning back to Angelica. "Let me assure you that we're investigating every lead we have."

"And how many leads is that?" Tricia asked.

"I'm not at liberty to say. But the ME did find cat hair on the clothes of the deceased."

"Well, there would be. I have a cat. Pammy stayed in my house for two weeks."

"We may want to take hair samples—just in case," Baker added.

"Feel free," Tricia said, disgusted. Then something occurred to her. "Have you informed Pammy's family of her . . . demise?"

Baker nodded solemnly.

"Has anyone stepped forward to claim her body? Have they decided on when to bury her?"

Baker pursed his lips. "They declined to take possession of the body."

"They what?" Angelica said with a gasp.

"I have no further information," Baker said.

Tricia and Angelica exchanged dismayed looks. How could any family fail to step forward and claim their dead? "Did they offer any explanation?" Angelica asked.

Baker shook his head. "Not that I'm aware of."

"What will happen to her?" Tricia asked.

"The body will remain in the county's custody for a limited amount of time, and then they will . . ." He paused, as though considering his words. "They'll dispose of it."

"You mean bury her in an unmarked grave?" Tricia asked.

Baker nodded. "It's not like they trash the indigent. It's done with dignity—just not a lot of flash. The state contributes some funds, but often local funeral parlors donate their services. Now, if you ladies will excuse me, I have work to do." He tipped his hat to them and exited the café.

They watched as he returned to his cruiser and took off, heading north.

Angelica was the first to speak. "I can't imagine what Pammy could have done that her family would abandon her . . . even in death."

"She did say something about hating them—and that the feeling was mutual. But I thought she had to be exaggerating." Tricia tried to swallow her distress. Okay, Pammy was never what she would've called a good or close friend, but to be abandoned so profoundly . . . Suddenly, Tricia had a better appreciation for her relationship with Angelica, despite their often silly differences.

She took a breath to regain her control. "Why was Captain Baker here so early?"

"Goodness knows. He probably doesn't have any leads but wants to look busy."

Angelica headed into her kitchen food prep station, where an array of vegetables was spread across the counter. She picked up a knife and began to slice a beefsteak tomato. "I've got to hire some help before I go crazy."

"You didn't answer my question. What did he want?"

"I think he came here just to annoy me."

"How?" Tricia demanded, frustrated with Angelica's lack of response.

"By asking the same questions he asked the other day. He's wasting his time and mine."

"It's a cop thing. They try to catch you changing your story."

"What story? I told him the truth. I don't have any hidden agenda, and neither do you."

"Did he ask about me?" Tricia asked.

Angelica nodded, set the tomato slices aside, and started shredding a head of iceberg lettuce. "He still can't figure out why you kept Pammy for two weeks."

"Well, he's got company there, because neither can I." Tricia chewed her lip for a moment. "I've got more news. Ginny is a freegan."

Angelica dropped the lettuce. "You're kidding."

"No. She told me yesterday. I've been thinking I should give her a raise. Then maybe she won't have to dig through garbage for her food."

"Don't you go and feel guilty about this," Angelica said, waving a lettuce leaf in Tricia's direction. "We pay our employees far better than any other booksellers in town. And we give them health care coverage, too."

"And more than one of the booksellers resents us for it," Tricia agreed.

"What Ginny's doing isn't illegal, and we're not responsible if people steal our refuse and then eat it." Angelica shuddered at the thought, set the lettuce aside, and started chopping a pepper. "Grab a knife, will you? I need to get those onions sliced for sandwiches."

"Sorry, I haven't got time. I've got an errand to run before I open the store." Tricia glanced at her watch. "If I get going now, I may just make it."

"What about me? I'm shorthanded."

"Call the employment agency."

"I have—every hour on the hour. Nobody wants minimum wage jobs—or those who are willing have been rounded up by Immigration. How's a small business supposed to survive these days?"

Tricia had no answers, and bid her sister adieu.

Ten minutes later, she stood outside the Stoneham Library's white-painted doors, admiring the untouched pumpkins that decorated the entrance. They weren't carved, of course, which was probably why they'd escaped being ruined by the neighborhood hooligans.

The library's door was unlocked at precisely nine. "Tricia!" Lois Kerr, Stoneham's longtime head (and only full-time) librarian, greeted Tricia like an old friend. "It's good to see you. What are you doing here so early?"

"Hi, Lois. I'm dropping off some books for the Friends of the Library's upcoming sale, and I wanted to do it before I opened my store."

"That's very nice of you. The revenue from that sale is a wonderful shot in the arm for us. It seems the library is one of the first line items to go when the Board of Selectmen need to trim the village budget."

"I'm glad to help."

Lois ushered Tricia inside and showed her where to stow the books in the library's small community room. It looked like other citizens of Stoneham had been as generous, for the room was very nearly stuffed to the ceiling along the back wall.

"Thank you so much," Lois said, then lowered her voice and leaned in closer. "I'm so sorry you've had to endure more unpleasantness."

Tricia nodded, but couldn't think of how to reply. At least, with Pammy being a nobody, the press hadn't descended upon Stoneham, as they had when the author Zoë Carter had died in Haven't Got a Clue's washroom.

"I understand the woman you found behind your sister's restaurant was a friend of yours."

"We were college roommates."

Lois *tsk*ed. "You must have been devastated."

"It was very upsetting," Tricia admitted.

Lois shook her head in sympathy. "And to think, she was in here only last week, making copies."

Tricia blinked. "She what?"

"Yes. As it happened, I was the one who helped her. Margaret was helping another patron check out books when your friend came in to use the copier. It jammed, and I had to clear the machine for her."

"Did you see what she was copying?"

"Some kind of journal."

"A diary?" Tricia asked eagerly.

Lois nodded. "Yes, perhaps it was."

"What did it look like? How many pages did she copy?"

"It had a red cover. I'm not certain how many copies she made. Maybe four or five pages. Is it important?"

"Possibly. Did she say anything else?"

"She asked me for directions to the post office."

Tricia stared at Lois for long seconds, her mind racing. "I have to go," she said, and turned.

"To the post office?"

Tricia looked back to see a grin breaking across Lois's face. "You could've been a detective."

"I don't think so," Lois said. "But maybe one day I might write a book about one."

Tricia smiled. "See you later, Lois."

The Stoneham branch of the U.S. Postal Service was located in a neat brick structure on the south end of town, its windows outlined in crisp white paint. A row of four small, cheerful-looking uncarved pumpkins sat outside the door. The Stars and Stripes flapped in the stiff breeze above her as Tricia entered the squat building.

Forty-something Ted Missile seldom wore his official Postal Service uniform. He often came to work in a polo shirt or a Patriots' sweatshirt. On the other hand, his boss, Postmaster Barbara Yarrows, could be counted on to be dressed in full regalia, from her regulation blue blouse down to her official uniform slacks or skirt. She was definitely old-school civil service, whereas Ted had taken the job after being laid off from a tool-and-die shop in Milford. Ted knew everybody in the village and greeted them by name. Barbara didn't. Tricia was glad it was Ted who stood behind the counter, and hoped he would be able to tell her what she needed to know.

Luckily, only one other person was inside the building. Tricia nodded a hello as the woman checked her mailbox, withdrew the contents, locked it again, and headed for the door.

"What can I do for you today, Tricia?" Ted asked. "Do you need a book of stamps? We've got a new 'dead entertainer' stamp out this week."

"Sure, I'll take a book. But I'll have one of those pretty flowered ones, instead."

"Coming right up," he said, and shuffled through the drawer, pulling out the correct one.

Tricia withdrew a ten-dollar bill from her wallet, which he accepted and made change.

"You want that in an envelope?"

"No, I'll just put it in my purse."

"Everything okay with you and your sister?" Ted asked, leaning across the counter and speaking low.

"Okay?" Tricia repeated, playing dumb.

"I mean, about that poor woman being found behind Angelica's new café the other day. You found her, didn't you?"

"Yes," she said, and sighed. It was expected that everybody in Stoneham knew her business and would ask about it—but sometimes it just got *old*. "Poor Pammy. I can't believe anyone would want to hurt her." Except maybe the person she was blackmailing, if that's what she was doing.

"She came in here the other day, you know," Ted said, bouncing on the balls of his feet.

"No, I didn't," Tricia lied.

Ted nodded. "Had a great big envelope filled with papers. Two ounces' worth."

"Ted," Barbara warned from the back of the post office.

"You wouldn't happen to know who the envelope was addressed to, would you?"

Ted looked over his shoulder. Barbara was pointedly

staring at him. Ted turned back to face Tricia and shook his head, but mouthed the words "Stuart Paige."

"The millionaire philanthropist?" Tricia whispered, in mock awe.

Ted nodded and whispered back, "It went priority rate. She even paid extra for delivery confirmation."

"Ted," Barbara warned.

"I understand Pammy got mail here, addressed to General Delivery," Tricia said.

"A few letters. There might be one here now," he said, and bent to paw through a stack of envelopes under the counter. "Yeah, here it is."

Tricia's breath caught in her throat, and she resisted the urge to snatch the letter from his hand. "I don't suppose you could give it to me? I was, after all, her best friend."

Ted shook his head. "No can do. It would be illegal."

"It might be something Captain Baker of the Sheriff's Department might want to see. He's in charge of the investigation."

"Oh, yeah, I hadn't thought of that."

"Maybe you should give him a call," Tricia hinted.

"Ted," Barbara said again, her voice growing more piercing. "There're several boxes that need to be taken out back. Could you do that now?"

Ted jerked a thumb in Barbara's direction. "She's a real witch, ya know."

"No," Tricia said, voice hushed.

"That's just between you and me," he whispered.

She nodded as Barbara called more stridently, "Ted!"

"See you later, Ted. Bye, Barbara." Tricia headed for the door.

*   *   *

As Tricia started back to her store, she reflected on everything she knew about Pammy's activities just before her death. She'd made copies of several pages of the diary, and the diary's cover was red. Big deal. She had no clue as to where the diary was or how to prove the copied pages had been delivered. Had Baker found a delivery confirmation receipt among Pammy's things? If not, where was it? Could it have been in her purse? Tricia could ask Captain Baker, but she still didn't feel she had enough evidence to present to him. And for all his kind words so far, was he likely to accept her word? Ted could back up her story—but so what? No one could prove that Pammy had sent Paige copies of the diary pages. The fact that Lois saw her make copies, and she asked for directions to the post office, and then Ted had weighed and stamped an envelope destined for Stuart Paige, didn't mean the two events necessarily *had* to be related. At least, Tricia had read enough legal thrillers to know a judge would likely rule in that direction.

And who had written the letter to Pammy that she'd never picked up at the post office?

The voice on the phone had said, "Give back the diary."

Again Tricia was faced with the same question: What diary? And give it to whom? The caller hadn't been clear about that, either. Maybe she was supposed to find the diary and the next call would tell her what to do with it. If that was the case, all she could do was wait and see if another call came in. And since the other calls had come at night, she had the whole day to kill before that would happen.

Unless the caller got antsy.

Tricia pulled her car into the Stoneham municipal parking lot and parked it. She was sure that the only books she'd seen in Pammy's car's trunk when Captain Baker had asked her to inspect the contents had been their college yearbooks.

Tricia had once had a little girl's diary bound in pink floral fabric with a little silver lock. Angelica had found it, broken it open, and not only read every page, but relayed its contents to the entire family at Thanksgiving dinner.

She pushed that unproductive thought away, grateful her relationship with her sister had improved since those days.

During the two weeks Pammy had been her guest, Tricia hadn't seen her friend read anything—not a newspaper, not a book, not even the back of a cereal box. In fact, now that she thought about it, why had Pammy been so keen on keeping the box of books? Perhaps to resell? But nothing in the box had been of any real worth. It was probably only the diary that had been valuable—and only to the person who wrote it, or perhaps wanted to destroy it because of its contents.

Tricia locked her car and started walking toward Haven't Got a Clue. Where had Pammy gotten the diary? Dumpster diving? Possibly. It wasn't likely she prowled used bookstores, despite the fact Stoneham was full of them. Most of the booksellers had a specialty: romance, military history, religion . . .

Ginny was waiting outside the door to Haven't Got a Clue—on time for the first time in days. She held a bulky plastic bag and stamped her feet on the concrete, trying to keep warm. "I was beginning to wonder where you were," she said by way of a greeting. "I didn't see your car in the lot, and when I called your cell phone, there was no answer."

Tricia sorted through her keys. "Sorry. I must have it turned off. I had some errands to run." She unlocked the door and entered the store, with Ginny following close behind.

"Give me your coat and I'll hang it up in back," Ginny said.

As she straightened up the pile of bookmarks next to the register, Tricia wondered if she ought to call Captain Baker and tell him about the letter at the post office. She was sure to talk to him again sometime soon—maybe she'd just wait.

She tidied the stack of Haven't Got a Clue shopping bags, and had run out of busywork by the time Ginny came back to the front of the store.

"What's Mr. Everett's schedule for the rest of the week?" Ginny asked.

"Coming and going, I'm afraid. There's a lot to pull together fast if you're planning an impromptu wedding."

"Why don't they just elope?" Ginny grumbled.

"I'm sure they feel this will be the last marriage for each of them. They want their friends to witness it, especially since they have no family."

"I guess."

Mr. Everett knew everyone in town. Would he have known Stuart Paige? Paige didn't have a long history in Stoneham, but he was well known throughout the state. Still, Mr. Everett was the soul of discretion; he wouldn't speak of Paige's reckless past if he knew of it . . . but Frannie Armstrong might. Frannie was the eyes and ears of Stoneham—more so than even Ted Missile.

As it happened, Frannie chose that moment to walk past Haven't Got a Clue on her way to the Cookery. In one hand she clutched her purse and a sack lunch; in the other, a bulky wire cage, no doubt the Havahart trap she'd spoken of the day before.

"Oh, look, Frannie's struggling with that cage. She's been trying to catch a stray cat. I think I'll go help her."

"I can do it," Ginny volunteered.

"That's okay," Tricia said, hurrying around the register and heading for the exit. "Be right back."

"Whatever," Ginny said, as Tricia flew out the door.

She hurried down the sidewalk to catch up with Frannie. "Here, let me help you," she said.

Frannie gratefully surrendered the cage. "Hi, Tricia. This thing isn't heavy—at least it wasn't for the first couple of blocks. But then it seemed like it weighed a ton."

"Think you'll catch Penny today?" Tricia asked as Frannie fumbled with her keys.

"I sure hope so. I hate to think of that poor little cat out in the cold at night. The weatherman says a cold snap is coming down from Canada in the next few days. We might even see a little snow."

"Not until the leaves are past peak, I hope. I'm praying for an onslaught of tourists to arrive any day now."

"I hope so, too. But then there's the Milford Pumpkin Festival on the weekend, and Stoneham will be as quiet as a cemetery at midnight." Frannie opened the door and Tricia followed her into the darkened store. In a moment, the lights were on and Frannie had removed her jacket. "Need any help setting up this cage?" Tricia asked.

"Thank you. I sure hope the first bus is late. Angelica won't be pleased if I'm not ready to open right on time." She glanced at the clock. "Which is in three minutes."

"I can get things ready here at the register if you want to go load the trap and set it up outside."

"Thanks, Tricia."

"It's my pleasure. I want to see little Penny go to her new home."

Frannie paused. "I will put an ad in the *News*—just in case some poor child is missing her kitty. But I'd be lying if I didn't admit I hope no one will claim her."

Frannie had lived alone for a long time. She deserved a little feline pal. "Go on, set up the trap," Tricia said, and gave her friend a smile.

A Granite State bus passed the store's display window, heading for the municipal lot, where it would disgorge its load. Several customers had entered the store by the time Frannie made it back to the sales desk. She rubbed her hands gleefully. "By tonight I might have my very own kitty. I've never had a cat before. My family are all dog lovers, ya see. But I fell in love with your Miss Marple, and now I want one of my own."

"I'll cross my fingers for you."

Frannie looked toward her customers and raised her voice. "Y'all just let me know if you need any help." One of the women nodded and went back to her browsing.

"Frannie," Tricia started, "you've been around these parts a lot longer than I have. What do you know about Stuart Paige?"

Frannie shrugged. "Just what I've read in the papers."

That wasn't what Tricia wanted to hear.

"Although," Frannie added, almost as an afterthought, "it's been said that he was a real womanizer when he was in his early twenties."

Now that was more like it. "Oh?" Tricia prompted.

"I'm sure you've heard about that accident where he was driving his father's Alfa Romeo, crashed it into Portsmouth Harbor, and some woman died."

Why did everyone seem to remember the make of the car more than the name of the victim? "Yes, I did hear that."

"Apparently she was the love of his life. When she died, he turned over a new leaf. Got religion, so to speak, although I don't think he joined any official denomination. But he decided to change his ways and do good in the world."

That sounded like a great plot for a 1950s movie. In fact it was . . . *The Magnificent Obsession*, with Rock Hudson and Jane Wyman. But did that sort of thing happen in the late 1980s? Tricia wasn't so sure. As her grandmother often said, "A leopard doesn't change its spots." There had to be more to the story than that.

If Frannie didn't know, then probably no one else in the village did.

Rats!

A customer ambled up to the register with several heavy volumes. Tricia wrapped the order while Frannie rang it up and made change. As soon as the woman turned her back on them and headed for the door, Frannie picked up where she left off. "I heard Mr. Paige has been staying at the Brookview Inn. In fact, he's taken a room long term. They say he's got some kind of business deal brewing. I'll bet Bob Kelly knows about it."

"And wouldn't tell me if he did."

"That's true. Bob is very loyal to Chamber members."

"But would Paige be a member? He doesn't have a business, or even live here in Stoneham."

"Yet," Frannie added. "I wouldn't know about new members since I left the Chamber. It's always possible Mr. Paige's cooking up something good for the village. Maybe he intends to help people who've lost their jobs. You know, open some kind of light manufacturing plant, or something. Bob was always trying to entice someone to locate a new business here."

That was a possibility, Tricia supposed. Now, could she get past Paige's keepers to talk to the man? "What do you know about his entourage?"

"I don't think he's got bodyguards, if that's what you mean. But I know he travels with at least one or two people—one of them is a secretary or something. Keeps the riffraff from bothering him."

Would Tricia be considered riffraff?

"I wonder if Eleanor could get me in to see him." Tricia envisioned Eleanor at her reception desk at the Brookview Inn. Plump, and in her mid-sixties, she was the soul of the place. She made sure everyone who stayed there enjoyed his or her visit.

"What do you need to see Stuart Paige for?" Frannie asked.

Should she tell Frannie about Pammy trying to crash the Food Shelf's dedication ceremony? Then again, Frannie probably knew all about it.

"My friend Pammy tried to talk to him the day she died. I was just wondering if he knew her."

"I heard about that," Frannie said.

Of course!

Frannie sighed. "But I doubt Eleanor would bother a guest just to satisfy your curiosity. People who stay at the Brookview expect exceptional treatment—and Eleanor sees to it they get it. Even though she considers you a friend, I'm sure her first loyalty would always be to her guests."

"As it should be," Tricia reluctantly admitted.

"That said, there's no reason you can't ask," Frannie said with the hint of a smile on her lips. A customer stepped up to the register. "Can I help you?" she asked.

Tricia noticed the wastebasket under the counter hadn't been emptied. She signaled to Frannie that she would take it out back. She disarmed the Cookery's security system, stepped outside, and looked around. The trap sat neatly to one side, with a heaping bowl of cat food and a water bowl inside the cage. *Come on, Penny!* The Cookery's Dumpster and her own stood side by side in the alley. There was nothing in them to interest one of the local freegans. In addition to speaking to Stuart Paige, Tricia needed to speak to the freegans as well. Had Ginny contacted any of her scavenger friends?

There was only one way to find out.

Tricia emptied the wastebasket, reentered the Cookery, reset the alarm, and saw Frannie was still tied up with customers. Replacing the wastebasket, she waved good-bye to Frannie and headed back to her own store.

Ginny was inundated with customers, and it was more than an hour later when Tricia finally had a chance to speak to her. "I was wondering, have you'd had time to talk to any of your"—she glanced to see if any of the customers was within earshot—"you-know-what friends about Pammy yet."

Ginny shook her head. "No. But we're meeting up with a bunch of them tonight in Nashua. Want to come along? They all agreed it would be okay."

"Definitely. Where and when?"

"I brought a change of clothes so that Brian could pick us up here at seven."

"That doesn't give us any time to have dinner."

"We'll eat on the way."

Tricia felt her cheeks redden.

Ginny laughed. "Don't worry; we're not going to eat what we find tonight. We'll stop and get something along the way."

"Okay. But I've got one question: What does one wear to go Dumpster diving?"

ELEVEN

 By six thirty, business had slowed to a crawl, and Tricia decided she'd best change for her first, hopefully only, food-salvaging expedition. She slipped upstairs to her loft apartment and fed Miss Marple before retreating to her bedroom closet, where she dug out her grungiest jeans and an old sweatshirt, found a pair of sneakers she thought she'd tossed long ago, grabbed her fanny pack, and was ready to go. She and Ginny closed the store a few minutes early so they'd be ready for Brian, who pulled up outside of Haven't Got a Clue at precisely seven.

Ginny climbed into the front seat of his SUV and Tricia got in the back.

"Hey, Tricia," Brian called, "glad to have you with us. Although I have to admit I never thought you'd have the guts to do this."

"Neither did I," she agreed as she buckled her seat belt.

"I'm hoping some of your friends will talk to me about Pammy Fredericks."

Brian checked his side mirror before he pulled away from the curb. "Don't be surprised if they don't."

"Where are we heading?" Tricia asked.

"Nashua. There's better pickings in a bigger city."

They lapsed into idle chitchat for the twenty-or-so-minute ride to the city closest to Stoneham. Tricia's stomach began to knot with each passing minute. Did Brian and Ginny expect her to climb into a Dumpster, paw through rotting, fly-ridden garbage in search of a few potatoes, maybe a loaf of bread, or some dented cans with no labels?

The lights of Nashua were straight ahead, and Tricia found herself swallowing over and over again as dread filled her. What about the germs—the stench? Whatever had possessed her to ask Ginny to take her along on one of their scavenging outings? Oh, yeah, she wanted to talk to Pammy's new friends.

What kind of friends picked through trash and then ate it?

Good grief, she'd almost forgotten she'd been on the receiving end of two meals made with trash, although, much as she hated to admit it, the food had been good, a testament to Pammy's culinary abilities.

Brian pulled the car into the parking lot of a convenience store.

"Is this where we're going to start"—Tricia struggled to find an appropriate word— "picking?"

"Nope. I came here to get a sub. If I get a foot-long, we can share it. What do you like, Tricia, turkey or ham?"

"Turkey, please. Although I'm really not very hungry."

"What do you want to drink?"

"Water."

"I'll have a Coke," Ginny said.

Tricia dug in her fanny pack for her wallet. "Let me give you some money for—"

Brian shook his head. "Nope. You've helped us a lot in the past year. This is on us." He opened the driver's-side door and hopped out of the car.

"This is a big night for us," Ginny said, watching Brian enter the store. "It's the only night of the week we eat out anymore."

"Eat out?" Tricia repeated dully.

"Yeah, it's a big deal for us to even get a sub these days."

In minutes, Brian was back, holding a paper sack cradled in his left arm. He opened the car door and handed the bag to Ginny, who began doling out bottles and little packets of mayonnaise and mustard.

"I had the clerk cut it up into several pieces." He eyed the rearview mirror, looking at Tricia in the backseat. "Maybe it's the lighting, but Tricia looks a little green. I don't think she's too hungry, babe."

Ginny laughed. "Tricia, you're not going to get poisoned. And you won't get sick. And you won't have to go into the Dumpster. I don't."

"You don't?"

"I do the dirty work," Brian said, and pulled at the shoulder of his sweatshirt. "I wear layers. If I get grubby, I can just peel them off, and into the laundry they go."

"We've got gloves and a big bottle of hand sanitizer," Ginny said. "Brian hands us what looks salvageable and we hold on to it until we get back to the car."

Tricia let out a whoosh of air. "Thanks for the heads-up. I feel a lot better about this."

Ginny laughed. "I thought you might. Now, have a piece

of sandwich. It could be a long evening." She handed Tricia a couple of napkins and a slab of the sub.

Minutes later, Brian collected the papers, stuffed them into the sack, and deposited them in the trash receptacle outside the convenience store. Soon after, they were back on the road.

"We're meeting up with our friends behind one of the smaller grocery stores. The bigger stores are open twenty-four hours, and they don't like us poking through their garbage."

They pulled down a side street and parked. "We walk from here," Brian said.

They got out of the car and locked it. Brian stepped around to the back of the SUV, unlocked it, and took out two big backpacks, several canvas shopping bags, and three pairs of gloves, handing them around so that they each had something to protect their hands. He and Ginny donned the backpacks. "Follow me," he told Tricia, his breath coming out in a cloud.

He turned and headed back to the main thoroughfare, leading the way, leaving Ginny to walk side by side with Tricia. Up ahead, Tricia could see several people standing under a light pole on the far side of the street, two of them with battered helmets and bicycles that sported canvas saddlebags on both front and back.

"'Bout time you guys got here," said a familiar female voice from the shadows.

As they approached, Tricia realized with a start that the voice belonged to Eugenia Hirt—Libby Hirt's daughter. No wonder the head of the local Food Shelf hadn't wanted to talk about the freegans. Her own child was one!

Eugenia looked androgynous. She was dressed in black slacks, a black jacket, and black shoes, and a black-and-white bandana covered her blond hair, which was apparently pinned up. She might've passed for a cat burglar. "Hi, Tricia," she called brightly. "Bet you're surprised to see me here."

"A little." Okay, that was a big, fat lie. She was shocked.

"Have you met my dad?" Eugenia asked.

Good grief! Her father was a freegan, too?

A slim, balding man with graying blond hair, probably in his late fifties and also dressed all in black, stepped forward with his hand extended. "Hi, Tricia. Joe Hirt. Eugenia's told me all about you—or at least your dining preferences. The cold tuna plate or cottage cheese with a peach half, right?"

Tricia shook his hand and managed a feeble laugh. "We are what we eat, eh?"

Tricia noticed the bicyclers standing behind him. "This is Lisa Redwood, and Pete Marbello," he said.

They chorused a less-than-enthusiastic hello, and Tricia nodded in greeting. She had never met Lisa before, but Pete looked familiar, though she couldn't place where she might've met him.

"What's the game plan for tonight?" Brian asked.

"We hit this Dumpster," Joe said, jerking his thumb over his shoulder, "and then we try the Italian market down the street." As the oldest, Joe was obviously their leader. The others fell into step behind him, with Tricia and Ginny bringing up the rear.

"Is there some significance to everyone wearing all black?" Tricia asked.

"Doesn't show the dirt," Ginny said. "It does give us a little anonymity, too."

They stepped from the sidewalk into a parking lot. A

mercury vapor lamp overhead cast a bluish glow over the large green garbage receptacle. Tricia wrinkled her nose and sniffed, grateful for the chilly night. She caught an unmistakable whiff of something vaguely sour, but not entirely off-putting.

"Who wants the honors?" Joe asked.

"It's my turn," Pete said. Brian stepped forward and gave him a leg up, as though he was about to mount a horse, and Pete climbed into the Dumpster. He landed on a pile of black plastic trash bags, piled high, sinking down so that only the top half of his body was visible. He pulled a flashlight from his pocket, grabbed a bag of trash, and loosened the twist tie that held it closed. Next, he shone the light into the bag. "Jackpot!" he called, and lifted a loaf of bread into the air. "The sell-by date is tomorrow." He tossed the bag down to Brian, who distributed the booty among them all, including Tricia.

"I really don't want—"

"Shush!" Ginny warned her.

Pete had already opened another bag, wrinkled his nose, and twisted the tie once again. "Paper trash." He grabbed another bag, and another, until he'd gone through most of them. By the time he was done, they'd collected the bread, nearly two dozen potatoes, several heads of what Tricia would have said was questionable lettuce, eight or ten jars of pickles, eleven boxes of crackers, and half a dozen soft tomatoes.

Pete jumped down from the Dumpster and joined Lisa. "Not bad for the first hit."

Joe pointed toward the other side of the lot. "Come on. The evening's getting away from us." Everyone followed.

"This is your chance to talk to the others," Ginny whispered, giving Tricia a poke.

Pete and Joe were in the lead this time, with Brian and Lisa following. Tricia caught up with Eugenia.

"How do you like your first time out, Tricia?"

"It's . . . interesting," she said. "I wasn't sure what to expect. What will you do with all that food?"

"I don't take it to the diner, if that's what you're worried about. And my mom won't accept it at the Food Shelf, either."

"Do you eat it at home?"

"Dad and I do. Mom . . . well, she inspects everything really carefully before she'll touch it. And she washes the jars and cans with a bleach solution in case they've got germs. She's very picky."

"What got you interested in being a freegan?"

"The Food Shelf, of course. I've always known about people going hungry. You can't believe the waste that goes on in this world—and especially this country. Did you know that grocery stores alone throw out between two and three percent of their food every week? That doesn't sound bad until you realize it's like billions and billions of pounds of edible food that ends up in landfills."

Sadly, Tricia could believe it.

"Dad and I tried to be conservationists, too. We went hunting a few times—but were too squeamish to actually kill something and then eat it. Now we just shoot clay pigeons."

"I hear Pammy Fredericks accompanied you guys on several of your . . . forays."

Although her face was half hidden in shadow, Tricia saw the frown that had settled across Eugenia's mouth. "She wasn't a real freegan—she was a scavenger. She didn't care about keeping viable food out of landfills. She didn't care about making the planet a better place to live. All she cared about was money. Getting something for nothing—or getting something she hadn't earned or didn't deserve."

"And you got all that from a couple of conversations?"

Eugenia laughed. "That's all it took."

"What made you think she only cared about material things?"

"The way she talked. She kept saying she was going to come into a lot of cash—that she'd be set for life."

"Where was she getting this money?"

Eugenia shrugged. "Beats me. I didn't really care. I told Dad I didn't want her coming with us anymore. And the next thing you know, she was dead."

Tricia stopped in her tracks.

Eugenia paused and turned. "Hey, don't look at me like that. I didn't mean he killed her. I just mean he told her she couldn't come with us on another run. And as it turned out, she was dead before we went foraging again."

Tricia's dinner sandwich suddenly lay heavy in her stomach.

"Hey, come on, guys," Ginny called, and Eugenia started walking again. Tricia followed.

Eugenia was young. She wouldn't understand what— oh, God, did Tricia dare admit that she and Pammy were on the cusp of middle age?—life could force you to do.

She didn't like to think about it. Instead, she forced herself to think outside of the box.

Lisa looked to be five or six years older than Eugenia. Perhaps she had a different perspective on Tricia's ex-roommate.

Lisa, accompanied by her bike, walked beside Ginny. They laughed about something, their canvas bags swinging as they walked. They looked happy. They were young and carefree and, for a couple of minutes at least, Ginny seemed not to be bothered by the yoke of debt that bogged down her and Brian, something that seemed to preoccupy her during working hours.

Tricia picked up her pace to shadow them.

"Do you think we'll score any protein tonight?" Ginny asked Lisa.

"We got those steaks last week. There's a chance they didn't sell out what they had, and we'll score two weeks in a row."

Eating marginal meat? The thought made Tricia cringe.

"I marinated ours overnight, and they were fork tender," Lisa went on.

"We did ours on the grill. They were pretty good, but I think next time I'll try a marinade, too." Ginny seemed to sense someone dogging her heels and looked over her shoulder. She gave her boss a nod and turned back to Lisa. "Did you know Tricia was friends with Pammy—the old girl who got killed earlier this week?"

Old girl? Pammy was two months younger than Tricia!

"She came picking with us a couple of times," Ginny went on.

"I remember," Lisa said irritably. "How could I forget? The stupid cow never shut up."

Ginny tossed an uneasy glance over her shoulder and cleared her throat. "Tricia wants to know if we remember anything she could've said or done that might've pissed someone off—maybe got her killed."

"That woman pissed off the general population simply by breathing," Lisa said. "Why Joe ever let her join us, I don't know."

"How did Pammy know how to find you guys?" Tricia asked.

Lisa shot an annoyed look over her shoulder. "I'm sorry your friend died, but she was a bitch. She didn't have a clue about what we're all about."

"Which is?"

"We're making a statement. This country is awash in waste. For example, the U.S. accounts for four percent of the world's population, yet we consume almost a quarter of the world's energy resources."

Tricia had to bite her tongue to keep from saying, *Yada, yada, yada*. "That's no reason for someone to kill her," she said instead.

Lisa stopped, turning to face Tricia. Her expression held no warmth. "Pam Fredericks was a greedy user. She wanted more than her fair share of what we found, and she didn't stop at picking up food."

"What else was she looking for?"

Lisa pursed her lips, her eyes narrowing. She glared at Tricia for long moment, then turned and resumed walking.

"Lisa, what else?" Tricia insisted.

"Never mind," she called over her shoulder.

Tricia hurried to catch up. "Ginny?" she implored.

"I can't make her talk," Ginny whispered. "Try asking Joe or Pete."

"Are they likely to share anything she told them with me?"

"I don't know," Ginny answered. "Pammy wasn't well loved by our little group."

"Could she have made contact with any other freegans?"

"It's possible, but I don't think there are any others in Stoneham. And she didn't seem to stray too far while she was in town."

Lisa caught up to Pete. They conversed in hushed tones.

Was she telling him that Tricia wanted information on Pammy? If so, was he likely to clam up as well?

Joe and Brian veered off the sidewalk, down a side street.

"We're almost at the Italian market," Ginny said.

"What are we likely to find here, besides steak?"

"They don't toss out a lot of jars or cans. The meat we found last time was freezer burned, which means they tossed it in their freezer when the expiration date got too close, then they didn't end up selling it. But it was edible. It was still partially frozen when we found it. We keep a cooler in the car so we can keep perishables like that fresher."

Tricia found it hard to hide her revulsion.

"Don't let the others see you making faces," Ginny warned, "or they're likely to ask you to go back to the car."

"It's hard for me to understand why you're doing this."

"We've been over it before."

"I know. I'm sorry. I'll be on my best behavior for the rest of the evening. I promise."

Once again, a bright light shone over the Dumpster, bathing it and the small parking lot in a soft glow. This time it was Brian who did the dirty work and climbed into the large metal receptacle.

"Don't you worry about rats?" Tricia whispered to Ginny.

"Why do you think I don't jump in the Dumpster myself?"

The others stood around, waiting for Brian to make a judgment call on the contents of the trash bin. He opened a black trash bag. "Anybody want stale cookies?"

"I'll take them," Lisa said, and he tossed the bag down to her.

"Having fun?" Eugenia asked Tricia.

"It's certainly a learning experience."

"There's some skanky lettuce here, but the celery looks passable," Brian said, and tossed rubber-banded bunches down to Joe, who distributed it around the group.

"I hope we find more usable vegetables. I've got a hankering to make some soup tomorrow," Eugenia said, and stamped her feet against the encroaching chill.

"Do you guys ever worry about being chased off?" Tricia asked.

"Sometimes it happens. Sometimes neighbors will call the cops, thinking we're trying to break in or steal something more valuable than veggies and jars of pepperoncini. The grocery stores could prosecute us for trespassing, but most of them don't want to draw attention to the amount of stuff they're putting into the waste stream."

"Have you ever done this during daylight hours?"

"I have," Eugenia admitted, "but it isn't as much fun. People can be cruel and say nasty things to you, too. I prefer to do it under the cover of darkness, but you need a really good flashlight."

"Do you ever jump in the Dumpsters?"

"Oh, sure. My dad and I have been doing this for years." She watched as Brian sorted through another bag of trash. "I'm sorry if I was short with you a while back. My mom wouldn't be pleased."

"Your mom's a great lady. I really admire the work she does for the Food Shelf."

"I do, too. About your friend . . . she tagged along with Dad the last couple of times we went out—probably because they're closer in age. You might want to ask him about her."

"Thanks, Eugenia." *And I'll give you a nice fat tip the*

next time I'm at the diner. Now she had to figure out how to get Joe away from the crowd and willing to talk.

"Jackpot!" Brian called, and brandished a bottle of virgin olive oil, which he held high over his head. "Looks like there're eight of them here."

"You're the one in up to your knees, so you get the extra one," Joe said.

Brian passed the bottles down to everyone.

"I think that's about all we're going to get here tonight," Brian announced, and climbed over the edge of the Dumpster.

"Where to now?" Tricia asked Ginny. "Do we go get coffee or something?"

"That kind of negates the reason we're out here," Lisa said snidely. "We're trying to leave a smaller carbon footprint—not pollute the world with more paper cups from take-out joints."

Tricia figured she'd better not mention the sub she, Ginny, and Brian had eaten before they'd joined up with this group—or the papers the sandwich had been wrapped in, the bag it came in, the plastic bottles they'd drunk from, and the disposable napkins that had all entered the convenience store's trash bin.

"There *are* restaurants that use china mugs, Lees," Eugenia said.

Lisa merely sniffed.

"We could try Hannaford," Pete suggested, changing the subject. "Last week we got those pineapples, oranges, and lemons that were in pretty good shape."

Joe shook his head. "I prefer to stick to smaller markets. Besides, I'm ready to call it a night."

"Well, I'm not," Lisa said sourly. "Besides, the gas Brian used to get here is too expensive to drive all this way and only look in a couple of Dumpsters."

"I think we'll call it quits, too," Brian said, backing up Joe.

"You guys just don't get it," Lisa said with a shake of her head, and mounted her bike. "Come on, Pete," she called over her shoulder. She shoved off and pedaled toward the main drag once more.

"Sorry, guys," Pete said with a shrug, got on his own bike, and started off after his girlfriend. "PMS or something, I guess. See you next week?"

"You got it," Brian said.

The five of them looked at one another. "Not much of a score tonight," Ginny said.

"I dunno," Eugenia said, and jerked a thumb toward the street, bidding the others to follow. "That olive oil alone was worth the trip. That size bottle retails for over ten bucks. You guys got three, and Dad and I got two—that more than makes up for the fuel we used to get here."

Ginny fell into step behind her, with Brian tagging along behind. That left Tricia right where she wanted to be—walking alongside Joe. "You've got a really great kid there," she told him.

"Thanks. We think so."

They walked for a few moments in silence before Tricia spoke again. "Did Ginny tell you why I wanted to tag along?"

"Something about wanting to see what your friend was up to. Sorry about your loss."

She nodded. "Thank you. I thought I knew Pammy. We'd been friends for a long time. But—when it came down to it, I really didn't know her at all. Did she tell you much about her life?"

"Just that she was broke, but she thought that was going to change."

"Yes, I've heard that from more than one person. Did she say how that was going to happen?"

Joe shook his head. "Seems to me she was the type of woman who always had a harebrained scheme she was working." He stopped. "Sorry, I didn't mean to disrespect your friendship with Pam."

Tricia managed a grim laugh, and they began walking again. "Don't worry. You're not the first one to think that about Pammy. She always had bad luck. Always seemed one step ahead of the repo man."

"It's sad, really. A woman like that. Very few friends, a family she was on the outs with."

"She told you all that?"

He nodded. "Do you know her family?"

Tricia thought back. In all the years she'd known Pammy, she'd never met any of her family. "No. But she always said they didn't have two nickels to rub together. I can't imagine why she thought she was about to come into money. She certainly didn't mention it to me."

He shrugged.

"And why was she hanging around Stoneham for so long?"

"The night I met her, she told me she wanted to attend the Food Shelf's dedication. The thing is, it kept getting delayed. Something to do with the HVAC systems. Libby could tell you why."

Was that why Pammy had stayed so long in Tricia's apartment?

"Libby told me Pammy was eager to see Stuart Paige at the Food Shelf dedication," Joe continued. "Coming into money—making a scene to meet a rich man. That almost sounds like a formula for blackmail."

"Yes, I thought of that, too," Tricia said. They resumed walking. "I didn't see you at the dedication."

"No, I had to work."

"And where's that?"

"A public relations firm here in Nashua."

"That's a bit of a commute—a whole fifteen, twenty minutes," Tricia said, and laughed.

"Ideally, I'd like to work in Stoneham, but there's not much in my line of work in a small town—except for people wanting freebies. And Libby would never leave Stoneham. I've got an old diesel Volkswagen that I converted to run on cooking oil. I get all I need from the Bookshelf Diner and a couple of fast-food restaurants between Stoneham and Nashua. It works out pretty cheaply, and I'm not dependent on foreign oil."

"Something I wish I could say. But then, I don't travel far from Stoneham these days, myself. In fact, I usually fill up my gas tank only a couple of times a month."

"You're a good citizen of the Earth."

Tricia laughed. "Thanks. And was Pammy? She apparently liked to recycle things. I understand she was an antiques picker at one time. My sister says she knew about and was good at restaurant food prep—not that she did it for Angelica for more than an hour or so before she was killed."

Joe shook his head. "I can't believe we've had three murders in Stoneham in the last year. It bucks the odds."

Tricia didn't want to get into the old "town jinx" discussion—especially since she'd been the one to find all three bodies—and quickly steered the conversation away from the topic. "I just can't imagine why she wanted to see

Stuart Paige. You mentioned blackmail. Did Pammy give you any hint of what she was up to?"

"Not a word. We mostly talked recipes. And don't forget, we were barely acquaintances. I only met the woman twice, when she came along on our forays."

"How did she do that? She and Ginny weren't pals, so I can't imagine her inviting Pammy along. In fact, she would've told me if she had."

"I'm pretty sure it was Pete who first invited her. I think she ran into him one night in back of the convenience store in Stoneham."

Pete—the one person Tricia hadn't had a chance to talk with on this little adventure. She couldn't even remember his last name. But Ginny would know. She'd ask her as soon as they got back to the car. If she could track Pete down, she might finally find out exactly what Pammy was doing in Stoneham. Then again, he might be as clueless as the rest of them. That thought didn't fill her with confidence.

She'd get no more out of Joe or Eugenia, and figured she might as well make small talk to kill the time until they got back to the car. "Tell me more about your job," Tricia said.

"I write press releases for a nonprofit. Public service announcements. The whiz kids get all the interesting assignments. I do a lot of volunteer PR for the Food Shelf, too."

It sounded pretty boring to Tricia.

Joe continued with his job description, but she only half listened, preoccupied with her disappointment at not finding out more about Pammy and her recycling lifestyle. Before she knew it, they were standing behind Brian's SUV. He'd already opened up the back, and he and Ginny were stowing their finds. Tricia handed him the canvas bag she held.

"You really need to get a more fuel-efficient car, Brian," Joe said.

"Yeah, yeah—but this thing's paid off. I can't afford a new loan—not with the house sucking up every spare cent we have."

"Don't start this argument again," Eugenia told her father, and gave Ginny a hug. "See you next week, if not before."

"Sure thing."

Eugenia leaned in to give Brian a quick kiss on the lips. He didn't seem startled by it, but Tricia could tell by Ginny's expression that she wasn't happy about it.

"Good night, Tricia," Eugenia called.

Joe waved a good-bye to them all, and he and his daughter continued walking.

Brian gave the button on his key ring a squeeze, and the SUV's doors unlocked. Ginny waited until they were in the car to speak. "You let her kiss you again."

"Hey, babe, we have a guest. Can't we discuss this at home?"

Ginny exhaled a snorting breath. Tricia was glad she wouldn't have to hear the argument that would probably break out the minute they dropped her off in front of her store.

They buckled their seat belts and Brian started the car, steering the vehicle away from the curb and heading for the main drag once more.

No one spoke for quite a while. Brian hadn't even turned on the radio to extinguish the tension.

The lights of Nashua were fading behind them when Tricia finally broke the quiet. "Thanks for bringing me along, guys."

"Did you find out what you needed to know?" Brian asked.

"Joe told me that Pammy started coming to these little

jaunts at Pete's invitation. Of course he told me this *after* Pete and Lisa left."

"Was it Pete?" Brian asked. "I thought it was Joe." He shrugged. "Guess I'm wrong."

A number of cars whizzed by in the opposite direction.

Tricia frowned. "Is there some way I can get hold of Pete? I'd like to talk to him—without Lisa being around. I think she took a dislike to me."

"She'd dislike anybody who was Pammy's friend," Ginny said.

"Why?"

"That woman was a terrible flirt. Just like Eugenia," Ginny grated.

Pammy had never given Tricia that impression. Or maybe it was just perceived that a woman alone was man-hungry.

"Do you have a number where I could reach Pete?"

"Sure," Brian said. "But you can look it up yourself. He works at the convenience store in Stoneham."

No wonder Pete had looked familiar—he'd probably waited on Tricia more than once. Had he found Pammy digging in that store's Dumpster? "I assume he works the day shift?"

"He works whenever he feels like it. His father owns the store."

Tricia felt the SUV accelerate.

"Why are you going so fast?" Ginny asked.

"There's a car speeding up behind me."

"So, let him go past," Ginny said.

Tricia looked behind her.

Brian pulled the car closer to the side of the road, but the car didn't go around them. Instead, it rode mere feet from the back bumper.

"What's this guy playing at?" Brian asked nervously.

"We've got an SUV—outrun him!" Ginny cried.

Brian steered back onto the road and gunned the engine. The SUV took off like a Formula One car, leaving the smaller car to eat its dust, until it was a couple of pinpricks of light on the darkened road.

"Yee-ha!" Brian called.

Suddenly another set of lights pulled onto the highway. Not just headlights, but blue flashing lights.

"Oh, no," Brian groaned as he braked the SUV. "Here comes a ticket. And a couple of points on my license."

He pulled over to the side of the road and hit the button on his armrest. The driver's-side window slid down, and he dug for his wallet so he could fish out his license. The Sheriff's Department cruiser pulled up behind them, its lights eerily piercing the surrounding landscape.

Another car whooshed past them, and Tricia could've sworn she heard someone yell from its window, "Suckers!"

TWELVE

Tricia let herself into the Cookery, then trailed through the darkened interior to the back of the store and the stairway that led to Angelica's loft apartment. Then she thought better of just appearing on her sister's doorstep—or threshold, or whatever you wanted to call it.

She reached into her pocket and withdrew her cell phone. She pushed the button that autodialed Angelica's number. It was answered on the first ring.

"Trish? Where are you?"

"Inside the Cookery. I wanted to let you know I'm on my way up. That is, if it's convenient." She hadn't seen Bob's car parked outside, but she didn't want to interrupt a romantic interlude—should one be going on.

"Sure, come on up," Angelica said cheerfully. "Are you hungry? I was just going to make some cocoa and cinnamon toast."

"Cinnamon toast?" Tricia repeated, brightening. "I haven't had that since I was a kid."

"Then you're in for a treat. I'll put another two slices of bread in the toaster. Hurry on up."

Angelica had unlocked the door, which was open for Tricia. She could already smell the heavenly aroma of the ultimate comfort food as she entered the hallway and followed it to Angelica's kitchen.

"Sit down," Angelica encouraged. She was clad in a pink robe and matching bunny slippers, with her hair hanging in damp ringlets around her shoulders. She'd been letting it grow out. Tricia wasn't sure that was a good idea, since Angelica looked great in short hair, but it did suit her when she wore it up, dressed in her vintage togs while working at the café.

Tricia peeled off her jacket and settled at the dining room table just as Angelica thrust a mug of cocoa at her. She could smell the nutmeg Angelica had no doubt just grated on the top. She took a sip, savoring the taste. Before she could swallow, Angelica settled a plate of cinnamon toast in front of her.

"Hey, you made this for yourself. I can wait for the new toast to pop up."

"Don't be silly. Eat. You're too skinny."

"Hey, I work at it."

"You may as well enjoy yourself. Life is too short to deny yourself anything. Particularly diamonds."

"Diamonds. Where did that come from?"

"Oh, I've been thinking about Mr. Everett and Grace. I think I'm going through marriage withdrawal," she said, and glanced at the ringless fourth finger on her left hand. "I have to figure out what to give them for a wedding gift. What are you giving them?"

"I haven't decided yet, either."

Angelica leaned aginst the island counter and took a sip of her cocoa. "What do you give the elderly bride and groom? A membership in AARP?"

"I'm sure one or both of them already has that."

"Do you think Grace is registered anywhere?"

"No. I'm sure they don't want or need anything."

"Maybe I could make some of the food. I've never made a wedding cake before."

"And when would you have time to do that?"

Angelica shook her head. "I'd make the time. Now, weren't you going out with those freegan heathens or something tonight? Tell me all about it."

"Yup," Tricia said, and took a sip of her cocoa. This was no ordinary hot chocolate. Besides the nutmeg, something else had to have been added. It tasted too rich, too thick, and . . . extremely fattening. And for once, she wasn't going to worry about it.

"I did go along with Ginny and her friends. So far, they haven't convinced me to bypass the grocery store checkout. I prefer to buy the food I eat, thank you. But I was surprised that some of the stuff they found didn't look all that bad."

Angelica wrinkled her nose. "Did they smell?"

"The Dumpsters? Not too bad. The chilly temperatures keep the odor down, but I wouldn't want to do this on a hot summer night. And I didn't see any rats, which was really good, because I'm sure I would've freaked out." She gazed at the little bubbles on the sides of her mug. "I feel so bad that Ginny and Brian feel they have to do this to keep their expenses down. That house they bought really turned into a money pit."

"I am so thankful I didn't end up with it. I think I've made the right decisions since I came to Stoneham, what with renting the storefront and then living above it. My accountant is pleased, at any rate."

"It's certainly been a financial drain for them. And added to that, Brian got a speeding ticket on the way home."

"What was he speeding for?"

"Somebody was fooling with us. Brian speeded up, and the next thing you know—"

"Been there, done that!" Angelica said.

"Sometimes I *do* feel like the village jinx." Tricia sighed. "I told Brian I'd pay for the ticket, but that won't help him if his car insurance goes up. I wish I could help them more."

Angelica frowned. "Tricia, will you stop feeling guilty? You've already done too much for Ginny. You pay her well above minimum wage; you pay for her health insurance; and you give her bonuses at the drop of a hat. What next? Are you going to adopt her?"

"Don't be absurd."

"Well, really," Angelica said, scowling. "Tricia, you are just too nice for your own good."

"Ginny has been an exceptional employee. She didn't know the mystery genre when I hired her, but she's done enough reading and research to—"

"Fake it!"

Tricia exhaled a long breath. "Possibly. But the fact remains, she's an asset to me. When you were having employee problems at the Cookery, you wanted to steal her from me."

"Where did you get that idea?" Angelica asked, offended.

"Ginny told me."

Angelica let out several short breaths, as though she didn't know what to say. "She must have misinterpreted our conversation."

"What part of 'I'll give you a dollar more an hour than Tricia is paying you' did she misunderstand?"

Angelica opened her mouth to answer—apparently thought better of it—and shut it again. Her scowl deepened. "She wasn't supposed to tell you."

"Sorry, but she felt no loyalty to you."

"And I paid her for a week's work," Angelica groused.

"Which she more than earned. You know your profits rose that week."

"Maybe," Angelica grudgingly agreed. "Nevertheless, your profits would be higher if you didn't share the wealth so generously with your employees. You're not running a charity, you know."

Tricia's accountant had voiced the same opinion on more than one occasion. "You're one to talk. You pay Frannie well, too."

"Well, she deserves it."

"Let's get back to the main subject."

"Which I've forgotten at this point," Angelica said. "Oh, yes, what did you learn on your little field trip?"

"Not as much as I'd hoped. Pammy was considered a flirt. Eugenia Hirt didn't like her, which makes me think Pammy might have batted her eyes at the girl's father. Ginny thinks Eugenia is a flirt because she kissed Brian on the lips. And that Lisa I met was so crabby she might turn red and walk sideways."

"Eugenia's last name is Hirt? Like Libby Hirt?" Angelica asked.

Tricia swallowed a bite of toast, and nodded. "Libby's her mom. Her dad works at a PR firm in Nashua. Sounded deadly dull. I wonder why he got into Dumpster diving. I should've asked him that. Wouldn't you know, I talked to everyone but the person who invited Pammy to come along on these scavenging trips. His name is Pete Marbello, and he works at the convenience store on the highway. I'm going to give him a call tomorrow." She glanced at the kitchen clock. "And if I want to be half awake tomorrow, I'd better get home now."

She grabbed her cup, gulped the last of her cocoa, and rose from her seat.

"I'll walk you to the door," Angelica said, and popped the last bite of her toast into her mouth.

Angelica followed Tricia down the stairs and through the darkened shop. "Come by the café for lunch tomorrow. Jake's making potato-leek soup—from my recipe, of course."

"Okay. See you then."

Before Tricia could exit, Angelica pulled her into a hug and planted a kiss on her forehead. "Be good—and if you can't be good, be careful," she said, and closed the door behind Tricia.

She walked the ten or so feet to her own store and let herself in, threading through the shop and up the stairs to her own loft apartment.

Miss Marple was behind the door, and scolded Tricia for leaving her alone for so long.

"Well, I'm home now, and it's time for bed," she told the cat.

As though agreeing with that statement, Miss Marple turned and led the way through the apartment to the bedroom that overlooked Main Street.

As Tricia reached for the light switch, she noticed the light blinking on her phone—indicating she had missed several calls. No doubt her crank caller. She didn't feel up to listening to the messages and flipped off that light, then headed for the living room to do the same.

She'd just bent to turn off the last light when she heard what sounded like a *thwok* in the room ahead of her. She extinguished the lamp. The apartment was silent. But she had heard something. Fumbling in the dark, she stayed out of the line of the row of windows that faced the street. Sure enough, several small holes dotted one of her windows in a characteristic pattern she recognized: a small entrance hole with a much bigger exit hole—classic BB shots. Not exactly a lethal weapon, but maybe the shooter had wanted to scare rather than hurt her. After all, she hadn't even been in the room when the shots had been fired. If someone had wanted to hurt or kill her, they could've done it as she walked from the Cookery to her own store.

Tricia kept to the far side of the line of windows and stared into the darkness. Lights blazed in the windows of the top floors of the buildings across the street. Like her, some of the shopkeepers lived above their stores; the rest of the space was rented out as apartments or offices. She didn't for a minute believe one of her neighbors would pull such a stupid stunt, and there were no preteen boys or even teenagers living on Main Street—just the demographic that would own such a firearm. All those buildings sported metal fire escapes, as her own did. Someone could have climbed a fire escape, broken into an office and gotten onto the roof, taken a few potshots—and was probably already long gone.

She hoped.

For some reason, she wasn't really afraid—more annoyed, perhaps. Someone had decided to crank up the fear factor. If the person on the phone could shoot at her windows with a BB gun, they certainly could have done so with a high-powered rifle. And thanks to the Supreme Court, any crank with a desire to start his own well-armed militia had the go-ahead from the country's top lawmakers.

She should probably call the Sheriff's Department and report this. But at this time of night, she'd have to deal with some deputy pulled off patrol. She glanced at the glowing numerals on her bedside clock. She didn't want to wait the hour or more it might take for one to arrive, and decided instead to just call Captain Baker in the morning.

Tricia sidled along the wall, reached for the drapery pull. Before she did, she peeked out the window one last time . . . and saw a dark shape scurry into the shadow-filled doorway of Booked for Lunch. Could it be the shooter?

Heart pounding, she watched and waited.

A car rolled by, its headlights cutting through the darkness and then receding into the gloom.

Suddenly the figure darted out—its arms raised above its head—and hurled something round into the street.

The pumpkin exploded onto the asphalt. Tricia stared at the resulting mess, entranced—and missed seeing where the figure went.

She watched and waited as another car drove past, skirting what was now just refuse.

After a good five minutes with no other sign of the vandal, she pulled the cord and the curtains closed across the bank of windows. Even with them closed, Tricia decided not to turn on her bedside lamp. As she undressed and got ready for bed in the dark, she kept thinking about the demolished jack-o'-lantern, wondering if the shooter and the vandal could be the same person. She also contemplated the holes in her bedroom window, and worried what her caller's next move would be.

THIRTEEN

"Ms. Miles," Captain Baker said firmly, "you should have called the Sheriff's Department as soon as someone shot at your windows. We're here to protect the citizens of Stoneham."

Tricia glanced out the front window of Haven't Got a Clue to where Baker's cruiser was parked. "I've always wondered about that. The other towns around here all have their own police departments. Why does Stoneham depend on the Sheriff's Department for protection?"

"The Board of Selectmen dissolved the Stoneham Village Police during the early 1990s, when the village was going broke. They never voted to reinstate it. But that's beside the point. You should have called us last night."

"What for? By the time a deputy arrived, the shooter would've been long gone." Tricia sounded a whole lot braver than she'd felt the night before, and she'd spent a good part of the night lying in bed and worrying. "Besides," she continued, "I haven't had a very warm reception from the Sheriff's Department in the past."

"I know about your past difficulties with Sheriff Adams. That's why *I'm* investigating Pamela Fredericks's murder. I want you to call my office—day or night—if you have anything to report. If there's an emergency, they can get hold of me in a matter of minutes."

Tricia exhaled a breath. "Okay. As a matter of fact, I do have something else to report. For the last couple of days I've been receiving"—she hesitated; they weren't really threatening calls—"annoying phone calls."

Baker's eyes narrowed. "How many have you received?"

Tricia shrugged. "Eight or ten." Her voice grew softer, as though she expected a rebuke. "Maybe more."

Baker looked ready to explode. "I don't suppose you saved any of them," he managed through gritted teeth.

"Just one. It's on my home answering machine."

"Is that a different number from the shop?"

"Yes."

"I suppose you're listed in the phone book as well."

"Just under my last name and first initial. But it's a P for Patricia, not T, and everyone around here knows me as Tricia."

"It doesn't matter, if the caller knows your address. Now, do you mind if I listen to this call?"

"Not at all. I'll show you the holes in my window, as well. If you'll follow me."

Baker grabbed his hat from the store's sales counter and followed Tricia to the back of the shop. Miss Marple scampered ahead of them. She wasn't about to be left behind with Ginny when she could follow Tricia upstairs and perhaps have an extra helping of cat cookies.

Tricia unlocked the apartment door and preceded Baker

inside, with Miss Marple scooting in ahead of both of them. She jumped onto one of the kitchen stools and gave a sharp "*Yow!*"

"You don't need a treat right now," Tricia told her, and the disgruntled cat sat on her haunches and glared at her owner.

Baker looked around the converted loft space. "Nice."

"Thank you." Tricia held out her hand, indicating the way. "The window with the BB holes overlooks the street."

Tricia led the way to her bedroom, glad she'd made the bed, and even dusted the nightstand, earlier that morning.

"Nice place," Baker said, eying the space, his glance landing on the queen-sized bed, where it seemed to stay for far too long.

"The window," Tricia prompted, indicating the glass across the way.

Baker shook his head, becoming all business once again. He moved to the window to examine the damage, and then shifted his gaze to take in the rooftops across the way. "The perfect vantage point."

"My thoughts exactly."

"You ought to keep your curtains shut for the time being."

"I did close them last night."

He reached for the traverse cord. "Daytime, too," he said as the drapes closed. The light grew dim, and the room seemed to shrink.

"I also saw something else last night."

"Oh?"

"The person who's been smashing pumpkins."

"When was this?"

"Just after the shots were fired. I couldn't tell if it

was a man or a woman—or a teenager. Just that the person was"—she paused, realizing what it was she'd seen the night before, but that hadn't registered until this moment—"chunky."

Baker frowned. "A fat vandal? You're saying it wasn't a kid?"

Tricia shrugged. "They say that thirty-three percent of today's youth are overweight-to-obese," she offered. "The person was dressed all in black. He or she raised the pumpkin over his or her head and then—*splat!*"

"*Splat,*" he repeated with no inflection.

She nodded.

"I want you to know I have looked into this pumpkin vandalism, and I can tell you that not one parent or homeowner in Stoneham has reported any stolen or smashed pumpkins."

"No one?" she repeated in disbelief. "Then why . . . ?"

"I have no answer. Now, where's that answering machine of yours?" Baker asked.

"It's actually part of my phone." Tricia led the way back to the kitchen. She stepped over to the counter and pressed the Play button.

"Tricia? It's Russ. I'm sorry about the way things went the other night. I still care about you. I think we should talk. Please call me."

Beep!

Tricia stared at the Play button her finger still hovered over. If she'd known that message was there, she would never have played it for Captain Baker.

He cleared his throat. "I take it that wasn't the message you wanted me to hear."

Tricia pressed the Delete button. "No, it wasn't."

"And this Russ is?"

"Russ Smith, the editor of the *Stoneham Weekly News*. We used to be . . . friends."

Baker nodded. "I see."

Tricia wasn't about to let on that the message had rattled her. She pressed the Play button again. This time, the draggy voice came out of the little speaker, sounding tinny and not at all threatening in the electric light of her drape-drawn day.

"Where's this diary? Do you have it?" Baker asked when the message had ended.

"I have no idea! I don't know what diary the person is talking about, and I certainly don't have it. The caller might be referring to a diary belonging to Pammy Fredericks. But if she had one, I never saw it."

"There wasn't a diary with her personal effects in her car, either."

"She did leave a box of books here, but they were pretty old—mostly mainstream paperback fiction. I gave them to the Stoneham Library for their used book sale."

"You what?"

Tricia shrugged. "They weren't worth anything. I mean, Pammy was dead. What good were they to her?"

"You should have told me about them," Baker said sternly. "We could have gone through them, maybe found something to help us in our investigation."

"Captain, I sell used books—take it from me, they were yard-sale castoffs, or something she got from digging through someone's garbage. They weren't worth anything."

"When was the sale?" he demanded.

"It won't happen until the end of the month."

"Then maybe it's not too late. Perhaps the head librarian can help me."

"Lois Kerr is great, but there must have been twenty or thirty boxes of books in her conference room. I doubt she'd remember which box I brought in."

"Would you remember?"

Tricia hesitated. The box had been nondescript, but she might remember some of the titles. "Maybe."

Baker grabbed her by the elbow and hauled her toward the door leading to the stairs and the bookstore beyond them. "Come on. Let's go."

"But I have a business to run!"

"I have a murder to investigate, and I need your help to do it."

Tricia grimaced and yanked back her arm. "You sure know how to sweet-talk a girl."

Lois Kerr stood at the threshold of the Stoneham Library's conference room and frowned. "As you can see, Captain Baker, our patrons have been very generous with their donations for our fund-raiser."

Generous wasn't the word. Since Tricia had dropped off Pammy's box of books several days before, an additional twenty or thirty cartons of old books had been added to the small room.

"I'm afraid I don't remember which box was yours, Tricia," Lois admitted.

Captain Baker did not look pleased. He sniffed the air, wrinkling his nose at the scent of old paper and mildew. "Ladies, you have your work cut out for you."

"What do you mean we have our work cut out for us?" Tricia demanded.

"You're going to dig through this pile of books until you find those that belonged to Ms. Fredericks."

"Excuse me, Captain, but I have a meeting with Select-man Tim Powers in exactly ten minutes. And as you can see"—Lois waved a hand at her neat tweed suit—"I'm simply not dressed for the task."

"Neither am I," Tricia protested.

"I pressed this myself," Baker said, jerking a thumb at his uniform blouse, "but it looks like I'll have to get it wrinkled. Your home is right above your shop, Ms. Miles; you'll be able to change as soon as you get back, if need be. And the quicker we find that box of books, the quicker you'll get to return to your store."

Lois flashed an embarrassed smile. "I'll just leave you two to your work," she said, and backed away from the conference room.

Tricia exhaled a long, annoyed breath, her gaze travel-ing up and down the stacked cartons. "We'll have to move all these boxes to get to the stuff that was donated before Wednesday."

"How do you know your box isn't in the front row? I think you should look at each and every box to make sure it hasn't been relocated since you dumped it off."

"I did not dump the box here. I brought it in and placed it on the pile. I thought I was doing a charitable thing, not hindering your investigation."

Baker opened his mouth to say something, and then closed it, apparently thinking better of it.

"Why don't we start sorting through the piles? The sooner we get at it, the sooner we can both go back to work."

He was trying and—if she was honest with herself—succeeding at treating her with more respect than Sheriff Adams ever had.

Tricia pushed up the sleeves of her sweater and sighed. "Okay."

She stepped into the conference room and grabbed the first carton of books, staggering under its weight.

"Hold on," Baker called, rushing up to her and taking the box from her. "I didn't mean you should have to cart all these boxes around by yourself. I'll put them on the table and you can go through them, okay?"

Chivalry was not dead after all. "That would be fine," Tricia said.

They set to work. One by one, Captain Baker shifted the boxes, Tricia unfolded the interlocking flaps, looked inside each one, and pushed it aside.

"I'm really sorry you're losing your morning to this," Tricia said after ten minutes had gone by and they'd shifted at least as many boxes. "I really didn't think the books would hold any value for you. They're just old books."

"Is that how you feel about the books in your shop?"

"Of course not. They're mysteries."

Baker laughed. "Ms. Miles, I do believe you're a snob."

Tricia looked up sharply. "I am not."

"Then why don't books other than mysteries intrigue you?"

"I never said that." She folded the flaps in on another box, pushing it aside on the table. "I do read other genres. My sister has been working on a new cookbook. I'm helping her edit it. I can also repair books—although I haven't had the time to do it since I opened my shop. Not only have I read the classics, from Shakespeare to Tolstoy, but every Harry Potter book, too."

"I stand corrected," Baker said, the hint of a smile gracing his lips, and placed another box of books on the table beside her.

Tricia opened the box, took out several books, and looked through the contents. She spied a copy of *The Three*

Roads by Kenneth Millar—otherwise known as Ross MacDonald—and flipped open the cover, thumbing to the copyright page. She froze, her heart pounding. Yes! A first edition. The dust cover had a couple of nicks and wrinkles, but it was in very good condition—something a collector, not unlike herself, would covet.

She carefully set the book aside. Would Lois let her buy some of these books before the sale? She'd have to ask . . . and, she decided, she'd pay a bit more attention as she went through the rest of the boxes. There could be many more surprises.

"You forgot to put that book back in the box," Baker commented.

Tricia feigned surprise. "Did I?"

"Yes."

Tricia met his gaze. "I don't think so. May I have another box, please?"

Baker took the box she'd just pushed aside, set it on the floor by the other cartons she'd already inspected, and picked up a new one for Tricia to look at. She opened the flaps. "And what is it you read for pleasure, Captain Baker?"

"Certainly not mysteries. They're a little too close to what I do for a living. When I read, I want to relax, not feel like I'm doing homework."

"Then I take it true crime is out, too?"

"Definitely. Don't laugh, but I actually do read cookbooks."

"Why should I laugh? Most of the greatest chefs in the world are men. Probably because it's women who have to do the drudge work at home."

"Ah, you're a feminist, too?" he asked.

She turned a level glare at him. "Some people don't like that word."

"Do you?"

"I think it's rather a tribute."

"Why's that?"

"Let's just say I don't like to see women treated as second-class citizens. How do you feel about reporting to a woman?"

The captain's expression grew somber. "My boss was elected to the job. If she'd come up through the ranks . . ." He didn't have to say any more.

Tricia finished with another box. "What do you make?"

He leaned in closer. "I beg your pardon?"

"What kind of food do you like to cook?" she clarified. "Barbecue?"

He frowned. "Now who's making assumptions?" He didn't wait for a reply, and plowed ahead. "As it happens, I'm rather good at baking. After all, my name *is* Baker."

"What do you bake?"

"Bread, mostly. My grandmother taught me. Do you cook?"

"Not unless I have to. My sister got all the cooking talent in our family. That's why she opened a café."

"And has a cookbook about to be published," he added. "From Penguin. In June. *Easy-Does-It Cooking*," he recited from memory.

Tricia laughed. "Exactly."

She pushed aside yet another box. The captain moved it to the discard pile and gave her another.

"By the way, Captain; did you get a call from the Stoneham post office?"

"No. Why?"

"Because, they're holding a letter there addressed to Pammy, in care of General Delivery."

"Why didn't you tell me this before?" he asked sharply.

"I only found out yesterday. I did encourage the clerk to call you. I guess he didn't feel it was necessary. I hope he hasn't had it returned to its sender."

"I'll check into it as soon as I leave here. Thank you for mentioning it."

Tricia nodded and opened the flaps on the next box. She recognized several of the titles. "This is it."

Baker whirled round. "Don't touch the books."

"Why not? I've already handled them. And it's unlikely you'll find any decent fingerprints. Besides, it was Pammy who handled these books before me, not my mysterious caller."

"Just the same," he said, taking custody of the box and moving it away from her. He carefully folded the carton's flaps back in.

"Since you intend to take those books away, don't you think you should make a donation to the library?"

"My tax dollars are my donation."

"Yes, but the library wouldn't have to hold book sales if our tax dollars better supported it."

"Hey, you're a bookseller. The library is your competition."

"I deal in mostly used, out-of-print, and hard-to-find mysteries. Collectors are my prime customers. Libraries serve a large portion of the rest of the population."

"Excuse *me*."

He lifted the box. "I'd better take these to the main desk and leave Mrs. Kerr a receipt. If we find nothing, the books will be returned."

"After the sale, no doubt."

"Possibly." He paused in the doorway. "I want you to keep me posted on your unknown caller. And if you find that diary, I want to be the first to know about it."

Tricia snapped to attention and saluted smartly. "Yes, sir!" She relaxed. "Now, may I be excused?"

Baker wasn't amused. "I'm serious, Ms. Miles. Whoever thinks you've got that diary is likely to come after it—*and* you. Next time he or she won't use a BB or pellet gun."

Much as she didn't want to admit it, Tricia had a feeling he might be right.

FOURTEEN

Mr. Everett stood behind the cash register, waiting on a customer, when Tricia returned to Haven't Got a Clue. It had been a couple of days since he'd reported in, so she was surprised to see him. She waited until he'd bid the customer a cheery good-bye before she stepped up to the cash desk.

"I didn't know we'd see you today. How are things shaping up for the wedding?"

His jovial smile faltered. "Not very well, I'm afraid. Grace had her heart set on being married at the Brookview Inn. Unfortunately, they have two other parties already booked for Saturday, and three baby showers on Sunday. I didn't realize there were so many expectant mothers here in Stoneham."

"Oh, dear. Can you wait a week?"

He shook his head. "We've already booked a cruise, and need to board ship on Monday. I'm just not sure what we'll do now."

"Can't you have the ceremony after you return?"

Mr. Everett's eyes widened in indignation. "Ms. Miles, it wouldn't be proper. I would never sully Grace's reputation in that way."

"I'm sorry," Tricia apologized. "It was a thoughtless suggestion. Please forgive me."

He nodded. "We won't speak of it again."

That still left the problem of the wedding location.

"What about Grace's house? It's lovely, and her living room is certainly large enough to accommodate all your guests."

"That's true, but we've already arranged to have work done while we're on our honeymoon. Grace is having the entire downstairs repainted and new carpet put in. They've already started preparing the rooms. We've been relegated to the upstairs parlor to read in the evenings."

Tricia looked around her store. Except for where Pammy had doused a customer's foot with coffee, the rug was in good shape. If they pushed back the chairs in the reading nook, there would be plenty of room for the wedding party and guests.

"Why don't we hold the wedding here?"

Mr. Everett's eyes flashed, and a small smile crept onto his lips. "Here? Really?"

He hadn't fooled her one bit. He'd been hoping she would offer Haven't Got a Clue. And if they celebrated with a wedding brunch, she could still open in the afternoon. Besides, Sunday was the last day of the Milford Pumpkin Festival. As Frannie had said, Stoneham would be dead while thousands of people celebrated the wonders of orange squash right down the road in the next town.

"I would be happy to play hostess for your wedding on Sunday. In fact, I think it's a marvelous idea."

"Thank you, Ms. Miles. I'm sure Grace will be especially pleased when I tell her. Do you mind if I use the telephone?"

"Go right ahead," Tricia said. "I'll just go hang up my coat."

But before he could do so, the phone rang. Tricia let Mr. Everett answer it. She hung up her coat and soon returned to the front of the store. "Ms. Miles, it's the Cookery's Ms. Armstrong, for you."

Tricia took the receiver. "Frannie?"

"I've caught Penny!" Frannie cried with delight.

"That's wonderful."

"Yes, but what do I do now? I'm all alone here at the Cookery. She's frightened, and Angelica doesn't want her in the store. What should I do?"

"Do you have things set up at your house? A litter box, bowls, et cetera?"

"Oh, yes, but I can't leave the store to take her home."

Angelica had her hands full at Booked for Lunch, so she couldn't return to take care of the Cookery. Since both Ginny and Mr. Everett were working that day, that left only one solution. "Would you like me to watch over the Cookery while you take Penny home?"

"I'd only be gone a half hour at most," Frannie said, her words a plea.

"Grab your coat, and Penny, and I'll be right over."

"Oh, Tricia, you are a lifesaver!"

"See you in a minute." Tricia hung up the phone.

"Am I to presume you'll be at the Cookery for the foreseeable future?" Mr. Everett asked solemnly.

Tricia sighed. "At least the next half hour, I'm afraid."

He nodded. "Ginny and I will take care of things here."

Tricia didn't bother to retrieve her coat, and instead headed out dressed as she was.

Frannie had retrieved the Havahart trap, with its howling occupant, and her coat, and practically flew out the Cookery's door the moment Tricia arrived. "Be right back," she assured Tricia, and took off at a trot.

No sooner had the door closed on her than it was opened again, and several customers entered. One hundred and fifty-six dollars later, they departed, and a familiar face crossed the threshold. Pete Marbello hefted a box and frowned at Tricia. "What are you doing here? This isn't your shop."

"No, it belongs to my sister."

He looked around the store. "Where's Frannie?"

"She had an errand to run. Can I help you?"

He stepped up to the register, letting the heavy box bang onto the glass-topped counter.

"Hey," Tricia protested.

"It's just books," he said. "Frannie's been buying them from me for the last few months. I don't suppose you know anything about cookbooks?"

"Not really."

"Damn." He pursed his lips, staring at the carton. "Can I leave them here for Frannie? Could you ask her to call me?"

"Sure." But she wasn't about to let him leave before she asked him a few questions of her own. "I understand your father owns the convenience store up by the highway."

"Yeah. The greenest store in the county," he said with pride. "You noticed the different trash cans out front, didn't you? For paper, glass, and plastic."

"I can't say as I have. But I'll be sure to look next time I'm there."

"That was my idea. I sort all the trash that goes into the Dumpster, too. We recycle more than the rest of the retailers around here. We only use recycled plastic bags in the store, too. If I had my way, we wouldn't use plastic *or* paper, but people are conditioned to expect them."

"What would you put their purchases in?"

"Customers should bring their own reusable bags. We sell them, but not enough people buy or use them."

"You're really serious about all this, aren't you?"

"Yeah, and you should be, too," he said, the weight of the chip on his shoulder coloring his voice.

"I have tried the cornstarch bags, but they aren't strong enough to hold books. The bags I use are made from recycled plastic, and for big orders, I have paper bags with handles."

"That's better than most of the other booksellers," he grudgingly admitted.

Tricia indicated the box of books. "Have you become a picker?"

"Sort of. I'm trying to get enough money together to start a recycling plant."

"That's pretty ambitious."

"You'd be surprised what can be recycled. My plan is to buy a flatbed truck, put an ad in the local papers, and offer a free service to pick up old appliances, like refrigerators, old cars, then scrap 'em. If I can hook up with the county, I should be able to clean up the environment—and financially, too."

"Tell me more," Tricia said, and leaned forward on the counter, trying to appear more interested than she was. How on earth was she going to get Pammy into the conversation?

He droned on and on. At last he mentioned the freegans, and she jumped at the opportunity to interrupt. "I understand you met my friend Pammy Fredericks digging through the convenience store's trash, and that you invited her along on several of your Dumpster-diving expeditions."

"Yeah," he admitted with a snarl. "I thought she was a kindred spirit, but it turned out she had a one-track mind. Always bitching about coming into money—or *not* coming into it. At least not fast enough."

"Yes, that's what Joe Hirt said, too. Pammy didn't tell me what her big plans were. Do you know?"

He shrugged. "Something about someone paying her big bucks for what she knew. She had some kind of proof."

"A diary?" Tricia suggested.

He frowned. "I dunno. Maybe. I didn't pay much attention to her. She wasn't really one of us. All she cared about was getting something for nothing. The world is better off without people like her. Takers. What did she ever give back to anyone?"

It was Tricia's turn to frown. His plan to scoop up scrap metal and resell it didn't sound all that altruistic, either, especially given the freegans' goal of living a less material existence.

"Pammy didn't deserve to die the way she did—suffocating in garbage."

He shrugged. "One less moocher sucking up our air and using our resources."

Tricia straightened. She'd had enough of him. "I'll tell Frannie to give you a call about these books," she said, letting him know he was being dismissed.

"She's got my number," he said, a sneer entering his voice.

Tricia watched as he left the shop. She glanced inside the carton of books. They looked to be in pretty good shape. Where had he gotten them? There weren't many yard sales at this time of year. She bent lower and sniffed. A bit musty, perhaps, but they didn't reek of the soup found at the bottom of a Dumpster or trash bin.

Pammy had spoken a little too freely about her diary and what she hoped to gain from it. Despite Pete Marbello's assessment of her, she did not deserve to be killed. More and more it sounded as though she was blackmailing—or attempting to blackmail—someone. But who? There was only one logical choice: Stuart Paige.

But Tricia had nothing but suspicions. She didn't even have the diary. Without it, there was no reason to talk to, let alone confront, the man.

Whoever killed Pammy might just get away with murder, after all.

Frannie was gone much longer than Tricia had anticipated—almost two hours. "I'm sorry I'm late," she apologized as she wiggled out of the sleeves of her coat. "When I got Penny home, I called the vet to make an appointment for her. They said they had an opening, and to bring her right in."

"I wish you'd called," Tricia said, looking at her watch. It was past Ginny's lunch break, and Mr. Everett would be holding down Haven't Got a Clue by himself.

"I'm sorry, Tricia. I should have. But the only day I have off is Sunday, and the vet isn't open then."

True enough. "I forgive you. But I'd better get back to my own store in case Mr. Everett needs to leave. He and Grace have a lot of plans to make before Sunday."

"Isn't it exciting—getting married at their age? Maybe there's still hope for me," Frannie added wistfully.

Tricia scooted around the sales desk, letting Frannie take her place. "Talk to you later."

Frannie waved. "Thanks again!"

Haven't Got a Clue was mobbed with customers, and

despite its being late, Ginny had not taken her lunch break. Mr. Everett stood by one of the back shelves, helping a customer, while Miss Marple observed the chaos from her perch on the shelf behind the register.

Tricia grabbed the stack of books Ginny had already rung up, and bagged them. "Here you go," she told the customer. "I'm so sorry I'm late," she whispered to Ginny.

"If you were helping anyone but Frannie, I wouldn't be so accommodating," Ginny said. To the customer she said, "That'll be forty-three eighty-five." The woman handed over her gold card and Ginny swiped it through the credit card machine.

"Anything happen while I was gone?"

"We've been very busy. Grace called to thank you. So we're holding a wedding here on Sunday?"

"Uh-huh." She hadn't offered to let Ginny get married at the store; would she feel slighted? "Does that upset you?"

"Of course not. It was nice of you to offer. But it's a good thing they're planning a small affair."

Definitely no hurt feelings there.

The credit card machine spit out a piece of paper, the customer signed it, and was on her way.

Tricia picked up the conversation where they'd left it. "I'm not sure of the logistics on this wedding. I may need your help getting things set up. I wonder if I should rent chairs, or if the caterer will handle that. If you could come in early Sunday morning, to help set things up, I'd be glad to pay you for your time."

"You'll do no such thing. Mr. Everett and Grace are my friends, too, you know. I'll do whatever I can to help make their day a happy one."

Tricia smiled. "I knew I could count on you."

Ginny glanced at her watch. "Yikes! It's twenty minutes past my lunch break."

Tricia flushed with guilt. She hadn't yet made any headway on putting together a break room for Ginny and Mr. Everett in her storeroom. Another task undone. Luckily, the day was bright and sunny. No doubt Ginny's car would be warm enough for her to endure another lunch break, but the weather wouldn't hold much longer.

Guilt, guilt, guilt.

Ginny retrieved her coat and grabbed a book from the store's paperback bargain shelf. As she opened the door to leave, Grace stepped into Haven't Got a Clue. "Hello, Ginny!"

"Hi, Grace. Bye, Grace!" Ginny said with a smile, and exited.

Grace hurried to the sales counter. "Hello, Tricia. I can't thank you enough for letting William and me get married here on Sunday. And I promise we'll be out of your hair in time for you to open at precisely noon."

"Don't worry about it, Grace. If we have to open later, we'll open later. I want you two to have a nice send-off. Besides, Milford's Pumpkin Festival is this weekend. We'll be lucky to have any customers at all on Sunday. How are your plans coming along?"

Grace beamed. "I've engaged a caterer, a photographer, and a florist. I've got my dress, and I'm on my way to the Stoneham Patisserie to order the wedding cake."

"Nikki's going to make your cake?"

Grace nodded. "I hope so."

Angelica had mentioned she might like to do it. Oh, well. Tricia made a mental note to mention it to her sister before she started pulling out pans and recipes.

"How about the guest list? Do you know how many people you'll be inviting?"

"I've narrowed it down to twenty. Do you think the store can accommodate that many people?"

"Oh, sure. I've hosted book signings with more than that." But not by much. "We don't have a photographer here in Stoneham. Did you have to go to Milford or Nashua to find one?"

"But of course we have a photographer here in the village. Oh, I admit he doesn't do it professionally anymore, but he accepted the moment I asked. And he refuses to take any money for it. I shall have to figure out a nice gift to give him when we return from our honeymoon."

"Who is this mystery man?" Tricia asked, intrigued. Could Bob Kelly have once owned a photography business? He seemed to have his fingers in every other pie in town.

"It's Russ Smith."

"Russ?" Tricia echoed, a bit more loudly than she would've liked. The one man in Stoneham she had no desire to see, and now he was an integral part of Mr. Everett and Grace's wedding. Could her luck get any worse?

She struggled to get her voice under control. "How nice."

Grace's smile widened. "Have you two thought about tying the knot?"

Tricia clenched her fists, and hoped to keep the anger out of her tone. "No. Sadly, Russ and I are no longer together."

Grace's face fell. "Oh, dear. I hope his being at the wedding won't be too upsetting."

"Of course not," Tricia lied. "We're adults. And we parted amicably."

Ha!

Grace brightened. "Thank goodness. It could have been very awkward."

Tricia ground her teeth together, but managed a reasonable facsimile of a smile.

Grace looked up to see Mr. Everett across the room. She caught his eye and waved.

His fingers fluttered a shy wave in return.

Grace looked back to Tricia. "Aren't I terrible—distracting William while he's at work?"

"I think it's very sweet. You both are."

Tricia suddenly remembered the peck on the cheek Stuart Paige had given Grace at the Food Shelf's dedication. "Not to change the subject—but I will. How well do you know Stuart Paige?"

"Oh," she said, taken off guard. "Casually. My late husband was a good friend of Stuart's father. Of course, I saw Stuart many times over the years, but it wasn't until he started his charity work that we really became acquainted."

"I've heard about his more rebellious days. And, of course, about the accident."

The joy left Grace's eyes. "It was very unfortunate. Though the good he's done can never erase what happened, there's no doubt he's dedicated his life to trying to make amends for past indiscretions."

Should she push Grace even further?

Tricia took the chance. "So you believe he's a good man?"

Grace answered without hesitation. "Yes."

Good now. But what if what Pammy knew about the man had happened years before? Would he want to keep another incident from his past quiet—and would he do anything, including murder, to make sure of it?

"I'd best let William know that things are shaping up for our big day, and then I'll be on my way," Grace said. "If you'll excuse me, Tricia."

"Of course."

Tricia turned away, disappointed. She hadn't learned anything new—except for Russ being at the wedding ceremony, and she didn't want Grace to know how she really felt about it. But after all, they were adults, and she *could* be with him in the same room for two or three hours without exploding—or falling apart.

Ha, again! Fall apart? He might fall apart if she clocked him, and that's exactly what she wanted to do.

Must distract myself.

Goodness knows, she had enough to think about—Pammy's death, the missing diary, setting up Ginny's break room, as well as the impending nuptials.

She didn't need another thing to think about.

The phone rang.

Tricia grabbed it. "Haven't Got a Clue. This is Tricia; how can I help you?"

"Oh, Trish—wonderful news," Angelica said.

Tricia looked out the window to see her sister on her cell phone, waving at her from the window of Booked for Lunch.

"Wonderful news!" Angelica continued. "Grace Harris has hired me to cater her wedding. And guess what? You're going to help me!"

FIFTEEN

"Isn't it exciting! My first catering job," Angelica gushed.

"How could you even think of taking on this wedding?" Tricia scolded. "You're shorthanded. Where are you going to find the time to keep two businesses afloat *and* make hors d'oeuvres for twenty people by Sunday?"

"Oh. I hadn't thought about that. Well, I can always round up all my friends to help."

"Such as?"

"Well, Frannie, of course. Maybe Ginny."

Tricia shook her head. "Much as Ginny loves Mr. Everett, I doubt she'd be willing to spend her off hours helping you make money."

"Oh, well, I could *pay* her."

"You can ask."

"And, of course, I'm depending on you," Angelica pressed.

"In case you hadn't noticed, I can't cook."

"If you can follow directions, you can cook."

Tricia watched as a couple of tourists entered the little café.

"Gotta go now. Talk to you later!" Angelica said, and disconnected.

The bell over the door jingled as another two customers entered her own store. Tricia put her worries out of her mind, plastered on her best smile, and said, "Welcome to Haven't Got a Clue. Let me know if you need any help."

The day whipped by. Customers came and went, spending freely. And, thanks to Craigslist, Tricia managed to hunt down a small refrigerator which was to be delivered the next day. Now she just needed to get a microwave and a table. And maybe a radio. And then she'd consider painting the drab room. Did she need more lighting, too? Establishing a break room was going to be more complicated than she'd anticipated. Still, she wanted happy employees.

By the time seven o'clock rolled around and Tricia closed Haven't Got a Clue, she was exhausted. Her plan for the evening was to make a sandwich, drink a glass of wine, and *read*. She would not think about Pammy. She would not think about Russ being at Mr. Everett's wedding. She would not think about Angelica's threat that she was going to have to help make hors d'oeuvres for twenty people by Sunday.

She'd just settled down with *A Graveyard to Let* by Carter Dickson when the phone rang. Miss Marple, comfortably ensconced at Tricia's side, glared at the offending instrument on the end table. Tricia picked up the receiver with apprehension. Would it be her annoying caller?

"It's just me," Angelica said. "Have you eaten yet?"

"A cheese sandwich."

"I've got leftover soup from the café, and I'm on my way up." She disconnected.

The last thing Tricia wanted was company. Still, she hauled herself off the couch and met her sister at the apartment door. Angelica held a stuffed brown paper grocery bag in her arms, and a canvas tote was slung over one shoulder, resting on her back.

"What have you got there?" Tricia asked.

"Cookbooks. I've made out a preliminary list of appetizers, and I thought the two of us could go over it."

"I don't care about that kind of stuff," Tricia insisted.

Angelica leveled a penetrating glare at her. "You wrestled over the catering list for your own wedding for over two months. Who better to help me with my sample menus? I need to have something to show Grace tomorrow if I'm going to pull the food together for this wedding on Sunday."

In a matter of minutes, Angelica had the soup warming, the aroma filling the entire kitchen. She'd also covered the kitchen island with cookbooks dedicated to either hors d'oeuvres or breakfast meals. While Angelica served up the soup, Tricia looked over the scribbled sheets of paper with lists of appetizers. "Any one of these is good, Ange. Just let Grace pick what she likes."

"As it's a morning wedding and reception, I thought I should stick to brunch-type foods. Strudel, little bagels, mini quiches, fresh fruit, et cetera," Angelica said, and sat down at the island.

"Yeah, yeah." Tricia picked up her spoon and began to eat her soup.

Angelica glowered at her. "You could show a little more

enthusiasm. I mean, this is your employee's wedding we're talking about."

The phone rang. Tricia ignored it, spooning up more soup.

It rang again. And again. Since Angelica was already present, it could be only one other caller. Okay, maybe two if she counted Russ—and she *didn't* want to count him.

"Aren't you going to answer that?" Angelica asked.

It stopped ringing.

"Um, there's something I haven't mentioned to you. Someone's been calling me, demanding that I give back Pammy's diary."

"What diary?"

"Your guess is as good as mine. She left a bunch of books here with me, but there was no diary among them."

"Where do you think she got the books?" Angelica asked.

"I don't know. An estate sale, perhaps. She could've found them in the trash on one of her Dumpster-diving ex-peditions. Who says she acquired them all from the same place? And anyway, it's the diary that someone wants, not the rest of the books."

"Why would anyone think you've got the diary?"

"Probably because Pammy stayed with me for two weeks. It wasn't in her car or her suitcases. I'm probably the last hope that person has of finding the book."

"But you don't have it."

"No, and I searched this apartment pretty thoroughly, too." Miss Marple jumped up on one of the stools, as though to let Angelica know that she had helped in the hunt.

"Did this person threaten you? Maybe you should tell Captain Baker about the calls."

"I already did. And besides, they haven't been threatening, just annoying."

"Still . . . they could escalate into threats. What did Captain Baker say?"

Tricia shrugged. "To keep him informed."

"And will you?"

"Of course. He seems a lot more amiable than Sheriff Adams ever was. Maybe because it's a career for him—not just politics."

Angelica frowned, looking around the kitchen. "Let's assume Pammy did hide the diary here."

"I told you, I've looked."

"Did she have access to your storeroom?"

Tricia shook her head. "I keep it locked in case any curious customers make their way up the stairs."

"Me, too. Would you believe someone peed in the Cookery's stairway on Sunday?"

"I told you Frannie should have help at the store."

"How would Frannie have stopped someone from peeing in my stairwell? The restroom was probably occupied and someone just didn't want to—or couldn't—wait."

"I hope you didn't make Frannie clean it up."

"She's managing the store now—tidying up is part of the job."

Tricia shook her head. "That's not what I would call 'tidying.' And can we get back to the subject at hand—the missing diary? How are we going to find it?" she said, and pushed her empty soup bowl away.

"Have you looked in your store? What better place to hide it?"

Tricia sprang up from her stool, the sudden movement sending Miss Marple flying. "Of course! Pammy could've ditched the diary when she left here on Monday. She went downstairs ahead of me. By the time I locked the apartment door and followed, she might've been down there almost a minute. That would've been plenty of time to hide the diary among the books in my store."

"And how are we supposed to find it? Look on every shelf, read the spines of every title you've got? There must be ten thousand books to sort through."

"It can't hurt," Tricia said, and headed for the door.

"Can't it wait until tomorrow?" Angelica begged. "I've been on my feet all day. And don't forget, I need to start making appetizers. Besides, the light isn't all that great down there."

"The light is perfectly fine in my store."

"Only if you're a mole. You ought to invest in more track lighting."

"And ruin my original tin ceiling? It was the only thing I kept during the renovation. Are you going to help me or not?"

"Well, I didn't say I wouldn't."

"Good, then let's go!"

"I'll rinse these dishes and put them in the dishwasher, and meet you downstairs," Angelica said.

An hour later, the idea of searching the shelves didn't seem like such a good idea. Angelica had brought her cookbooks back down and left them by the door before she attacked a set of shelves in the back of the store. She'd amassed a pile of books around her and was reading the cover flap on the one in her hand. "Hey, this Dorothy Sayers sounds like a good author. Have you ever read *Gaudy Night*?"

Tricia sighed and sat back on her heels. "Only ten or twenty times. I thought you didn't like period pieces."

"I'm open to all fiction, although I prefer cooking and decorating books. I'm reading this wonderful book right now—"

"We're supposed to be looking for the diary, remember?" Tricia interrupted.

Angelica poked her tongue out at her sister.

Tricia reseated herself in a more comfortable position and resumed her search. Red cover. No words on the spine. She squinted in the bad light. Perhaps Angelica was right. Perhaps she did need to add more lighting so that customers could better see the bottom shelves.

"How long are we going to keep up the search?" Angelica asked.

"Until we find it."

"What if it isn't here?"

Tricia didn't want to think about that. If the diary wasn't hidden in Haven't Got a Clue, it could be anywhere—if it still existed. And what was she supposed to tell the voice the next time it called? "Sorry, but I don't have it. Never did. Don't know where it's at. Please stop bothering me."

That and five bucks would get her a double latte cappuccino with hazelnut and cinnamon at the Coffee Bean across the street.

Tricia pulled out another two or three books, noting that none of them had any dust on them. Mr. Everett was truly serious about his dusting. Thinking of Mr. Everett reminded her that he and Grace were about to get married, and that he'd need a week off right at the peak of the fall foliage season, when Stoneham would be filled with tourists.

"Red cover," Angelica muttered. "No type on the spine." She held up a book, waving it in the air. "It's not a diary with a lock, Trish. It's a journal."

Tricia's head snapped around. "You found it?"

"I'm almost as good as Saint Anthony when it comes to finding lost items. Remember, it was me who found the missing cookbook after Doris Gleason was—"

"Don't remind me," Tricia interrupted, holding up a hand to stave off another round of "I told you so," which Angelica had probably been about to make.

Tricia crawled across the space between them until she was inches from her sister. She made to grab the book, but Angelica held it out of her reach. "Hey, I found it, I should be the first to read it."

Tricia scowled but sat back, extending her arms behind her, palms down, on the floor.

"Uh-uh-uh!" Angelica tut-tutted, pointing at the circle of books around her. "Don't get comfortable. You can put these back while I read aloud."

"You took them out—you put them back."

Angelica looked down her nose at Tricia and cleared her throat. Then she grabbed the reading glasses that hung around her neck on a chain. She stared down at the book. "Hmm. Somebody obviously wanted to get rid of this thing. Look." She held the book out for Tricia to see.

The edges of the pages had been singed.

"Looks likes someone tried to burn it and changed their mind, or someone tried to burn it and someone else rescued it. Wow, there must be some juicy stuff inside." Angelica opened the cover and turned to the first page. "The first entry is dated August seventh, twenty-one years ago." She frowned. "The author would not win points for penmanship."

"Read!" Tricia commanded.

Angelica squinted at the cursive handwriting. "*Bunny and I went shopping on Saturday, but nothing in my size fit. I knew then that I was probably pregnant. Just my damn luck.*" She looked up. "Oh, Trish, this is delicious. A scandal on page one."

Tricia frowned. "Being pregnant is hardly a scandal, even in the nineteen eighties."

"How do you know? Maybe this woman was a society maven."

"We don't even know who the author is. Unless there's a name on the flyleaf."

Angelica looked at the inside front cover. "No such luck, honey." She flipped through several pages, skimming the handwriting. "Oh, my, I may have been wrong. This looks deadly dull. Here's a weather report: *Rainy and gloomy today. I think I'll clean out the kitchen cabinets. That ought to keep me out of trouble for at least the afternoon.*" She pulled a face. "I've changed my mind about reading this. Here." She handed off the book. "You can have it. Pick out the more salacious parts and give me a capsule update."

Tricia flipped through the pages. "Fine. I've got nothing better to do tonight."

Angelica struggled to her feet. "Oh, yes, you have." She nudged one of the books on the floor with the toe of her shoe. "I told you, I'm not putting these away. I'm going home." She headed for the shop's front exit, and picked up her bag of cookbooks. "Good night, dear sister. See you tomorrow."

Tricia, too, pulled herself to her feet, and crossed the store to lock the door behind Angelica. She didn't want to put the books away either, but if Mr. Everett was going to be scarce for the next couple of weeks, she didn't want to overwork Ginny.

Twenty minutes later, Tricia and Miss Marple headed up the stairs, the formerly missing journal in hand. As Tricia entered her loft apartment, the phone began to ring. "Not again," she groaned. She let the answering machine take the call. Sure enough, it was the same voice. What that person wanted, she now had. She waited until the caller hung up before she turned down the volume on the phone. She poured herself a glass of wine and sat down on the comfortable leather couch in the living room. Miss Marple deigned to accompany her, settling herself on Tricia's lap.

The phone rang three more times while Tricia read the contents of the journal. Angelica was right: most of it was pretty dull. Its unmarried author chronicled her pregnancy—the morning sickness, the expanding waistline—and her firm determination to hook the baby's father; she wasn't prepared to settle for just child support. Not surprising, the love of her life was not about to leave his comfortable lifestyle for the likes of an unwanted lover. And not once in the hundred or so pages of rather sloppy cursive handwriting did the author ever mention the name of the baby's father—let alone her own. What good was this as an instrument of blackmail? But someone thought the journal was worth killing for. And now that someone was hounding Tricia for it.

Well, "hounding" was a strong word for the relatively benign calls she'd received so far. If so, maybe that was why the threat wasn't explicit, nor the calls all that frightening.

The author's water had just broken, but Tricia was yawning, and decided she could wait until tomorrow to read the rest and find out the sex of the baby. Miss Marple had fallen asleep long before, and was startled to awareness when Tricia's hand slipped and she nearly dropped the journal on the cat. Miss Marple stretched her legs and jumped from Tricia's lap, heading for the bedroom.

"I'm with you, Miss Marple."

Tricia set the journal aside and turned off the living

room lamps. As she entered her bedroom she paused, looking over her shoulder to see the book once again.

If the journal's contents weren't worthy of blackmail, could there be something else about the book that warranted further investigation? She crossed the darkened living room to retrieve it.

In her bedroom, she turned on the bedside lamp, sat down, and examined the book in greater detail. There was nothing special about it. It hadn't been expensive and was probably purchased in a discount store. She held the book by its spine and shook it. No loose pieces of paper fell out. No secret compartment revealed itself.

She thumbed through the pages, picking up where she had left off. The next entry wasn't as drab and/or hopeful as the previous hundred or so pages. The tone had changed to hysteria.

I can't believe I gave birth to that—that thing! All my plans—all my beautiful plans for a wonderful life—are gone. I don't even want it. Bunny talked to Social Services this morning, and thank God I can dump it into the foster care system. I'm signing away all my rights. If anyone asks me about it, I'll tell them it died. I'm just so disgusted!!!

Tricia slammed the cover shut and tossed the journal onto the night table. Talk about disgusted! The author's self-serving dreams of a pampered life must have turned into a nightmare when the child was born with some kind of birth defect. Or maybe it was a Down syndrome child.

It wasn't the author who earned Tricia's pity, but the poor baby. The author hadn't even mentioned if it was a boy or girl—just *it*.

Tricia rose to her feet and began to pace, Miss Marple watching her every move.

As far as she could see, Pammy had been killed for noth-

ing. The author had never mentioned names. She'd given
the child up. There was no indication where the author
lived. Without more information, it would be impossible to
prove if Paige—or the Pope himself—was the father of the
illegitimate child.

Maybe she should just give the caller what he (or she?)
wanted.

Better yet, she'd call Captain Baker and turn it over to
him.

Tricia glanced at her bedside clock. It was too late to
call tonight, but she'd do it first thing in the morning.

That said, she wasn't sure she was ready to give up the
journal. She could copy it, but that wasn't the same as actually having it in her possession, despite whatever danger
her caller represented. Yet keeping it was foolhardy. And
how would she convince her unknown caller that she'd
given it to the Sheriff's Department? Should she hold a
press conference? Perhaps she could give the journal to
Baker with the stipulation that he report his findings to the
media. Would he? Well, perhaps her acquaintance Portia
McAlister, from Boston's News Team Ten, would help. Of
course, Pammy's murder wasn't big enough for the Boston market, but maybe Portia knew someone at the *Nashua
Telegraph*.

Tricia made another circuit of her bedroom. There was
no way she was going to ask Russ for a favor, not the way
they'd left things. *He'd* left things, she reminded herself.
She hadn't instigated their breakup, and so what if he'd
called her to smooth things over? He was probably wracked
with guilt over the way he'd treated her.

She considered that idea. No, he wouldn't feel guilt. He
didn't seem capable of any real, *strong* emotions. And besides, what good was a weekly newspaper, when the current

issue would come out the next day—and had been printed days before? Anything she could contribute wouldn't be released for another eight days.

Yes, she'd give the diary to Baker—but only after she'd made a copy of it.

Just in case.

SIXTEEN

 Tricia left a message for Captain Baker at eight the next morning. She glanced at the clock as the phone rang ten minutes later. A public servant who arrived at work on time—more or less—and immediately returned his calls. Very refreshing.

Tricia held the phone tightly as she considered how she wanted to phrase her situation. "I'm ready to talk," she said, expecting a scolding.

"Talk about what?" Baker asked.

"About everything I *think* I know about Pammy Fredericks's death."

"Is this new insight since we spoke yesterday, or have you been holding out on me?"

"What information would I be withholding?"

"I don't know—perhaps the names of the local freegans. I haven't had much luck tracking them down."

Should she confess she'd joined the freegans on one of

their Dumpster-diving expeditions? That was probably the prudent thing to do, but would it get Ginny into trouble?

She sidestepped the question. "As a matter of fact, I've got the diary my caller has been demanding. It was here in my store, mixed in with my regular stock. I want to turn it over to you."

"I'll be right over," he said, and hung up.

"Right over" was relative, since he had to drive at least thirty miles to get there.

Tricia decided to kill time by heading down to the store. She'd had a run on best sellers and needed to restock—and that meant order forms and faxing. As usual, Miss Marple was keen to start the workday, and accompanied her down the stairs to the shop.

The phone rang at eight thirty, and Tricia picked it up. "Haven't Got a Clue. We're closed right now, but we'll open at—"

"Tricia? It's Frannie."

"Hi, Frannie. You're lucky you caught me in the store."

"I already tried your home and cell numbers. You ought to turn that cell phone on once in a while, ya know."

Tricia laughed. "Everybody tells me that. What can I do for you?"

"It's Penny," Frannie said, and her voice cracked.

"What's wrong?"

"She doesn't like me." Frannie began to sob.

"Hey, now. How do you know she doesn't like you?"

"She spent all of last evening hiding behind the couch. I couldn't even coax her out with cat food, kitty treats, or even a catnip toy."

"That's not surprising," Tricia said. "You've only had her a few hours. She doesn't know she can trust you, yet."

"Well, of course she knows me. I've been feeding her for weeks."

"You've been leaving out bowls of food for weeks. She doesn't know it was you who did it."

Frannie sniffed. "What can I do to make her like me?"

"Nothing."

"What?" she cried, aghast.

"Let her get used to her new home. Let her come to you on her own terms."

"Is that what you did with Miss Marple?"

"Yes. And with every other cat I've had. You'll see. She'll warm up to you in a couple of days."

"Are you sure?"

"Positive."

"Okay."

Tricia moved the phone away from her ear as Frannie blew her nose loudly.

"I wish I didn't have to leave her alone all day," Frannie said. "Do you think there's any way Angelica would ever let me bring her to the store?"

"Not likely. Besides, Penny needs to get used to her new home before you even think of bringing her to the store."

"But would you ask Angelica about it? I'm sure you could get her to change her mind."

No one's powers of persuasion were that good.

"I'll ask," Tricia agreed, "but don't get your hopes up."

"Oh, thank you, Tricia. You're a peach! Talk to you later."

Tricia replaced the receiver. It would be a cold day in hell when Angelica let Frannie bring a cat into the Cookery. Still, she'd keep her promise, and ask. It was the least she could do.

By the time Captain Baker arrived at Haven't Got a

Clue, Tricia had finished her chores and had a fresh pot of coffee waiting, and there was still plenty of time to talk before the store opened or her employees arrived.

She handed the journal to the captain.

"And you say you found it here in the store?" he asked.

Tricia nodded. "Actually, my sister found it. Pammy must have stashed it among my stock on the morning she left—the day she died," Tricia clarified. "I read through it, and it appears to be a woman's journal through her pregnancy. Pammy told a couple of the locals she was about to come into a lot of money, and she was very interested in talking to Stuart Paige."

"Just who did she tell?"

Tricia shrugged. "I'm not sure I remember exactly who told me," she fudged.

Baker studied her face for a long moment. Was he psychic? Did his cop's intuition tell him she wasn't being entirely truthful?

Finally, he spoke. "I haven't had any luck finding any of the local freegans. I've talked with Mr. Paige, and he assures me he never spoke to Pamela Fredericks."

"Pammy may have thought he was the father of this woman's baby, but there's no way to prove it. The author didn't name names—not even her own."

Baker flipped through the pages, reading snatches of it before thumbing through to other passages.

Tricia decided not to mention she'd copied its contents on her all-in-one printer earlier that morning. Those pages now resided in the bottom of the cedar chest in her bedroom.

Baker frowned. "I don't suppose there are any useful fingerprints on it anymore. You say your sister handled it, too?"

"Sorry, but we did."

"Did she read the contents?"

Tricia shook her head. "She thought it looked pretty tame. She was right—that is, until the last entry. The author gave up the child, and from the looks of it, then tried to burn the book."

Baker continued to page through the journal, only half listening to her.

"Captain, I hope you'll announce to the media that you've got the journal or diary or whatever my elusive caller wants to call it. If he knows it's in your custody, he'll probably leave me alone."

He snapped the book shut. "Not if he thinks you read it."

Oops! Tricia hadn't considered that.

"Are we sure it's a man who made the calls? It could've been a woman. You can get those voice-altering devices at places like Radio Shack," Tricia said.

"I'll keep an open mind," Baker said, giving her a wry smile.

Tricia couldn't help but smile as well. Unlike his boss, he *had* listened to her. At least he hadn't ridiculed her assumption about Pammy and Stuart Paige.

The ghost of a smile touched Baker's lips. "What?"

"What, what?" Tricia repeated.

"You're smiling."

"I am? Oh, I'd better stop, then," she said, and tried to keep a straight face, but it was impossible. She laughed and realized she probably looked like an idiot. And heavens—what if he thought she was flirting with him?

Good grief, she realized—she *was* flirting with him. She covered her mouth with her hand, and this time she was able to wipe the smile from her face. She looked up and into his green eyes. Haunting eyes—like her ex-husband's. The man she'd never really gotten over.

"I apologize, Captain Baker. I was thinking about something funny, and this situation is anything but funny."

"I agree. But there's nothing to apologize for. I'm surprised you're able to keep a sense of humor after what you've been through—not just the death of your friend, but what you've gone through in the past year."

True enough.

"I've been reading mystery books since I was a little girl. I never, ever expected to know a murder victim, and now I've known three. It's terribly upsetting. Pammy and I weren't close, but we had history together. I'd like her killer to be found and brought to justice."

"Justice?" Captain Baker asked with a laugh. "That's not something I see too often in my line of work."

"But you're a man of the law."

He sighed. "Yes." He looked down at the book in his hands. "I'd better get back to the office and read this," he said, reaching for his hat.

"I made a fresh pot of coffee. You could sit in the reader nook. It would at least be quiet—for the next hour, that is."

"I've got an office with a door. It'll be quiet enough. But thank you."

Tricia nodded and walked him to the door.

"Unless I have more questions, your part in this investigation is now done. Is that clear?" he said.

"What do you mean?"

"Sheriff Adams doesn't think you'll be content to . . ." He hesitated.

"To mind my own business?"

"I didn't say that."

"But that's what you were thinking."

Baker sobered. "I don't know you very well, Ms. Miles—"

"Tricia," she insisted.

"But from what I've already seen, you might be as stubborn as a terrier. I wouldn't want you to get hurt pursuing avenues of investigation better left to the Sheriff's Department."

"I'm flattered you're concerned about my personal safety," she managed, trying not to bite her tongue.

"It's my job to protect and serve." His tone was definitely verging on condescending.

She shook her head and pursed her lips. "You had to go and ruin it, didn't you?"

He looked baffled. "Ruin what?"

"Here I thought I'd been dealing with a reasonable member of the Sheriff's Department, and you had to revert to being a jerk just like your boss."

Baker straightened in indignation. "I—what?"

Tricia pointed toward the door. "Go. Now. Before we both say something we'll regret."

Baker opened his mouth to say something, apparently thought better of it, and closed it. He seemed to do that a lot. His grip on the diary tightened. "Good-bye, Ms. Miles."

He stalked off to the door, yanked it open, and exited.

Nobody told Tricia what to do. Not Angelica, not Bob Kelly, and certainly not Captain Baker of the Hillsborough County Sheriff's Department.

The problem was . . . she had no plans to defy him. There were no other avenues she could investigate on her own.

Unless . . . If Baker went directly back to his office to read the diary, she might have time to track down Stuart

Paige and ask him about Pammy herself. She hadn't re-membered to tell Baker about the envelope Pammy had mailed to Paige.

Tricia glanced out the store's large display window, watching as Baker got into his cruiser. There was still time to flag him down and share that piece of news.

He started the engine and pulled away from the curb, heading north. Should she call him, leave a message about the envelope?

She might have . . . if he hadn't gotten snarky.

Stubborn as a terrier, eh?

What was it Frannie had told her days before—that Paige was staying at the Brookview Inn, just south of the village?

Tricia glanced at her watch, and grimaced. Half an hour before Ginny or Mr. Everett showed up for work. It would take Baker almost half an hour just to get back to his of-fice. She'd still have time to go to the inn and try to talk to Paige. Although if what Frannie had said was true, the inn's receptionist, Eleanor, wasn't likely to help her get in to see the man. Maybe she could bluff her way in.

It wasn't much of a plan, but it was all Tricia had.

No matter the season, the Brookview Inn always looked lovely. Since it was October, corn shocks, gourds, and pumpkins decorated the long porch that ran across the front of the white-painted colonial structure. And no smashed jack-o'-lanterns, either. Tricia didn't linger to enjoy the view, however, and jogged up the front steps and through the main entrance.

The parking lot had been full, and the noise coming from the restaurant adjacent to the reception desk told Tricia that some kind of breakfast business meeting was still in session. As usual, Eleanor was seated behind the check-in desk. Trust her to be the most dedicated employee on the face of the planet. Didn't she ever take a potty break?

Before Tricia could make a hasty exit, Eleanor called her name.

"Tricia, it's so good to see you. What's it been, three—four months?"

"Hi, Eleanor. Yes. I've had a great summer at the store. Not much time to attend Chamber meetings or even go out to dinner."

"Yes, it's been a long time since you and Russ have been in here."

Tricia cringed at the sound of his name, and Eleanor was quick to notice. "Uh-oh, trouble in paradise?" she asked.

"Russ and I have decided to . . . cool our relationship." That sounded a lot better than saying she'd been dumped. And surprisingly, the whole village didn't know about it yet. Well, they would now.

"I'm so sorry. You made such a nice couple."

"I'm keeping busy."

"Yes, we are, too. The inn is booked to capacity. It's a real coup for us, since there aren't a lot of accommodations in Milford—we're always packed straight through the Pumpkin Festival."

"I'm sorry I have to keep the store open and will miss it."

"Me, too, for the most part. But I'm taking off a couple of hours so I can enter the pie contest. I won third place two years ago, and I'm going for first this year. But talking about the festival isn't what you came in for. What can I do for you?"

Should she offer the truth?

Why not?

"I'm here to see Stuart Paige."

Eleanor shook her head. "I'm afraid he's tied up right now."

Frannie was right. Eleanor was good at protecting her guests from unwanted visitors.

"He's in the dining room, giving a speech to the Chamber of Commerce."

"What? Why didn't anyone tell me?"

"They always meet here on the second Friday of the month. The breakfast portion of the meeting is already over. Since you're a member, I don't see why you can't go in there. Perhaps you can introduce yourself to him when he's finished speaking."

"Thank you, Eleanor. I think I will." And Tricia marched across the lobby. The French doors to the restaurant were open, and Tricia slipped into one of the empty chairs at the closest table. Paige stood at a lectern. His amplified voice sounded rather husky as it resonated through the restaurant's sound system. Tricia recognized a number of her fellow bookstore owners, as well as members of the Board of Selectmen. Sitting at the table closest to the lectern was Russ, jotting down notes on his ever-present steno pad.

Paige's tone changed ever so slightly, and Tricia realized she'd entered just as he was about to wrap up his speech.

"In conclusion, building the Robert Paige Memorial Dialysis Center here in Stoneham will bring new life to the village. New construction, new jobs, new residents, and an influx of tax revenue for Stoneham. It's a win-win situation, and I hope you'll all elect to be a part of it." He collected his notes. "Thank you for inviting me to speak here today—it's been a pleasure."

The room erupted into applause, and Bob Kelly, clad in his green Kelly Realty sports jacket, rose to lead the ovation. So that was why Paige was still in town—to drum up support for another of his pet projects.

Paige's handlers crowded around him, ushering him away from the front of the room, with Bob following in his wake. Bob would no doubt stick to Paige like glue—unless, of course, Paige's entourage interfered. They'd done so after the opening of the Food Shelf. She stood, moving to the side of the room to intercept the man. She might have to ask her questions on the fly.

The applause died down, and already other business owners were up and out of their seats, headed for the exit.

One of Paige's handlers sidled close to his boss, and whispered something in his ear. Paige listened, nodded, and then spoke to Bob, who looked disappointed.

The handler snagged Paige's jacket sleeve, and steered him toward the exit.

Adrenaline coursed through her, making Tricia feel jumpy as she waited the interminable seconds it took for Paige to navigate through the crowd.

"Mr. Paige—Mr. Paige!" she called through the din of overlapping voices. She waved, trying to draw his attention, but Paige's handler looked right through her, still guiding his employer through the thinning ranks of Chamber members.

"Mr. Paige," Tricia called again, falling into step behind her quarry. "What was in the envelope Pammy Fredericks sent you last week?"

Paige abruptly halted, his head jerking around to take her in. "What did you say?"

Tricia caught up. "The Sheriff's Department is investigating Pammy Fredericks's murder. I think they'd be very interested to know what was in the envelope she sent you."

"Envelope? I don't know what you're talking about."

"Mr. Paige," the handler insisted, grabbing his employer by the elbow once more. "We're going to be late for your ten thirty meeting."

"She made copies of pages from a woman's diary. A woman who wrote about her pregnancy and intended to strong-arm the father of her baby into marrying her—that is, until the child was born with birth defects. Pammy mailed those pages to you several days before her death."

Another gray-suited flunky stepped behind Tricia, grabbed her by the elbow, and propelled her forward. "Not the time and place for this, honey," he growled. "You're outta here."

"Let me go!" The hand on her elbow tightened. At least she was going in the same direction as Paige, heading for the Brookview's front entrance.

"Mr. Paige! Mr. Paige!" she cried.

Paige was on the top step, and turned back to look at her. Shots rang out, splintering wood and shattering glass.

The flunky let go of Tricia's arm, pushing her aside. He made a flying leap at his employer, knocking him forward, and the two of them tumbled down the inn's wooden steps.

"He's hit!" came a voice.

A stream of suited businessmen and businesswomen emerged from the inn's open doorway, led by Bob Kelly, whose green jacket stuck out like a flag, while Paige's handlers dragged the wounded man to the side of the inn and out of the line of fire.

"What happened?" Bob demanded.

"Someone fired shots at Mr. Paige—my God, at me!" Tricia cried.

Instead of stopping to make sure she was all right, or

even reassure her, Bob barreled down the stairs after Paige
and his entourage. "Stuart! Stuart!"

"Someone call nine-one-one," a voice behind Tricia
shouted.

Russ was suddenly beside her. "Tricia, what happened?"

"Is he dead? Is he dead?" another voice yelled.

Tricia's knees felt weak as she grabbed the banister to
keep from stumbling down the stairs. Somehow, she took
off after Bob, with Russ right behind her.

A pasty-faced Paige sat on the ground behind a linen delivery truck, his bloodied right hand clasping his left shoulder. His crisp white shirt was stained scarlet. Although
gasping for breath, he managed to speak with his flunkies,
one of who was on a cell phone. Meanwhile, Bob hovered
over them all like a worried mother hen.

The cell phone flipped shut. "The sheriff and ambulance
are on their way," the gray-suited man announced.

"Can I get you something? Something cold to drink?
Something hot?" Bob blathered.

The flunky in brown pushed him aside. "Why don't you
take care of crowd control?"

Bob nodded like a bobblehead. "Sure, sure."

Again he pushed past Tricia, heading back for the inn's
entrance.

Tricia surged forward, but a hand held her back.
"Tricia!"

Russ! "Let go," she growled, and pulled away. She
crouched next to Paige. "Had you been threatened before
this happened? Who'd want to kill you? Does it have anything to do with those pages Pammy Fredericks sent you?"

Paige opened his mouth to speak, but Tricia was yanked
upright before she could hear what he said.

"Hey!"

"Stand back, ma'am. Give the man some air," said the flunky in brown.

"I tried to stop her," Russ said, sounding like a tattletale.

The wail of a siren cut through the cool autumn morning, and moments later the Stoneham Fire Department's rescue unit pulled alongside the inn's entrance. The EMTs jumped out, equipment in hand, and jogged to intercept Gray Suit.

Tricia and Russ were shunted off to one side, forced to stand with the rest of the rubberneckers. Their attention was riveted on the wounded man, but Tricia stared at the wooded area across the road from the inn. It hadn't been developed. In addition to trees, the area was thick with brush—the perfect hiding place for someone with a rifle.

"Is that where the shots came from?" Russ asked.

She nodded. She was in no mood to look at—let alone speak to—him, and moved aside, skirting the crowd to stand on the other side of the inn's driveway.

Once a couple of deputies had arrived, Bob managed to wrangle his way back to the mob surrounding Paige. No doubt he was already pondering the bad press that this incident would generate, and thinking about damage control.

"He's going to be all right, right?" he badgered.

"His wounds aren't life threatening," an EMT told him, "but to be on the safe side, we're going to take him to the trauma center in Nashua."

Another Sheriff's Department cruiser pulled up outside the inn, and Tricia was surprised Captain Baker wasn't behind the wheel. Good. That would buy her more time.

She decided not to wait for the ambulance to take off, and walked purposefully for her car in the back parking lot. If she could arrive at the hospital before the captain, perhaps she could sneak in to see Paige before the sheriff's deputy could interrogate the philanthropist.

"Tricia, wait!"

She turned and stopped. Russ. Again.

"Tricia!" he called again, and caught up with her. "What were you asking Paige? What's with the envelope you mentioned?"

So, he had heard her. And, typically, he was more interested in the story than in her. He hadn't been this interested on Tuesday before he'd dropped his bombshell about leaving Stoneham.

Her anger boiled over. But instead of coming up with a scathing retort, she settled on simplicity. "Leave me alone."

He reached for her arm, but she wrenched it away. "Come on, we've been friends a long time."

"A year. We were friends for a year. We're not friends anymore."

"Tricia!"

She pointed at the crowd still milling around the Sheriff's Department cruisers and the ambulance. "Go get your story. You need the practice if you're going to be a big-time crime beat reporter once again."

Russ glared at her for what seemed like a long time, and then he turned to stalk back down the driveway.

Tricia watched him for a couple of seconds before she started for her car. As she walked, she pulled her cell phone out of her purse, and punched in the preset button to dial Ginny's cell phone. She picked up on the second ring.

"Ginny, it's Tricia."

"Where are you? The store was supposed to open five minutes ago!"

"I had an errand to run. I'll be right there. By the way,

didn't you once tell me that Brian has an aunt who works at the medical center in Nashua?"

"Sure. Her name's Elsie Temple. She works at the reception desk in the ER."

Bingo!

"Is there any chance you could pull in a favor for me?"

"I can try," Ginny said warily. "What do you have in mind?"

SEVENTEEN

Brian's Aunt Elsie wrung her hands nervously. A woman of fifty or so, her neatly coiffed hair was a dull jet black, with not a gray root in sight. "If anyone but Ginny had asked me to do this, I'd have said no right on the spot," she said, bending to look beyond Tricia, checking for feet in the bathroom's four stalls, and any eavesdroppers. Finding no one there, she handed a visitor's badge to Tricia.

They'd had to meet in a second-floor ladies' room, well out of the way of any security cameras—just in case. Tricia had no desire to get this nervous wreck of a woman fired.

"If anyone asks who you're here to visit, say Smith. Seems like we've always got at least one in the ER at any given time. And for heaven's sake, don't let on who gave you the badge."

"I won't. And I promise I won't cause a disturbance. I only want a chance to talk to Mr.—"

"Don't tell me the patient's name. The less I know, the better. Holy smoke," Elsie nearly whimpered, "I can't believe I'm doing this."

Tricia peeled off the backing and applied the sticker to her jacket. "I'd better go. Thank you."

Elsie nodded, grabbing a paper towel from the wall dispenser and soaking it in cold water. She wrung it out before applying it to her forehead.

The ladies' room door closed behind Tricia, who felt like six kinds of a creep, but she had to get to Paige before Captain Baker did.

Was it possible she could find a dirty laundry bin and rustle up a lab coat? No, without a hospital name badge, she'd be outed in a heartbeat. Playing the visitor card was her best shot to get in and out of the ER without a hitch.

Head held high, Tricia made her way back to the emergency room lobby, looked around, and confidently strode through the doors into the patient-care area.

The ER reminded Tricia of a giant horseshoe, with patient cubicles grouped around center workstations filled with computer terminals. Patient names were written on whiteboards outside each cubicle. It had been at least ten minutes since Paige had been brought in. Since his injuries weren't life threatening, he wasn't liable to be rushed into surgery . . . she hoped.

Thanks to her visitor's badge, nurses and technicians passed by her without a second glance. Good. She passed the last cubicle on the first side, and started down the row to check out the others. Intent on reading the patient names, Tricia almost bumped into a man in a gray suit. Too late she recognized him as part of Paige's entourage.

"What are you doing here?" Gray Suit growled.

"I—I . . ." Caught—and without even finding Paige's cubicle. "I need to speak with Mr. Paige."

"Now is hardly the time." Gray Suit looked around, grabbed Tricia's elbow, and steered her toward the exit. Now she'd not only be shown the door, but probably be turned over to hospital security.

Gray Suit guided Tricia through the ER lobby, right past security, and out the Emergency entrance.

The cool air felt rather refreshing as Gray Suit kept Tricia moving down the sidewalk and away from the hospital. Finally he stopped and let go of her arm. "Paige won't tell you anything," he said at last.

"But you don't even know what I want to ask."

"I heard what you said back at the inn. You asked about an envelope from Pam Fredericks. He never saw it. I'm paid to make sure he *doesn't* see things like that."

"What happened to the envelope?"

"It was turned over to one of Mr. Paige's attorneys."

"Does the Sheriff's Department know about it?"

Gray Suit shook his head.

"Were you aware Pammy Fredericks was murdered?"

Gray Suit looked up sharply. "No, I wasn't. I don't pay attention to what happens in hick towns. But that explains why we didn't hear from her again."

"Don't you find it strange that Pammy attempted to blackmail Mr. Paige and then was found dead a day or so later?"

"Not at all. Sounds like she was bad news."

"A case could be made that someone in Mr. Paige's organization—say, a bodyguard like yourself—might be responsible for her death."

Gray Suit laughed. "Hey, lady, I ain't no James Bond, and I'm definitely not licensed to kill."

Tricia studied his face. He was probably no older than thirty; muscular, with sandy brown hair and dark eyes. Could he be a reader? No, too young. More likely a moviegoer.

"Now that you know about Pammy's death, you ought to report receiving that envelope to Captain Baker of the Hillsborough County Sheriff's Department."

"I'll consider it."

At that moment, a Sheriff's Department cruiser pulled up to the side of the building. Sure enough, Grant Baker sat in the passenger seat.

"And here he is now. I hope you'll do the right thing," she told Gray Suit, "because if you don't, I will."

Baker got out of the car, making a beeline for Tricia and Gray Suit.

"What are you doing here, Ms. Miles?" he demanded.

"I came to see Mr. Paige after he was shot." She jerked a thumb in Gray Suit's direction. "This gentleman works for Mr. Paige. We were just discussing the envelope Pammy Fredericks sent to Mr. Paige last week."

Baker's eyes narrowed. "Envelope? What envelope?"

Tricia explained how Lois Kerr had seen Pammy making copies of the diary, and then immediately afterward she'd gone to the post office, where Ted Missile had seen Paige's name on the envelope.

"Why didn't you tell me this sooner?" Baker demanded.

"Maybe if you hadn't called me a terrier, I would have."

Gray Suit smirked.

"You know very well I meant you were probably stubborn—and now you've proved it."

Tricia balled her fists, willing herself not to haul off and smack the captain.

He'd already moved on. "And you are?" he asked Gray Suit.

"Jason Turner."

"What happened to this envelope?" Baker asked.

"She's right," Turner said with a nod in Tricia's direction. "The package did come to Mr. Paige's office. He never saw it. It's now in the hands of one of his attorneys."

"I'll need the name."

Turner gave it to him. Then he went on, "Look, I need to be inside with my employer. I'll be available for any other questions you have." He fished inside his suit jacket, came up with a business card holder, and handed the captain one of his cards.

Tricia watched him walk back through the emergency room entrance.

Baker stepped around to block Tricia from following. "Wasn't it just a couple of hours ago I told you to stay out of this investigation?"

"Shouldn't you be asking me about the shooting? I was a witness. In fact, what if those shots were intended to kill me—not Paige?"

"I doubt it," he said, and frowned.

Appalled at his disregard for her safety, Tricia felt her mouth drop open. "You're just as useless as your boss."

She turned, but Baker grabbed her by the arm. "Okay, what did you see?"

"Nothing."

Baker pursed his lips. "I'm not going to tell you again: stay out of this investigation."

She glared at him. "You're not my mother." And with that, she stepped off the sidewalk and marched toward her car—angry at him for bringing out the worst in her.

Moments later, Baker jogged to catch up with her. "Ms. Miles, please wait."

Tricia halted, still fuming.

Baker removed his trooper hat, holding it in front of him like a scolded child looking for mercy. "Ms. Miles, let me apologize. We seem to have gotten off track today."

An apology? From a member of the Sheriff's Department?

"I'm sincerely worried that you could get hurt if you continue to poke around and ask questions about Pamela Fredericks's death. As I understand it, you and your sister were nearly killed in a car accident last fall when you got involved with an unsavory character. And you were physically assaulted last spring. I don't want to see a repeat of either scenario."

Tricia found herself looking into Baker's sincere green eyes, and felt herself melting once again.

Damn those eyes!

She swallowed. "I don't know anything more about Pammy's death—or what she did in the hours before she died—than I've already told you."

"Will you please promise me that you'll stop looking into this?"

"How can I promise that? I run a store where every piece of stock involves a mystery. If somebody tells me something, of course I'm going to be curious about the implications. I can't deny my nature, Captain."

Baker exhaled an exasperated breath. "You can be curious all you want. Just don't act on that curiosity. Please!"

Tricia shrugged. "I'll try."

Baker squeezed his eyes shut, his lips pursing. Was he about to explode?

"I think you should ask Mr. Turner where he was at the time of Pammy's death," Tricia said. "How do we know he didn't decide to shut Pammy up after she'd tried to blackmail his boss?"

Baker sighed. "What would his motivation be?"

"Protecting his employer."

"I will definitely speak with him—and his employer, whenever he's available. Now, please put this out of your mind."

"Pammy Fredericks was my friend."

"You said she was 'sort of' your friend," Baker reminded her.

"Nevertheless, we had a twenty-four-year history, even if we weren't particularly close. And what headway have you made in the case?"

"I'm not at liberty to talk about it."

"In other words: none. How about the shooter at the inn? Have you scouted out the woods across the road from the inn?"

"My men are doing that now."

"What are the odds it's the same person who shot at my bedroom window?"

"Of course, we can't rule that out. Yet from what I understand, Mr. Paige was not shot with a BB gun or air pistol."

"Well, of course not. Although as far as we know, they haven't dug a slug out of him yet."

"As soon as I talk to the doctors, I'll know more." Baker set his high-crowned hat back on his head. "Good day, Ms. Miles."

"Good day, Captain Baker."

He turned away, and Tricia continued on to her car. Thinking . . . thinking.

Turner knew the contents of Pammy's envelope. Baker would probably know the contents of that envelope within the hour. She wanted to know, too. Pammy had wanted money to keep the paternity of the journal author's child quiet. Paige was the object of her blackmail scheme.

That explained why Pammy had been killed, but not who had done it. All attention would be riveted on Paige or his associates, as it should be.

End of mystery, at least from Tricia's point of view.

Maybe.

She unlocked her car and climbed in. It was just as well. She had a wedding to host on Sunday, and losing Mr. Everett to his honeymoon during prime leaf-peeping season, she'd be too busy to think about Pammy's death.

It was all for the best.

Why did she have a niggling feeling that she had missed something?

That niggling continued into the early afternoon. Tricia rang up a thirty-nine dollar and eighty-five cent purchase for three Rex Stout mysteries while on autopilot. She kept turning over in her mind what little she knew about Pammy's interactions with Paige and the freegans; neither Gray Suit nor Ginny's friends had been willing to share much.

Ginny staggered to the register, dumping a stack of old books, most missing their dust covers, on the counter for what looked to be the best sale of the day. "This lady here sure is a fan of Ngaio Marsh."

"Yes, I can see," Tricia said with delight, and quickly totaled up the sale. Two hundred and twenty-seven dollars and fifty-five cents. Not a bad afternoon at that.

Ginny bagged up the books and sent the customer on

her way before looking at her watch. "Almost lunchtime. I'm having celery dipped in one hundred percent virgin olive oil."

"Your take from the other night?"

Ginny laughed. "They were the best things we found that night."

"I've been thinking a lot about our Dumpster-diving expedition," Tricia said.

"Sorry you had to come on such a dull night."

"It was very interesting. If nothing else, you have a diverse group of friends."

"I wouldn't exactly say we're *all* friends. But we work together well."

"Tell me, is Lisa always so annoying?"

"Yes. Pete and Brian have been friends since they were kids. Unfortunately, Lisa now comes with the package. She's the only militant freegan in the group. Well, Eugenia thinks *she* is because she once ate vegan for an entire month, but Lisa wouldn't agree."

"I noticed she hardly spoke to Eugenia. They aren't friends, either?"

Ginny frowned. "It's all so complicated—like a soap opera, really. See, Pammy annoyed Eugenia by telling her she knew about her biological parents, and that for a price she might reveal that information."

"What?"

"I thought I told you all this."

"No. Please go on."

"Well, Eugenia's a bit sensitive about being adopted. Her parents didn't tell her until she was about twelve. Mrs. Hirt told her that her biological mother had died and had never named a father on the birth certificate. Eugenia never thought about tracking down her biological parents until

Pammy came along and dangled information in front of her. Eugenia was all upset and told Lisa, who was a real bitch about it. She told Eugenia to hold the drama and get her head together, or see a shrink or something."

"Full of compassion, that one," Tricia commented.

"You said it. Lisa also thinks it's great that somebody's going around ruining all the kids' carved pumpkins. She said there was never such a waste of good farmland as that used for raising pumpkins. She says it's a crop that can't be used for anything but frivolity. I've got to admit that in a way she's right. Still, what doesn't get sold can always be used as compost."

Tricia rolled her eyes, and Ginny laughed but soon sobered. "Anyway, Mrs. Hirt was—" Ginny gave a wry smile. "Well, she was *hurt* that Eugenia would even want to find out about her biological parents."

"Doesn't every adopted child at least wonder about their birth parents? And what kind of proof did Pammy offer?" Tricia asked, thinking about the diary.

Ginny shrugged. "I only got the story thirdhand. Eugenia and I aren't really chummy. But apparently Pammy knew some deep, dark secret about Eugenia, something the poor kid never told anyone about. She was practically hysterical when Pammy casually mentioned it."

"Mentioned what?"

"Lisa didn't know. Eugenia may have been upset, but she wasn't willing to share what she was upset about—at least not with Lisa."

Had Eugenia told her father all this? She'd said she'd asked him not to allow Pammy to join them on their Dumpster-diving expeditions. And conveniently soon after, Pammy was dead.

Sweet little Eugenia a murderer?

No. Tricia refused to believe it.

And yet . . .

"How did you guys get tied up with Eugenia and her father?"

"Brian and Pete have known him since they were little kids. He coached soccer . . . or was it softball?" She frowned. "I'm not really sure. But we've been going out on our expeditions with Eugenia and Joe for at least a year, if not two."

"This morning Captain Baker asked me if I knew any freegans."

Ginny's eyes widened. "What did you tell him?"

"I skirted the question. But it might be a good idea for you or one of your friends to talk to him."

"What for? We don't know anything about Pammy's death."

"Are you sure?"

"I trust those guys—with my life."

"Even Lisa?"

Ginny didn't answer.

"If he asks me again—point blank—I can't lie."

"No, I guess you can't. I'll call the others and see what they want to do."

"Maybe you could all talk to Captain Baker at once."

"Maybe," Ginny said, without conviction. A customer entered the store, and Ginny jumped to attention. "Can I help you find something?"

Tricia looked through the shop's big display window. From this vantage point, she couldn't see the Bookshelf Diner, where Eugenia worked. What deep secret had the poor girl hidden all her life? What did Pammy know about her, how had she found out, and how cruel was she to threaten the kid?

But Eugenia a murderer? No way. Tricia had met her parents and deeply admired her—apparently adoptive—mother. Besides, Eugenia couldn't possibly have the physical strength to pick Pammy up and toss her into the garbage cart. It had to be a man who did that.

That brought her back to Stuart Paige, who also didn't look physically capable of killing Pammy. And anyway, maybe the idea hadn't been to kill Pammy at all. Someone had gotten angry at Pammy and probably decided to scare her. From what the technician had said the day Pammy died, she'd struggled to free herself from the garbage cart before suffocating.

It could have just been a tragic accident. Someone trying to scare someone who'd used scare tactics and blackmail for her own profit. Which brought Tricia back to Jason Turner. He seemed to enjoy being a bully.

Tricia sighed. She simply didn't have enough information. Eugenia might like her as a customer, but she wouldn't reveal to Tricia whatever secret she'd hidden her entire life. Nor was it likely her parents would speak about whatever it was Eugenia found so shameful.

Once again, Tricia found herself back to square one.

EIGHTEEN

 Lunch came and went. The UPS man delivered the little refrigerator and microwave Tricia had ordered off the Internet. The employee break room would soon be a reality. The next steps were to find a table, something to act as a counter, and some reasonably comfortable chairs.

Ginny was as excited as a child on Christmas morning. "Do you mind if I take the appliances upstairs and get them set up?"

"Oh, they're much too heavy for you to cart up the stairs."

Ginny waved off her protests. "No, they're not. If you could see what I've lifted and carried these past few months while working on our house, you'd know I could've been a successful stevedore."

Tricia laughed. "Where did you come up with that description?"

Ginny thought about it. "I don't know—some book I read. I've been reading a lot of classic mysteries lately."

"Yes, I know. And I think it's wonderful. But there's nowhere to put them yet."

"I'll just take them out of the boxes and set them on the floor. I can come in early one day and we can set them up. When we get some furniture, that is."

"I don't want you to get hurt. If they're too heavy, don't mess with them. Maybe I can get Bob to help us take them up. He ought to be good for something."

Ginny giggled and took off for the back of the store.

Business picked up, and Tricia waited on several customers, helping them find their favorite authors and ringing up the sales. In between, she was preoccupied with thoughts of how to approach furnishing the break room. She was staring out the window, looking at nothing, when a Sheriff's Department cruiser pulled up and parked right outside Haven't Got a Clue. She watched as a tight-lipped Captain Baker emerged from behind the driver's seat, slammed his regulation hat onto his head, and marched for the door.

Ginny reappeared and stood behind Tricia. "Uh-oh. This looks like trouble."

Baker opened the door, letting it slam against the wall, stepped inside, and let it bang shut before he advanced on the sales register like an angry bull.

"Where are they?" he demanded, shoving the red-covered diary at Tricia.

"Where are what?"

"The missing pages. There are at least two sheets—four pages—missing."

"There are?"

"Would I be here demanding you return them if I didn't think so?"

"I don't know what you're talking about."

He opened the book to the middle. "Read the last sentence on this page and see if it makes sense to you."

Tricia scanned the cursive text at the bottom of the left-hand page. *I've asked him for money so that I can*—her gaze traveled to the top of the right-hand page—*and I'm not about to make waves. That would insure I never get him back again.*

Tricia frowned. She must have been tired when she originally read that segment of the journal. Otherwise she would've noticed that the sentence didn't make sense. Unless the writer had been fatigued herself, and lost her train of thought. She noticed the diary's signature threads were loose, as though pages had been ripped out. Funny she hadn't noticed that before—maybe because the lighting in her living room wasn't as bright as it could be.

Tricia handed back the journal. "What makes you think I took the page or pages out?"

"You were the last one to have the book in your possession."

"But why would you think I tore them out? Isn't it more likely Pammy would've done it herself? Or how about the diary's original owner?"

"Someone did it. If the diary was found here, perhaps the missing pages are here, too."

Tricia straightened in indignation. "What do you propose? To tear my shop apart looking for them?"

"It's an option."

She stood tall. "I don't think so."

He stood taller. "I can get a warrant."

It was all Tricia could do not to explode. "Captain, Pammy was unsupervised in my store for less than two minutes—more like one minute—before she left here on

Monday. She only had time to hide the diary. My sister and I took nearly every book off the back shelves before she found it. Pammy could've had those pages in her suitcase or her purse. And don't forget, she tried to confront Stuart Paige at the Food Shelf's dedication after she left here. Isn't it likely she would've had them with her?"

"No. Because if he or his associates took them from her, she'd have no leverage for blackmail."

"No one ever said Pammy was the brightest light on the Christmas tree."

Baker had no rebuttal. Instead he turned to Ginny. "Why didn't you tell me you were a freegan?"

Ginny looked like a deer standing in headlights. "You never asked."

He turned on Tricia. "You knew I was looking for freegans. Why didn't you tell me your employee was one?"

Ginny had already used up the best excuse. "I didn't think they could help you. I've already talked to them, and—"

Baker lost it. He yanked his hat from his head and threw it on the counter, startling both women. "When are you going to get it through that head of yours that I'm running this investigation, not you?"

"How did you find out about Ginny?"

"The convenience store owner told me."

Ginny's eyes blazed. "Did he also mention his son is one of us, too?"

Baker spoke through clenched teeth. "No, he didn't." He looked down at the journal still clutched in his hand.

"What's your next move?" Tricia asked. "You've tracked Pammy's movements the morning of her death. She could've dropped off those pages at any one of her stops."

"Yes. I suppose I'll have to go back and interview every-one who spoke with her that day."

Tricia pointed to her watch. "Time's a-wasting."

This time it was Baker who looked like he wanted to slug somebody. Instead, he jabbed his index finger in Ginny's direction. "I'm going to call for another deputy to come and question you. Stay here. Don't talk to any of your friends. Do you hear me?"

Ginny's head bobbed, her eyes still wide.

"I'll talk to you later," he told Tricia, then grabbed his hat, and stormed out of the shop.

Ginny winced. "Are you actively trying to make an enemy out of him?"

Tricia shook her head, almost as angry as Baker had been. "We started off on the right foot, but things have gone downhill since Monday. Maybe it's my destiny to never get along with law enforcement. Me, who's a fan of police procedurals."

"Maybe you should have gone into police work instead of bookselling. For you, it would be just as dangerous as owning this bookstore."

Tricia chose to believe Ginny was kidding.

She glanced down the street and saw Baker enter the Happy Domestic, the first place Pammy had put in a job ap-plication. Next up would be Russ at the *Stoneham Weekly News*, and then Angelica at Booked for Lunch.

Was it possible Pammy had dumped the pages at the last place she'd visited before her death?

"Watch the shop, Ginny. I've got to go see Angelica."

"Sure thing. But what am I going to say to the dep-uty who comes to interview me? Do you think I need a lawyer?"

Tricia shook her head. "Just tell the truth. You'll be

okay." She headed for the door. "I'll be back as soon as I can."

Tricia jaywalked across Main Street and entered Booked for Lunch. The place was a madhouse. Every table was full, as were the stools at the counter. Angelica waited on a table of four while a strident voice at the counter called, "Miss! Miss!"

Angelica looked up and saw Tricia. "See what that guy wants, will you?"

Tricia jumped behind the counter. "How can I help you, sir?"

"More coffee," he said, shoving his stained cup toward her. She reached behind her and grabbed a coffeepot from the warmer. "Not decaf, you idiot!"

Tricia looked down. Sure enough, the pot's handle was orange. "Sorry." She switched carafes and poured. "Do you need creamer with that?"

"Of course I do," he snapped. "Why doesn't the owner hire competent help? First that stupid waitress, and now you."

It took all Tricia's resolve not to pour coffee on his lap.

A little bell rang from somewhere in the vicinity of the kitchen.

"Miss, I could use a refill, too," said a voice at the other end of the counter.

Tricia poured, and offered everyone else a refill.

Angelica rushed to the counter to grab a bottle of ketchup. "What are you doing here—not that I care. I can use the help." She grabbed a jar of mustard, too.

The little bell rang again; twice this time.

"Captain Baker says there're pages missing from Pammy's diary. He'll probably be here any minute to search the place."

"Not until I close! And why would he think she left the pages here?"

"This was the last place she visited before she died. Have you seen anything that looks like diary pages?"

"Miss, where's my ketchup?" a voice demanded.

Tricia threw an angry glare at the offending customer. "Remind me why you wanted to start this business."

"I'm shorthanded, and they want their food when they want it—not when I can get it to them."

"Captain Baker also found out Ginny is a freegan. He was furious because I didn't tell him."

A little bell rang madly from the kitchen.

"What *is* that?" Tricia asked.

"Jake's got my two burgers and fries up. Can you go grab them? They're for table four."

"I've got my own business to run, you know."

"Please?" Angelica pleaded.

Tricia turned. If their father could see the two of them working as waitresses—after all the money he'd spent on Ivy League colleges—he'd have a fit.

She collected the plates and delivered them to table four, grateful Angelica had hung a little numbered ceramic tile above each table. After she'd collected ketchup and mustard for the table and had been assured the couple needed nothing else, she went behind the counter once again. No one was screaming for anything, so she crouched down and began her search.

Though the café had been open only a little over two weeks, Angelica had accumulated a wide assortment of junk behind the counter. Condiments, jumbo coffee filters, packages of napkins, a case of cocoa mix, coffee, nondairy creamer, order pads, a box of pens, odd dishes, silverware, and heaven only knew what else. What she didn't find were the missing pages of Pammy's diary.

"I'd like my bill, please," the counter's crab said.

Tricia looked up. Angelica was conversing with a foursome at table two. "Ange. Check needed over here."

Angelica didn't turn, but gave a backward wave.

"Miss," crabby insisted.

"Ange!"

Angelica turned, reaching into her apron pocket for her order pad. "Sorry, honey," she said, handing the patron his check. "We're shorthanded."

"I'd like to speak to the manager," crabby demanded.

"You're looking at her," she said, tearing another sheet from her pad.

"You ought to hire competent help," he said, glaring at Tricia.

"As I told you, sir, we're shorthanded. Tricia here came over just to give me a hand. Of course, if you'd like to apply for a job as a waiter, I'd be willing to look at your résumé."

The man grabbed the check, thumbed through his wallet, and yanked out a few bills, which he tossed on the counter.

Angelica picked up the money. "Hey, a fifty-cent tip. That's forty-nine cents more than I expected."

The customer stomped out of the café.

"Ange," Tricia whispered, "you shouldn't be so flip with your customers. You know the old saying, 'the customer's always—'"

"Right," Angelica finished. "Well, guess what—sometimes they're not right. Sometimes they're downright rude." She turned back to the people sitting at the counter. "Anybody need another round of coffee?" she asked cheerfully.

Nobody took her up on it.

She turned back to her sister. "How long can you stay, Trish? The lunchtime rush will be over in another fifteen or twenty minutes."

"I guess I could stay that long. But I'm totally incompetent as a waitress."

"It doesn't take a rocket scientist to bus tables. You can start with the stuff on the counter. Afterward, I'll give you a hand looking for Pammy's pages."

"Fair enough."

Tricia scooped up the dishes and took them to the kitchen. Before she could escape, Jake, the cook, had her wrapped in an apron with her sweater sleeves pushed up as far as they would go, and up to her elbows in suds, washing dishes. Just what she needed—dishpan hands.

But Angelica had been right about the lunch crowd. Within fifteen minutes most of the customers had left the café.

"Oh, Trish, you are an angel," Angelica said, swooping in with yet another load of dirty dishes. She scraped the leftovers into a plastic tub and handed the plates and silverware to Tricia.

Jake, who'd been cleaning the grill area, untied his apron. "I'm off to my second job," he said, and grabbed his jacket from the peg. See you tomorrow, Angie."

"'Bye, Jake."

The door slammed behind him.

"He's got a second job?" Tricia asked.

"I pay him better than average, but it's still not enough to make ends meet. I just hope he doesn't quit on me." Angelica handed Tricia a towel. "Dry off, and we'll see if we can't find those papers you're looking for."

Before Tricia could remove her apron, a voice called out from the dining room. "Ms. Miles."

"Oh, no," she groaned, recognizing Captain Baker's voice.

"Which Ms. Miles do you think he's calling?" Angelica asked.

"We'd better both go, although my being here is sure to make him angry—and he wasn't in a good mood when he left my store."

Angelica led the way back to the dining area. "Captain Baker, how nice to see you again." What an actress! She actually sounded pleased to see the man. "Did I tell you my cookbook, *Easy-Does-It Cooking*, is going to be published on June first?"

"Yes. More than once." He looked past her, and saw Tricia. "What are *you* doing here?"

Tricia indicated the damp apron still covering her sweater and the front of her slacks. "Helping my sister. She's shorthanded."

"Bull! You came over here to see if those diary pages were here."

"Well, you can rest assured they're not," Angelica said. "If they were, I'd have seen them in the last four days."

"I did take a peek behind the counter, but couldn't find them," Tricia admitted. "And if I had found them, of course I would have turned them over to you. I want you to find Pammy's killer before someone else gets hurt or dies."

"Do you mind if I have a look?" Baker asked.

"You'd better say yes, Ange. He's already threatened me with a warrant."

He shot a blistering glare in Tricia's direction.

"Of course you can look," Angelica said. "But if you tear the place apart, you're going to put it back the way it was." There was no arguing with *that* tone.

Baker's hostility backed off a couple of points. "Thank you."

"Why don't you start under the counter?" Angelica suggested. He moved away. "Tricia, I think you should go back to your store now. Thank you for helping me with the dishes." She said it loud enough for Baker to hear her.

Tricia untied the apron and handed it to her sister, making a show of it. "You're welcome. If you get in a jam again, you know you can always count on me."

"I'll hold you to it," Angelica whispered. "And I'll give you a full report the minute he leaves."

Tricia nodded and headed for the door.

"We'll talk later, Ms. Miles," Baker told her again.

Not a threat, a promise.

NINETEEN

Tricia glanced at her watch. She'd been gone a lot longer than she'd expected—and with nothing to show for it but chapped hands. Another Sheriff's Department cruiser was now parked outside the Cookery, but its driver was inside Haven't Got a Clue—and so was a crowd of customers, with no one to serve them. A chagrined Ginny sat on one of the chairs in the nook while Deputy Henderson grilled her.

Tricia jumped behind the register. It took nearly ten minutes before she'd taken care of those ready to pay and be on their way, before she could finally leave her post to join Ginny.

Henderson slapped his notebook closed. "Thank you, Ms. Wilson. You've been very helpful."

"I don't see how. I told you, I don't know anything."

The deputy nodded to Tricia and headed for the door.

"Are you okay?" Tricia asked once the deputy had left.

Ginny nodded. "But my friends are going to kill me for dropping a dime on them."

Tricia couldn't help but smile at the phrase. Ginny must've picked it up from one of the mysteries in stock—or was she more street savvy than Tricia had believed?

"No luck finding those missing pages?" Ginny asked.

Tricia shook her head. "I didn't think I would." She thought back to her last encounter with Jason Turner. "Only one person I know read those pages. Jason Turner opened that envelope. He read the pages that Pammy mailed to Stuart Paige. But if Captain Baker is still looking for them, Turner must not have told Paige or the rest of his entourage what they said."

"What makes you think they're so important? I mean, if she took them out, maybe she *didn't* want Paige to see them."

Tricia hadn't thought of that. The references to the baby's father were vague—maybe deliberately so. Could Pammy have concocted the whole diary-blackmail scheme by writing a fake diary?

No. She wasn't that smart.

Could the missing pages point the finger at the real father, making the diary useless as a blackmail tool? That made a lot more sense. Had she destroyed them? Knowing Pammy, that didn't seem likely, either.

"How are you going to get this Paige guy to talk?" Ginny asked. "He doesn't know you. He's got no reason to tell you anything."

"That's true, but I've got nothing to lose by trying." Tricia glanced at her watch. Almost two o'clock. "I hate to keep asking you to cover for me, but—"

Ginny waved a hand in the direction of the door. "Go!"

Tricia went to get her coat from its peg at the back of

the store. But first, she made a brief stop in her apartment to pick up something—something that might be the key to getting her inside Paige's hospital room.

The medical center's brightly lit corridors were buzzing with activity. Scrubs-clad nurses came and went, monitoring equipment beeped and buzzed, and as visiting hours were in full swing, people in street clothes seemed to be everywhere.

Tricia thought the hospital might refuse to tell her Stuart Paige's room number, but when she asked at the lobby reception desk, they directed her to the third floor.

The door to Paige's room was open. She stepped inside. He lay on the bed, which was cranked up to a semi-sitting position. Eyes closed, he looked pale, and older than he had a mere six hours ago.

"Mr. Paige?" Tricia called softly.

The door to the private room's bathroom opened, and a figure stepped out. "What are *you* doing here? Get out!" Turner ordered.

"Jason?" came a feeble voice from within the room.

Tricia looked back to the rumpled figure on the bed. Paige's eyes were now open.

"I'm sorry, sir, but you have an unwanted guest."

Turner grabbed Tricia's elbow to usher her out.

"No, let her come in," Paige said, his voice weak.

Turner let loose, and Tricia tiptoed into the room.

"Please, sit down," Paige said, indicating the chair next to his bed.

Tricia took the offered seat. Why was it hospitals provided only uncomfortable chairs for visitors? She clutched her purse on her lap, unsure of what to say. Paige solved that problem.

"You were at the Food Shelf's dedication. And at the Chamber of Commerce breakfast this morning."

"I'm sorry I arrived too late to hear most of your speech."

His smile was weak. "I don't think you missed much."

"I don't know—a new dialysis center could be a boon for Stoneham."

"It will certainly be a boon to dialysis patients in the tristate area. A press release went out earlier today. It'll be on the news tonight, if you're truly interested."

Which explained why Russ had attended this particular Chamber meeting.

"And you are?"

"Tricia Miles. I own the mystery bookstore in Stoneham—Haven't Got a Clue."

"And do you?" he asked.

"Do I what?"

"Have a clue?" He leaned back against his pillow. "Jason has told me about the diary and the pages your friend sent to my office. Now you'll want to know about my relationship with Marcie Jane Collins—everybody else does."

Tricia swallowed. The woman who'd died when Paige had crashed his car into Portsmouth Harbor. "Did she have your baby?"

He blinked. "That's a new one. Everyone else wants to know about the night she died."

"I read the story on the Internet. M.J. died about a year after she gave birth to a child. A child she apparently gave up for adoption. Was it your child?" she asked again.

Paige sighed, looking even more tired.

"Sir, you don't have to answer this woman's questions. You don't even have to put up with her being in this room," Turner said.

Paige waved a weak hand to quiet his employee. "It's

going to come out eventually. I'd rather tell my story to this young lady than to a TV reporter."

"Sir, we can issue a statement. There's no need to—"

"Jason, why don't you go get a cup of coffee and leave us alone for about fifteen minutes?"

Turner looked ready to protest, but nodded. He backed up. "I'll be just outside if you need me," he said, then turned and left the room, closing the heavy door behind him.

"He's very protective of me," Paige said.

"I can see that," Tricia said. Fifteen minutes wasn't much time, and she didn't want to waste it. "Had you ever met Pammy Fredericks?"

Paige shook his head. "I never saw the woman, but Jason tells me she called our offices several times. She mailed us some papers, asking for money or she'd reveal something about my sordid past." The ghost of a smile crept across his lips. "As if anything else could be as embarrassing as what everybody already knows."

"You were saying about your—" Had the woman been his friend, lover, mistress?

"M.J." He smiled. "She liked being called that. Like in the Spiderman comics."

"What did the papers Pammy sent you contain?"

"According to Jason, nothing. At least nothing with my name on it. Just ramblings about hooking 'him.'"

Tricia opened her purse, took out a folded piece of paper, and handed it to him. He took it, fumbled to straighten it out on his lap, and gave a shuddering breath.

"That's her handwriting, all right. Where did you get this?"

"Pammy hid the diary in my shop. I made a copy of it before I handed it over to Captain Baker of the Sheriff's Department."

Paige nodded. He pointed to the date in the top left corner. "See this? At the time the diary was written, I was out of M.J.'s life—had been for at least a year or so."

"Yes, I understand you two had broken up for a while."

He looked at her through narrowed eyes.

"I read several accounts of your colorful past online," she explained.

He shook his head, perturbed. "I wasn't very stable in those days. I drove too fast—drank too much. She worked on my father's clerical staff." He was quiet for a moment, lost in thought. "After we started going out, Dad grew to love her. He hoped she'd straighten me out. Sadly, she only managed that in death. He didn't know she was almost as wild as I was, which was part of the reason we originally broke up. When we got back together, it was as if that wild streak in her took over. She didn't care about anything. We did a lot of foolish things together. Things I'm deeply ashamed of now." He sighed. "No matter what good I've done these last nineteen years, it will never make up for what happened that rainy night in Portsmouth."

"I read that the police theorized the car hydroplaned."

He nodded sadly. "We'd both been drinking. Truth was, at that point, M.J. drank more than I did. She said it helped her forget."

"Forget her child?"

He looked up sharply. "How did you know?"

"I read most of her diary. M.J. was very upset. I take it the child had birth defects. She called the baby . . . *it*."

"M.J. made the mistake of having an affair with a married man after we had parted ways—I never did know his name."

"What happened to the baby?"

"It went into foster care. The people who took it in eventually adopted it."

"Now you're calling the baby 'it,'" Tricia admonished.

"I'm sorry, but I don't know what sex it ultimately ended up being."

Tricia blinked. "Excuse me?"

"Didn't M.J. write about what was wrong with the child in her diary?"

"No."

"It was born with multiple sex organs. The baby needed gender assignment surgery. M.J. saw it as a punishment for her affair."

"The baby was a . . . hermaphrodite?"

He nodded. "I believe the more popular term now is intersex. To make things worse, M.J. suffered from postpartum depression. It wasn't as well understood in those days. Sometimes not understood today, either."

"You seem to know a lot about it."

"My foundation has contributed funds to study it, to find new medications that can help women in need."

Paige closed his eyes, and Tricia decided he'd had enough traumas for one day. She reached out to touch his arm. "Thank you for seeing me, Mr. Paige. I'm sorry I had to drag all this up for you again."

His smile was tepid. "I suppose I'll have to go over it with Captain Baker at some point in the future, but I don't understand what significance it can have to his case. Ms. Fredericks may have tried to blackmail me, but she never would've succeeded. I wouldn't have paid. The child wasn't mine."

Tricia shook her head. Pammy had probably figured blackmailing Paige was worth a shot, withholding the missing pages that would back up his claim of innocence. A paternity test would've cleared him in a heartbeat, but Pammy probably hadn't been smart enough to consider that, either. There could only be one reason she'd withheld those pages: they had to have named the baby's real father.

If Pammy had been smart, she would've destroyed the pages. But time and again Pammy had proven she wasn't that sharp. Unless she reserved the pages in some kind of backup plan in case Paige wouldn't pay. Could she have saved them to blackmail the baby's real father? But why? Unless that man had money or something else that would improve her life.

It just didn't make sense.

Then again, Pammy had never made sense.

Tricia noticed Paige staring at her. "Do you read mysteries, Mr. Paige?"

"Yes, as a matter of fact I do. Dick Francis is my favorite author."

"As I mentioned, I run a mystery bookstore in Stoneham. May I send you a few titles?"

"I'm missing several of his early books from my collection. Do you have a copy of *Bonecrack* at your store?"

"I sure do, and I'd be glad to send it over."

That would be very kind of you. Let me pay you for—"

"You'll do no such thing. It would be my pleasure to give it to you."

"You're very kind. Thank you." He handed her the sheet of paper.

"Would you like to keep it, as sort of a remembrance?"

He shook his head. "I don't like to remember M.J. from that last year of her life. I prefer to think about the days she worked for my father, before all the unhappiness consumed her."

Tricia nodded and rose from her chair. "Thank you for seeing me."

Turner stood outside the door, his expression dark.

"I hope you didn't upset the old man. It wouldn't be good for him."

"Actually, I'm surprised the hospital kept him here. The paramedic said his injury wasn't life threatening."

"No, but his kidney disease is. He's already had one failed transplant, and has been back on dialysis for years. So far they haven't been able to locate another donor kidney for him."

"Surely a man in his position—"

"Oh, I'm sure he could buy one from a living donor—but that's not his style."

Tricia remembered how pale Paige had been at the Food Shelf's opening. No wonder he'd stepped up his philanthropic gifts. If he felt his time was growing short, he might want to see the fruits of his generosity.

"I'm very sorry to hear that. I'll be sending over a book for him. I'll have it left at the reception desk. May I call you to be sure Mr. Paige has received it?"

Turner reached into his pocket and withdrew his business card holder once again. He handed her a card. "Please don't stir up any trouble." His concern was genuine.

"Believe me, I'm trying to stop trouble from erupting."

"Then you'd better be careful. Being in the middle of something you don't understand could get you killed."

"Is that a threat?"

He shook his head. "Just an observation."

*   *   *

It was nearing five o'clock by the time Tricia returned to Haven't Got a Clue. As usual, customer traffic had thinned. In fact, there were no customers in the store. Ginny leaned over the sales desk and looked up as the door opened and Tricia strode in. She'd been reading a copy of *This Old House* magazine.

"Looks pretty dead," Tricia said, indicating the lack of warm bodies in the shop.

Ginny nodded. "Thanks to the Pumpkin Festival, I don't think we've pulled in ten dollars in the last hour. How did it go at the hospital?"

"It went. I'm convinced Stuart Paige and his people had nothing to do with Pammy's death."

"How come?"

"He's too nice. And he's not well. In fact, I promised to send him a book at the hospital. How would you like to go home early tonight?"

Ginny frowned. "Didn't you say he'd been taken to the medical center in Nashua?"

"I'll give you gas money. If you go there and back, you should still be home at least a half hour earlier than usual."

Ginny nodded. "Okay. That'll give me time to slap some joint compound on the living room's new Sheetrock before dinner. Let me get my coat."

Two minutes later, Tricia had wrapped up a copy of *Bonecrack*, given Ginny Turner's card with instructions to call him when she arrived at the hospital, and sent her on her way. Tricia stared at the clock. She still had another hour and forty-five minutes before closing time. After that, she'd go upstairs, scrounge in the fridge, and settle down with a good book.

She glared at the phone. It wasn't going to ring. It wouldn't be Russ, calling to apologize for this morning. His phone message said he wanted to talk, but he hadn't called again. That meant he'd only been trying to smooth things over. To assuage his guilt, perhaps? And anyway, if he was the photographer at Grace and Mr. Everett's wedding, he could talk to her then. He probably knew about the new job by now. Maybe he'd even gloat.

Now she was being ridiculous.

Tricia glanced out the window. A light still glowed inside Booked for Lunch. Angelica was probably holed up in her café's kitchen, preparing the food for Grace and Mr. Everett's wedding. She hadn't called to tell Tricia the results of Captain Baker's search, as she'd promised. Or if she had, Ginny hadn't mentioned it.

Tricia picked up the heavy receiver on the old 1930s phone. She dialed the number and waited as the phone rang and rang. Twelve, thirteen, fourteen times before it was answered with a testy "What do you want?"

"Ange? It's Tricia. You said you'd call me after Captain Baker left your place."

"You caught me at a bad time. I'm working on the food for Grace's wedding."

"And?" Tricia prompted.

"Captain Baker didn't find a damn thing. I could've told him he wouldn't—but why listen to me?"

"I've been to see Stuart Paige. Lots to report, but it doesn't get me any closer to finding out who killed Pammy."

"Why don't you just let the captain work this out? I mean, why are you so interested?"

Tricia wasn't sure she could answer that question.

"Ginny said it's been dead here for the last hour. I'm

feeling discouraged. In fact, I may even close the store early tonight."

"Terrific. Then come over here and help me with these mini quiches."

"You know I can't cook."

"You just have to assemble ingredients; I'll do the cooking."

Tricia sighed. "Why not? I'll be over in about ten minutes."

"See you," Angelica said, and hung up.

Tricia hung up the CLOSED sign on the door, pulled the shades, and put the day's receipts in the safe. She checked to see that Miss Marple was asleep in one of the chairs in the nook before she grabbed her jacket and purse, and headed out the door.

Angelica was waiting for her, and let her into the darkened café. "Come on back to the kitchen."

With only the dim security lights on, the café's usually bright and cheery interior looked dated and unwelcoming. It was far more pleasing in the light of day. Tricia followed her sister to the cramped kitchen.

The work counter was littered with bags of flour, cartons of eggs, and mounds of what looked like seaweed on a platter. "What's that?' Tricia said, turning up her nose as she hung her jacket on a peg next to Angelica's.

"Thawed frozen spinach. You can squeeze it dry while I whip up the eggs. I've already got all the little pastry shells made. See?" Angelica pointed to the stack of mini muffin pans and their contents. "I'll bake and freeze these tonight, and then thaw them and pop them in the oven on Sunday morning, just before the ceremony."

Tricia's lip curled as she contemplated the mass of wet,

limp spinach. "Spinach for breakfast? What were you thinking?"

"These days, people don't eat enough fruits and vegetables."

Tricia sighed. "No matter how many veggies you put in a quiche, it'll never be a healthy food. You'll be putting Grace's guests in danger of a heart attack."

"Get on with your work," Angelica said.

"Okay, what do I do first?"

"Wash your hands. And scrub them like you were about to do surgery. There's a nailbrush on the sink. Use paper towels to dry them. And don't touch the rim of the garbage pail when you throw them away."

Tricia did as she was told, while Angelica cracked eggs into a large plastic bowl.

"Tell me all about what happened after you left here this afternoon," Angelica said.

Tricia told her tale as she squeezed cold, green juice from the spinach until her hands ached.

"I'm betting Pammy tore those pages out of the diary because they would've proved Paige wasn't the father of M.J.'s child. And knowing Pammy, if she couldn't wring money out of Paige, she might have tried to go after the baby's real father."

"That doesn't make sense," Angelica said, as she beat eggs with a big metal whisk. "Why would the real father care about the baby twenty years later? At this point in time, he might not even be married to the same wife. Hardly anybody lasts twenty-plus years of marriage these days. We're prime examples."

"But just say he was—that news could destroy his marriage."

Angelica shrugged. "So many people harp about the sanctity of marriage—but if it's so sacred, why is this country's divorce rate more than fifty percent?"

Tricia finished squeezing the last of the spinach. She dried her hands. "I'm convinced that Pammy left those pages here in this café."

"Don't get your hopes up. Captain Baker was pretty thorough in his search. He did everything but empty the bags of flour."

Tricia's eyes widened. "Where was Pammy working before I found her in the garbage cart?"

"Here in the kitchen. She was washing dishes."

Tricia looked up at the sacks of flour and sugar on the shelf above the triple sink. Most of them hadn't been opened.

"Let's go back to the day Pammy died. Jake had left for the day. You were busy out front with the last of the customers—or cleaning up or something, right?"

"That's right," Angelica agreed.

"So Pammy was here in the kitchen, all alone. What if someone called her out to the back of the café? If she had the pages on her, and she recognized the voice, she might have stuffed them into something really fast—if she wasn't prepared to give them up just yet."

"I told you," Angelica said patiently, "Captain Baker tore this place apart."

Tricia studied everything on the shelves above her. A big glass jar held white crystals. Sugar or salt?

"Why is that stuff up there in a jar—and what is it?"

"Sugar. I had ants just after I started stocking the place. I didn't want to spray chemicals around my food prep area, so I sprinkled some borax on the shelves and put my sugar in jars. I haven't seen an ant since."

Tricia reached for the jar. The lid did not want to come loose.

"Give it to me," Angelica said. Since the opening of the café, her nails had taken a beating, but her hands were bigger and stronger than Tricia's. She wrenched off the lid and shook the container. The sugar didn't want to budge. She grabbed a spoon from the drying rack, plunged it into the sugar, and stirred it around.

Nothing but sugar. No folded pages. No nothing.

"Rats! I was really hoping we'd found them," Tricia said.

Angelica replaced the lid and put the jar back on the shelf. "Too easy. And I'm sure Captain Baker looked in every other container in this kitchen, too. Those pages just aren't here."

Tricia wasn't about to give up.

While Angelica stirred the spinach into the egg mixture, Tricia took out the step stool and moved it to the shelving. Since Angelica seemed in an affable mood, Tricia decided to broach a potentially volatile subject. "Frannie has fallen in love with Penny."

"Penny?" Angelica asked, squinting down at her recipe.

"Her new cat." Tricia climbed to the stool's top step and steadied herself by grabbing onto the shelf. It was obvious everything had been moved, for Angelica liked order, and nothing was lined up to her usual standards. Cans of vegetables, tuna, and fruit stood next to a meat slicer and a food processor—everything you'd expect to see in a small working kitchen.

"She hates to leave the poor little thing all alone at home while she's at work all day. It could make for a neurotic cat."

"Well, she's not bringing it to the Cookery. I've made that clear. And I'm assuming she'd have to lug a carrier with her to work everyday. That wouldn't be good for the cat. Talk about making the thing neurotic. Can't she get it a friend to keep it company during the day?"

"Maybe," Tricia admitted, exasperated.

"If there's one thing the Cookery doesn't need, it's some kind of animal mascot," Angelica said, and it was obvious by her tone that the subject was now closed.

Tricia wasn't ready to quit. "Ange, what is your problem with people having pets? Just because *you* don't like them—"

"I'll tell you what's wrong with pets," Angelica said, shaking her whisk in Tricia's direction. "They die on you. You give them all your love for years and years, and then they go and die on you, and give you a broken heart." She finished the sentence with a sob, her eyes filled with sudden tears.

"Ange," Tricia said, with understanding, "have you lost a pet?"

Angelica wiped at her eyes with the edge of her apron. "Maybe."

"There's no maybe about it. Was it a dog or a cat?"

Angelica sniffed. "A toy poodle. His name was Pom-Pom. John, my second husband, bought him for me. When he left, all I had was my little Pom-Pom. He was the joy of my life. And then he got sick. Cancer." Tears cascaded down Angelica's cheeks, and her face scrunched into an ugly mask of grief.

A lump formed in Tricia's throat. "I'm so sorry, Ange. You never told me you had a dog."

"Well, why would I? It sounds so stupid to love a damn animal."

"No, it doesn't. Pets enrich our lives."

Angelica waved a hand in dismissal. "Anyway, after Pom-Pom died, I told myself I'd never put myself through it again."

"How many years did you have him?"

"Just three. He was such a tiny boy. I spent thousands of dollars on treatment, but it didn't help. It nearly killed me when I had to have him . . ." She couldn't finish the sentence.

Tricia wrapped her arms around her sister. "I'm sure he loved you. And you had three wonderful years with him."

Angelica sniffed. "Not nearly enough." Then suddenly she was sobbing into Tricia's shoulder.

Tricia patted her sister's back. "How long have you been denying yourself the love of a pet?"

Angelica hiccuped. "Fifteen years."

"Oh, Ange, I'm so sorry."

"I don't understand how you can allow yourself to love that silly little cat of yours, knowing you're going to lose her someday."

"It's painful to lose a pet. Especially for people like us, who'll never have children. But I like to think of the wonderful years Miss Marple has already given me, and I hope we'll have many more years together. Our pets give us unconditional love. Something we can't always count on with people," she added, thinking of both her ex-husband, Christopher, and Russ.

"It's been a long time since you lost Pom-Pom. And you've got a lot of love inside you. Wouldn't you like to share it with someone besides just me and Bob?"

Angelica pulled back and wiped the tears from her eyes. "Maybe. But my heart would be broken when that pet died, too."

"Yes, but if your heart breaks, at least you know it was *real* love that you felt." Tears filled Tricia's eyes, too. "I'm not saying this right. What I guess I mean is . . . why deny yourself any kind of love? You deserve it, Ange."

Angelica straightened up, took a stiff breath, and swallowed hard. "You know, maybe you're right. I was a wonderful mother to my sweet little Pom-Pom."

"Yes. And you could do the same for some other dog or cat. There are a lot of abandoned dogs and cats who need homes."

"I don't know if I'm ready to do this again just yet."

Yet? Pom-Pom had been consigned to doggy heaven at least fifteen years before.

"When you are, you should really consider contacting a shelter to make your choice. I'd be glad to help you with that."

"Well, I guess I hadn't thought that getting a new pet would actually honor Pom-Pom's memory," Angelica said softly. "No other dog could ever take his place."

"Of course not." Tricia patted Angelica's back one last time, and stood back. "And you know, if you gave her a chance, you might get to like Frannie's cat."

"Cats aren't as bad as I thought," Angelica admitted. "I actually kind of liked it when you and Miss Marple stayed with me last spring. She's really not a bad little cat at all."

Tricia smiled. "No, she's not."

Angelica cleared her throat and started beating the egg mixture with renewed vigor.

Tricia let out a long breath, feeling exhausted.

She let her gaze travel around the entire kitchen. Everything looked just fine . . . except for maybe the clock, which was a teensy bit crooked. No doubt Captain Baker had knocked it askew during his search of the premises.

She moved the step stool across the kitchen.

"What are you doing?" Angelica asked.

"The clock is crooked. It bugs me."

"And you always say *I'm* the picky one."

Tricia mounted the steps. As she grasped the clock, something slid out from behind it. "Eureka!" In her haste to get down, she nearly fell.

"Watch out!" Angelica cautioned.

Tricia scooped up the folded papers and spread them out on the counter. They were indeed the missing pages from Pammy's diary.

"Read, read!" Angelica encouraged.

Tricia scanned the words.

I'm so annoyed with Joe. At first he was angry about the baby, but I thought I'd wear him down. Libby can't have children, after all. Why should he want to stick with her when I can give him what he wants?

Tricia gasped. "Good Lord! Joe—Libby! She's talking about the Hirts."

"You think little Eugenia's father killed Pammy?" Angelica asked, aghast.

Tricia's mind whirled with the implications. "Oh, sweet heaven! Eugenia was the baby who needed gender assignment. No wonder she didn't want anyone to know her secret. Can you imagine how the kids at school would have teased her with that piece of news?"

"But she's been out of school for years," Angelica said.

"Public school, yes, but she's still taking classes at Daniel Webster College in Nashua."

"I'm sure she's practically anonymous at college. Unless you live on campus, most people are."

Tricia's mind whirled with the implications. "It had to be Joe who killed Pammy, don't you see?"

"That poor woman," Angelica said, shaking her head in sympathy.

"Who, Pammy?"

"No, Libby. Married to a rat. Well, what else is new? I've married four rats." Angelica nodded at the pages on the counter. "What are you going to do with them?"

Tricia sighed. "I certainly don't want to confront Joe Hirt. I'm going to let Captain Baker take care of that." She grabbed her purse from the counter and dug through it until she found the business card the captain had given her days before.

By the time the captain arrived more than an hour later, all the mini quiches had been baked and were nestled in plastic wrap in the café's large freezer.

Tricia and Angelica were sitting at the counter in the dining area, eating tuna sandwiches and spooning up Angelica's delicious potato-leek soup, when the cruiser arrived. Angelica let the captain in.

"Thank you for calling me, Ms. Miles. Somehow I had the impression you were going to try to deliver justice by yourself."

"Not me. Last time out, I got my nose broken. I'm content to stand quietly along the sidelines."

"I'm not sure I would have believed that a few hours ago."

"I'm sorry if you thought I was interfering. I simply wanted to make sure that whoever killed Pammy was found."

"Why don't you have a cup of coffee while you look them over?" Angelica suggested.

This time, Baker took her up on her offer, settling at one of the counter's stools. He quickly skimmed the pages. When he'd finished, he picked them up, waving them in

Tricia's direction. "This doesn't prove Joe Hirt killed anyone. All it says is that he fathered a child, with a birth defect, out of wedlock. I'll be speaking with him concerning
this, but we're still a long way away from proving he or
anyone else killed Pamela Fredericks."

"I suppose you're right," Tricia said. "But at least you
have one more piece of the puzzle."

He stood. "I don't want you to speak to anyone in the
Hirt family until this whole thing is settled. Do I make myself clear?"

"I wouldn't know what to say. But what if I run into
Eugenia at the Bookshelf Diner?"

"Stay away from her until this is resolved." Baker
glanced around Angelica's café, which looked a lot more
cheerful with all the lights turned on. "What's wrong with
eating here? It seems like a charming little place."

"Why, thank you, Captain Baker. Are you in a hurry?
I've got some wonderful potato-leek soup that's to die
for!"

"No, thank you, I've already had dinner. But it does
smell good."

"Suit yourself," Angelica said, and dug into her soup
once more.

Tricia walked him to the door.

"It goes without saying that you shouldn't talk about the
contents of the diary," Baker said.

But she already had. Ginny knew some of what the diary
held. Thankfully, Tricia hadn't told her what she'd learned
from Stuart Paige. And it would be best not to tell her that
Eugenia was the subject of the entire diary, since the two
young women were . . . kind of . . . friends. The same kind
of friends she and Pammy had been? More like acquaintances stuck with each other.

Tricia cleared her throat. "Of course, Captain. I don't want anything to interfere with your investigation."

"Thank you, Ms. Miles."

"Call me Tricia."

He nodded and smiled. "Tricia." He tipped his hat. "Good night."

Tricia closed the door, lingering as she watched the captain get into his cruiser and drive off.

"*A-hem!*"

Tricia looked over at her sister. "What?"

Angelica sported an absurdly smug expression. "Methinks you're sweet on that man."

Tricia frowned. "Don't be absurd. I'm merely glad he's not as obnoxious as his boss. And besides, now that he's got the missing diary pages, I'll probably never see him again."

The thought saddened her, but she wasn't about to admit it to Angelica.

"Sit down and finish your soup," Angelica said. "After all, now you can relax. No matter what happens next, it's totally out of your hands."

It certainly was.

TWENTY

 It was after ten when Tricia decided to put her book down and go to bed. Only then did she real- ize that for the first night since Pammy's death, she hadn't been bothered by her mysterious caller. Did that prove it had been Joe Hirt on the other end of the line? No one had shot at her windows, either. Eugenia had said she and her father shot skeet. Had Captain Baker thought to ask him about owning any guns? And had the captain spoken to Joe with Libby or Eugenia present? She hoped not. But if Joe had killed Pammy, everything would eventually be made public. Would the community rally around Libby? She'd worked tirelessly for more than two decades to help those less fortunate. She deserved better than to be the sub- ject of vicious gossip.

Everything will work out, Tricia told herself. But the un- easy feeling in her stomach wouldn't go away.

She turned off her bedside lamp and sat on the edge of

her bed, staring at the closed curtains. Miss Marple jumped up to join her and gave a hearty "*Yow!*"

"I don't like them being closed, either," Tricia said.

She petted the cat's head and scratched behind her ears, idly wondering how Frannie had made out with Penny. Miss Marple made herself comfortable on the bed, but Tricia didn't feel as settled as her cat. She got up and nudged the curtains where they met in the center of the window. Once again she saw a figure dart along the west side of Main Street. With hands raised overhead, the figure tossed yet another carved pumpkin into the center of Stoneham's main thoroughfare.

She thought she recognized that silhouette, and grinned. It wasn't only the freegans who donned black and slunk through the shadows like cat burglars. She wasn't sure what she would do with this new knowledge.

She let the curtain fall once again. "Oh, well, there's always tomorrow."

"*Yow!*" Miss Marple agreed.

Tricia awoke early the next morning, and decided to make use of the time by working in the storeroom. Ginny had moved the microwave and fridge to the second floor the day before, and Tricia was determined to whip at least one part of her mini warehouse into an employee break room.

The front of the storeroom overlooked the street, and contained shelves full of inventoried books, as well as twenty or thirty cases of books that still needed to be unpacked and sorted. The cavernous room also held the assorted furniture and bric-a-brac she hadn't wanted to incorporate into her apartment. Assessing the space, Tricia decided the back of the room could be sectioned off to make an agreeable space for Ginny and Mr. Everett to eat their lunches or just take a break.

She unearthed her old kitchen table and chairs, and a sideboard that would hold the microwave, and dragged them into place. Digging through a box of kitchen utensils, she found mismatched silverware, a napkin holder, and eight mugs. Only three of the mugs were chipped, and she tossed them. Next she scrubbed the old utility sink so they had a place to rinse their dishes.

It was nearly nine thirty when Tricia stood back to evaluate her work. The space needed some homey touches, but it would do for now. She had just enough time to take a quick shower before opening the store.

Tricia had finished pouring water into the coffeemaker and hit the On button when she heard a knock at the door. She answered it and found a red-eyed Ginny, who'd shown up for work a full five minutes early.

"Is something wrong?" Tricia asked.

Ginny shook her head and sniffed. "No." Her voice was strained. "Yes."

"Why don't you hang up your coat, and then come back and have a cup of coffee?"

Ginny nodded and shuffled toward the back of the store. By the time she returned, Tricia had poured the coffee. She handed Ginny a cup, and they moved to sit in the readers' nook.

"Now, tell me what's wrong."

"Every Friday night I balance our checkbook. Last night was no different. But things just aren't adding up. Brian works all those extra hours, and it's not showing up in the bank."

"Did you ask him about it?"

She shook her head. "I'm not sure if I want to know the answer."

What had Angelica said about rats?

Tricia decided to push. "What do you suspect—that he's seeing someone on the side?"

"Until last night, I never would've even considered he might cheat on me. We've been together since high school."

And maybe that was part of the problem.

"What do you think I should do?" Ginny asked.

Tricia chose her words carefully. The last thing she wanted was to give Ginny advice and then have it blow up in her face if Brian had a reasonable explanation for his actions. "I've always found the best thing to do in these situations is to talk things through." The way she had talked things through with Russ? By leaping out of her seat and fleeing from his house? By refusing to return his telephone calls?

Oh, yes, she was one to talk. But then, she wasn't in the dark about where their relationship stood. Russ had made it plain he was moving on.

Tricia took in Ginny's tear-swollen eyes and decided it was time to lighten the mood. "Hey, I've got a surprise for you."

Ginny sniffed. "For me?"

"The break room. It's finished. Well, almost."

Ginny brightened. "Do we have time for me to look at it before we open?"

"Sure."

Tricia led the way upstairs to the storeroom. She threw open the door. "Ta-da!"

Ginny entered before her, her mouth opened in awe. "When did you have time to pull this together? It was a mess the last time I was up here."

"This morning. I got up a little early. The fridge is plugged in, and I even tested the microwave. It does boil water."

"This is fantastic. Thank you, Tricia. You sure know how to keep your employees happy."

Tricia glanced at the microwave's clock. "Oops! We should've opened a full minute ago. We'd better go. I hope you won't sit in your car to eat your lunch anymore."

"No way. Maybe I'll bring in my old boom box. That way I can listen to music while I eat lunch or read."

"Go for it!"

Back in the store, Tricia unlocked the shop door, turned the sign to say OPEN, and headed for the register. Not thirty seconds later, the door opened, the little bell overhead jingling as Joe Hirt stepped over the threshold. He didn't look happy.

"Hello, Tricia."

Tricia's heart sank.

Joe nodded at Ginny. "Can I have a few minutes alone with your boss?"

"No, you can't," Tricia said. "Captain Baker told me I'm not supposed to speak to you."

"I'll bet he did. When was that? Right after you gave him Pammy's diary?"

"I really should go . . . do something," Ginny said nervously.

"No, please stay. Joe, you'll have to leave. I simply can't speak to you about any of this. I promised Captain Baker."

"You're finishing what your friend tried to do—break up my family," he accused.

"I turned the diary over to the Sheriff's Department. Anything else would've been obstruction of justice—a crime. And I really cannot talk about any of this with you. If you don't leave, I'll have to call the Sheriff's Department and have them remove you from my store."

His arms hung rigidly at his sides as he clenched his fists—not unlike Clint Eastwood in an old spaghetti western, about to draw and fire. "We'll speak again," Joe said grimly, then turned and left the shop.

Tricia let out a long sigh and leaned against the counter, feeling drained.

"What's he so pissed off about?" Ginny asked. "And why does he think you're trying to hurt his family?"

"I'm not supposed to talk about it to anyone."

"Not even me?" Ginny asked, hurt.

Tricia shook her head. "I'm sorry, Ginny, not even you."

Ginny sighed, her shoulders sagging. "I guess I have enough problems to worry about anyway."

They both looked up as the shop door opened. This time it was a real customer.

Tricia spoke. "Sometimes the best thing you can do when things aren't going well is to lose yourself in work. That's what I'm planning to do today."

Ginny drank the last of her coffee and tossed the cup into the wastebasket. "You know, we ought to use those china mugs I saw up on the sideboard in the break room—at least for you and me and Mr. Everett. We're wasting a lot of paper when we drink out of these disposable cups several times every day. And it would be better for the business's bottom line."

Trust Ginny to be worried about the store's welfare— if not the entire planet's. "I never wanted to bother with washing them," Tricia admitted.

"How about if I do it?"

"That would be great. Maybe later I'll go upstairs and bring some down, unless you'd like to bring in one of your own from home."

"I do have a favorite one—it's got a little gray cat on it. It reminds me of Miss Marple." At the sound of her name, Tricia's cat appeared and jumped on the counter, giving a *yow!* for attention. Ginny petted her, but even the damp nose nuzzling her hand didn't seem to lift her spirits.

"Hey, you're not supposed to be up here," Tricia scolded the cat. She picked her up and set her on the floor. Miss Marple walked away with her head and her tail held high.

Ginny took a deep breath, as though steeling herself. "I guess I'll ask if this customer needs help."

Tricia touched her assistant's arm, and nodded in reassurance.

With Ginny occupied, Tricia took out the disinfecting spray and wiped down the counter before she headed for the register, taking the paper cup and its tepid coffee with her. The phone rang. She forced a smile into her voice that she didn't feel. "Haven't Got a Clue, this is Tricia. How may I help you?"

"You didn't do as I said," came the voice. "You didn't give me the diary."

That damn voice again. And he/she/it had called the shop line, not her personal line.

"How could I? Besides, I told you, Joe, I can't talk to you. And I've told the Sheriff's Department about these calls. I wouldn't be surprised if they've already tapped my line to catch you." A lie, but the caller didn't have to know that.

"You'll pay for this," said the voice.

Tricia hung up the phone. She wasn't about to be intimidated by Joe Hirt. Instead, she picked up the receiver and dialed the Sheriff's Department. It took five minutes on hold before Captain Baker came on the line.

"I didn't think I'd be hearing from you again," he said.

"Neither did I, but Joe Hirt came to my shop this morning."

"That is a problem," Baker agreed. "I talked to him earlier, and I told him not to contact you."

"He also just called me with that stupid voice-altering device. This time on the shop line—not my personal phone."

"Probably because the caller knew you weren't in your apartment."

That was true. She thought about what he'd just said. "You don't think my caller is Joe Hirt?"

"It could be—but not necessarily."

"I told whoever it was that you were tapping my phones, and would catch him."

His only comment was a flat "Hmmm."

"What do you want me to do in the meantime?" Tricia asked.

"As I told you before; avoid the Hirt family—and keep your curtains closed at night."

"Yes, sir," she said with a bored sigh.

"Tricia, I mean it."

"And I'll do it."

"Thank you. And please feel free to call me with any new developments."

She thought about it. "Does this mean you don't think Joe is the one behind Pammy's death?"

"There's no proof he is."

"But the diary—" Tricia interrupted.

"Is just one piece of evidence. And don't you dare go looking for anything else."

"At this point, I'm totally clueless—and I don't mean that in a Paris Hilton kind of way."

"Well, stay that way." His voice softened. "At least in this instance. Otherwise, I think you're a very sharp lady."

Now who was flirting with whom?

Only . . . for some reason, she didn't mind.

"Thank you, Captain."

He cleared his throat, and when he spoke again, it was in his "cop" voice. "Keep in touch."

"I will. Good-bye." She hung up the phone.

Ginny wandered up to the cash desk. "What are you smiling about?"

Tricia immediately sobered, unwilling to share those particular thoughts and feelings. "Nothing."

It was a glorious fall day in Stoneham, which meant that most of her potential customers were probably in Milford for day two of the Pumpkin Festival. Still, Tricia was determined to enjoy the tiny part of the day she could access—her lunch break. She called Booked for Lunch and placed a take-out order, but instead of immediately picking it up, she decided to take a walk down Main Street.

She passed the Chamber of Commerce. Their new secretary/receptionist, Betsy Dittmeyer, was very sweet . . . in a noncommittal, bland sort of way. Gone were the colorful posters of Hawaii that Frannie had used to decorate the reception area. Instead, the walls were empty of any ornamentation. Not even a picture interrupted the stark order of Betsy's desk. Tricia missed Frannie as the face of the Chamber. Still, the Chamber's loss had been Angelica's gain, and Frannie had blossomed with the responsibility of running the Cookery.

Tricia stopped in front of Kelly Realty. The pile of pumpkins that had decorated the front of the building just days before had dwindled considerably. Surely his give-away program hadn't been that successful. Tricia opened the door to the office, a little bell jingling cheerfully over her head as she entered.

Bob Kelly sat at his desk, the *Nashua Telegraph* propped up before him, as he spooned soup from a plastic container—the same kind of take-out container Angelica used at Booked for Lunch. No doubt she'd been feeding him lunch since the day she'd opened. Okay, she cared for him. That was her lookout. But Tricia wasn't feeling as generous.

Bob looked up, dropping his plastic spoon onto the desk blotter. He yanked away the paper napkin that he'd had draped over his suit coat and shirt. "Tricia, what brings you here?"

"Hello, Bob. Sorry to interrupt your lunch, but I have a couple of questions I'm hoping you can answer."

He smiled and waved a hand, indicating she should take one of the two chairs in front of his desk. This was where he wrote his real estate contracts—and the leases he held on most of the buildings the booksellers occupied on Main Street. Tricia had sat in the very same seat when she'd signed the three-year lease on the building that Haven't Got a Clue now occupied. Later she'd found out she'd paid far more than any of the other leaseholders. That had set a precedent, escalating the prices on all the other leases—something that had not endeared her to the booksellers who had come to Stoneham before her.

"First of all, what do you know about the person who's been smashing pumpkins for the past week?"

"Why, nothing. I'm just as appalled as the rest of the citizens of Stoneham."

"Really?" Tricia asked. "Somehow I find that a little hard to believe."

Bob's mouth dropped open, his eyes growing wide in what looked like genuine anxiety. "Whatever do you mean?" he asked, his voice the epitome of concern.

"Cut the crap, Bob, I know it's you who's been smashing those pumpkins all over town. I saw you do it on Wednesday night, and again last night. I should go straight to Captain Baker and report you. I'm sure you've probably broken more than a couple of laws—including littering."

"I don't think I understand what you're getting at," he said in all innocence.

"I'm telling you I've seen you toss carved pumpkins into Main Street on two separate occasions. Only I wasn't sure until last night that it was really you, and I mean to report you."

"You can't do that!" he cried.

She nodded. "Okay . . . give me a reason not to."

Bob frowned, but didn't offer an explanation.

Tricia waited for at least thirty seconds before she spoke again. "Okay, then answer me one question: Why are you doing this? Do you have some kind of sick squash fetish?"

"I don't owe you any explanations," he grumbled.

So, he didn't deny it.

Tricia crossed her arms. "No, but what will Angelica think when I tell her about this?"

"Why do you have to tell her anything?" he asked, panicking.

"I think she should know what kind of man she's involved with. Someone who'd destroy a child's jack-o'-lantern . . ."

"I did not smash anybody's pumpkins but my own."

"You mean to say you carved all those pumpkins before you busted them all over the streets of Stoneham?"

"Of course I did. You think I want to get arrested for trespassing or stealing?"

"But you made a terrible mess. That costs the taxpayers money."

"The village did not order a street sweeper run. I . . . talked them out of it. Besides, most of the shopkeepers have cleaned up the messes in front of their shops."

"Of course they did. They didn't want their customers to slip in the slimy mess you made, and sue them. And that still doesn't explain *why* you did it."

Bob snorted a few anxious breaths before answering. "For the publicity—what else? It got Stoneham noticed by the *Nashua Telegraph*, didn't it?"

"There was a two-inch story buried in the 'Outlying Towns' section. And do we really want to be known as a village that harbors a pumpkin smasher? Come on, Bob, what's the real explanation?"

"Okay, maybe I'm . . . jealous." The man actually pouted.

"Of whom?" she demanded.

"Not whom, what. Every year that darn Milford Pumpkin Festival gets tons of publicity. People come to the town by the thousands to look at a bunch of stupid old squashes."

Tricia couldn't believe what she'd just heard, and burst out laughing.

"Hey," Bob protested. "It's *not* funny."

"Yes, it is." Tricia covered her mouth to stifle a smirk and had to clear her throat before she could speak. "Milford is a beautiful, picturesque little town—"

"So is Stoneham," Bob countered.

"Yes, but we bring in people twelve months a year, thanks to being known as a book town. Milford has their festival three days of the year. How could you possibly be jealous?"

"We ought to have some kind of festival here, too, and drum up some national exposure."

"Then go for it. Come up with something else. There are three other seasons and a lot of other possibilities you could choose from."

"Like what?"

"I don't know. Pilgrim Day."

"Plymouth, Mass., has that covered."

"Choose another fruit or vegetable, then. Maybe we could have a cauliflower festival, or how about okra?"

"We don't grow them locally," Bob groused.

He'd missed her sarcasm.

"Then how about a 'welcome-back-geese festival' next spring? Or why don't you get that nudist camp down the road to march in the Stoneham Fourth of July celebration?"

Bob's eyes narrowed. "Now you're teasing me."

Maybe she was. She leaned forward on his desk. "Do you really want the rest of the Chamber of Commerce, the Board of Selectmen, and the whole village to know what you've been up to?"

Bob stood, pulled in his overhanging stomach, and puffed out his chest. "Are you threatening me?"

"Not at all. I just want you to stop. And I want you to clean up the mess you've made."

"And what do I get out of the deal?"

"I never tell Angelica just what kind of a nutcase you really are." She shook her head. "I still don't know what it is she sees in you. But—there's no accounting for taste. And you do have *some* redeeming qualities," she said, remembering what Libby Hirt had said about him championing the Food Shelf.

Bob stared into his cooling soup. "Okay, I'll clean up the mess and I won't smash any more pumpkins."

"Good." Tricia rose from her seat. "I'm glad we came to this understanding, Bob. I really wouldn't want the rest of the villagers—and God forbid, the organizers of the Pumpkin Festival—to know anything about this. I mean, you're a respected man in this town. If only for Angelica's sake, I don't want people to think you're a total jerk."

"Thank you, Tricia." His face screwed into a frown as he thought about what she'd said. "I think."

"We'll talk no more about this, shall we?" she asked.

"Yes. Thank you." Bob rose from his seat and walked around his chair, offering her his hand.

She took it, resisting the urge to wipe it on her jacket afterward. "Well, I'd best be on my way. I've still got a business to run."

"Yes. Me, too."

Tricia gave him a big smile. "See you later, Bob."

"You, too, Tricia."

And off she went to pick up her lunch.

It was nearly three o'clock, and once again the store was empty of customers. If Tricia had better anticipated the slowdown, she could've had Ginny start inventorying the books up in the storeroom, but it was too late in the day for that.

The phone rang, and Ginny grabbed it. "Haven't Got a Clue, this is Ginny. How can I—" She paused. "Sure thing. Tricia, it's Frannie—for you." She held out the phone.

Tricia left the shelves filled with true crime titles she'd been alphabetizing, and picked up the receiver. "Hi, Frannie. What's up?"

"Oh, Tricia—I've been meaning to call you all day, but with one thing and another—"

"Don't tell me you made headway with Penny?"

"I sure did. Just like you said. I ignored her last night. It took a few hours, but eventually she came out from behind the couch. First she sat in the middle of the living room. Then, little by little, she moved closer to me. By the time the eleven o'clock news came on, she was sitting on my lap and purring like crazy."

"See, I told you."

"Yes, you did. And I can't thank you enough."

"It wasn't me. It was you. Sometimes you just need to show a little patience where animals are concerned." And people, too?

No, she was not going to think about Russ again. He'd made his decision. He could live with it. She was determined to do so, too.

Tricia heard the soft tinkle of a bell.

"Oops—got a customer. Gotta go. See you at the wedding tomorrow."

No sooner had Tricia hung up the phone than it began to ring again. Tricia picked it up. "Haven't Got a Clue, this is Tricia. How can I help you?"

"Tricia, it's Libby Hirt."

Good grief.

"Libby, I'm not supposed to talk to you or Joe or Eugenia until—"

"Why did you give that diary to the Sheriff's Department? Why did you have to drag up the past? Why couldn't you just destroy the damn thing?"

Tricia took a deep breath. She should hang up the phone. She should do as she had been told, and end the conversation. But the hurt in Libby's voice, the anguish, was like a stab in the heart. "Libby, I'm sorry. It's evidence in Pammy Fredericks's death."

"How? It doesn't prove anything."

"Did you know about Joe's affair with M. J. Collins?"

Silence. Then, "Not until last night. I wish he'd never told me. It destroys the faith I've had in him. It makes our entire marriage a sham. And what will it do to our daughter when she finds out the truth?"

"Perhaps it could bring you all closer together."

"Or it could destroy our family."

"Everyone seems to forget that Pammy Fredericks was murdered."

"Maybe she deserved it," Libby said bitterly. "Blackmail is an ugly game. Would she have bled Joe dry? And what about Mr. Paige?"

"Libby, I know you're upset and you don't mean what you just said."

"And just maybe I do."

She broke the connection.

Tricia hung up the phone. Was there something in the Stoneham water supply causing relationships to crash and burn? First she and Russ; Ginny and Brian might be on the skids; and now Libby and Joe Hirt—who, until yesterday, had apparently represented the village's most stable marriage.

And what was she going to tell Captain Baker, now that she'd spoken to yet another member of the Hirt family? There was no way she could set foot inside the Bookshelf Diner—and run into Eugenia—until this whole mess was resolved. In fact, if she was smart, she wouldn't step outside Haven't Got a Clue.

She forced herself to think about other things. With the wedding set for the next day, she had too much to do. The store needed a thorough cleaning. Although it was last minute, perhaps she should hire a cleaning team to come in—but did cleaners work Saturday evenings? What if she couldn't engage someone to come after store hours? And had anyone thought to rent chairs for the reception? Or maybe tall tables, so the guests had somewhere to park their plates of breakfast foods, champagne, and cake while they ate? She'd have to ask Angelica.

With less than sixteen hours to go, Grace and Mr. Everett's wedding seemed so far away—so normal and life-affirming. And Pammy was still—and forever would be—dead. Although she'd been on the outs with her family for years, it seemed doubly cruel they should decide not to claim her body. There'd be no commemoration of her life. And if Tricia took it upon herself to arrange one, would anyone show up?

Pammy had been shy and awkward when they'd met twenty-four years ago. She'd been shrewd and apparently heartless the last time they'd spoken. And she'd accused Tricia of not knowing how to have any fun. But was fun at someone else's expense enjoyable, or just spite?

Tricia preferred to think the latter.

Pammy was dead and, as far as Tricia knew, no one—and she would have to include herself—would mourn her.

A truly wasted life.

Though she had too many other phone calls to make, on impulse Tricia hauled out the phone book and called the Hillsborough County Medical Examiner's office. Maybe Pammy's family had reconsidered. Maybe plans were already in place for some kind of service, and no one had thought to call her. However, the person she spoke with at the ME's office only reaffirmed what she'd already been told by Captain Baker.

"What does that mean?" she asked, already knowing the answer.

"Eventually, the body will be buried at taxpayers' expense."

"Thank you." Tricia hung up the phone.

Buried in an unmarked grave. Did anyone deserve that?

Several customers entered the store. Tricia waited on them, all the while thinking of the phone calls she needed to make to ensure the wedding went off without a hitch. It was time to put Pammy out of her mind . . . forever.

Still, until her killer was caught, Tricia wasn't sure she could do that.

Everything felt unfinished. Like Pammy's life.

And Tricia hated that feeling of helplessness.

TWENTY-ONE

Tricia couldn't remember a day that wore on as long as that particular Saturday. The Milford Pumpkin Festival really *had* cut into business. The few customers she'd had that afternoon had regaled her with tales of the Great Pumpkin contest, the pumpkin catapult, the chili roundup, and the scarecrow contest. And oh, the food!

Rats, Tricia thought. *Maybe Pammy was right. I always miss out on the fun.*

Eleanor had indeed won first prize in the pie contest—Frannie had called back with that update. No doubt the blue ribbon would be framed and hung over her receptionist's desk at the Brookview Inn by the next morning.

Grace had called with an update about the wedding flowers, thanking Tricia profusely once again for letting them hold the ceremony in the store, and promised she would arrive early the next morning to help coordinate the last-minute details.

The thing Tricia hadn't been able to accomplish was hiring a cleaning firm. That meant the job was up to her. Oh, well . . . she tried to think of it as part of her gift to Grace and Mr. Everett. With Mr. Everett in short supply these last few days, the place had become dusty, so she commandeered his lamb's wool duster and started working on the shelves.

It was ten minutes until closing. Haven't Got a Clue had had no customers for at least twenty minutes when Tricia glanced at her watch. "Don't you just hate this time of year?" she asked Ginny.

"Yes. When the sun goes down, it's like the whole world closes up."

"I've been thinking of adopting winter hours—except between Thanksgiving and Christmas, of course."

"I would hate to see my hours cut, but you have to do what's best for the store," Ginny said sensibly. "Besides, it would give me more time to work on the house. I have this vision of the living room being finished in time for Christmas. I can already imagine a crackling fire in the fireplace, and our stockings hanging from the mantel. That is, if I can find someone to tell me the chimney is safe enough to light a fire."

Tricia laughed. "We'll stay open until seven tonight, but depending on how trade is on Monday, we might as well adopt new hours."

"What about the Tuesday Night Book Club?"

Tricia shrugged. "We might have to start an hour earlier. Hey, dinner at a decent hour. Now there's a plan."

Ginny laughed and began her end-of-day chores, emptying the coffeemaker's filter of grounds, and pouring the last of the coffee down the washroom sink. She was still in the back of the store when the door opened. Eugenia Hirt entered Haven't Got a Clue, her face dark with anger. "What's going on, Tricia?"

Tricia had been counting out the day's receipts, and closed the register's cash drawer. "I'm not supposed to speak to you or anyone in your family. Direct orders from Captain Baker of the Sheriff's Department."

"That's what my mother said. But something's going on, and nobody will tell me what it is. Everyone seems to think *you* know."

"Captain Baker said—"

"I don't give a damn what any sheriff's deputy said. You know, and *you will tell me*!"

"Are you threatening me?" Tricia asked.

Eugenia threw back her head, standing taller. "Maybe I am."

Tricia tried not to laugh. "Go home." She had to fight the urge to say *little girl*. "Your mother is very upset. See if you can make her feel better."

"Not until you tell me what was in that diary."

So, she knew about Pammy's diary. Had Pammy said something, or had she heard her parents arguing about it?

Before Tricia could answer the girl, the shop door flew open. Eugenia whirled. "Dad! What are you doing here?"

"Come on, honey. Let's go home."

Eugenia shook her head. "I'm not leaving until someone gives me some answers."

Ginny reappeared from behind a set of shelves. "What's going on?"

"Nothing," Tricia and Joe said in unison.

"Ginny, why don't you go home?" Joe suggested.

Ginny's face flushed. "Why?"

"Because it looks like Tricia, Eugenia, and I have some serious things to discuss. Things that you don't need to be a part of."

Ginny moved to stand next to Tricia. "I don't think so."

Tricia was grateful for the support, but her tightening stomach told her that Ginny might be safer if she left the store—now. "Maybe he's right, Ginny. I think you should—"

"No way," Ginny said. "I have a few questions of my own. Like why did you try to run Brian's car off the road the other night, Eugenia?"

"I don't know what you're talking about."

"The hell you don't. When we left you and Joe in Nashua on Wednesday night, you came up behind us and sat on Brian's bumper, trying to scare us. Why?"

Eugenia shrugged. "It was a joke. Can't you take a joke?"

"I didn't think it was funny," Ginny said.

"Neither did I," Tricia agreed.

Joe stepped around to the front display window and grabbed the cord, lowering the blinds. Miss Marple, who'd been dozing on the shelf behind the register, got up and stretched. Closing the blinds was usually the signal that dinner was close at hand.

"Why did you close the blinds?" Tricia asked, unease creeping up her spine.

"We need privacy," Joe said. "Ginny, get your coat and go."

"No!"

"I don't care if she hears our business," Eugenia said. "I want to know everything that's going on. I'm an adult. It's time you leveled with me, Dad. What was it Pammy said to you? Please, tell me!"

Joe sighed, all the weight of the world on his shoulders. "She tried to blackmail me."

"With what?" Eugenia insisted.

"Pam said if she couldn't shake down Stuart Paige, she would come after me."

"But Dad, Pammy threatened to tell the world at large about my . . . my birth defect. That would humiliate only me. What else could she have possibly known that would hurt our family?"

Tricia said, "Eugenia's not a child anymore. Tell her, Joe. Libby told me you two have already discussed it."

"Mom knows what?" Eugenia asked.

Joe offered his daughter his hand. She took it, her own visibly shaking. "Princess, we always told you your biological parents were dead. But that's only partially true. Your biological mother died in a car accident when you were still a baby, but your father is alive."

"You know who he is?" she asked, eagerly.

"It's someone you already know and, hopefully, love."

"Who? Please tell me!"

"It's . . . me."

Eugenia's mouth fell open, and for a long time she just stared at the man she'd always known as her adoptive father. "I'm really your little girl?" Her voice was barely a whisper.

"Your birth mother couldn't handle your . . . birth defect. She gave you up for adoption. I wanted you. I talked your mother—Libby," he clarified, "into taking you in as a foster child. I knew she'd fall in love with you—as I already had, even though I'd only seen you from behind the glass window in the hospital nursery."

Eugenia shook her head, her eyes filling with tears. "But Dad, you and Mom have been married almost twenty-five years. I'm twenty-one . . . that means . . ."

Joe bit his lip, and looked like he was about to cry as well.

"I never meant to hurt your mother. It just happened. And the thing was . . . I got you in the bargain. We both got you, and it kept us together. We loved you as you were—we loved you through all the surgeries. We will *always* love you."

They fell into each other's arms, tears streaking their cheeks. Tricia hardened her heart. This was all very nice, but it didn't answer who killed Pammy Fredericks.

The door opened, the little bell below the transom tinkling cheerfully.

Ginny whirled. "Brian! What are you doing here?"

He nodded toward Eugenia. "I followed her."

"Why aren't you at work?" Ginny asked, suspiciously.

"I've got some things to tell you, Ginny. I . . . kind of lost my evening job."

"You what?"

"Two weeks ago," he admitted.

Her eyes narrowed. "And just what have you been doing every work night for the last two weeks?"

"Looking for a new job," he said, his voice harsh.

"And what else?" Ginny asked, and turned her gaze on Eugenia.

"Okay, so I hung out a few nights with Gina."

"Gina?" Ginny asked, the color rising in her face. "Is that your pet name for her?"

Joe looked confused. "What's going on?"

"Nothing, Daddy," Eugenia said.

"Apparently there's a lot more going on than I thought," Tricia said.

"Me, too," Ginny agreed. She turned back to Brian. "And I'd like an explanation."

Brian walked back to the shop door, flipped the sign to CLOSED, and pulled down the door shade. "It might be better if we weren't disturbed."

Fear crept up Tricia's spine. Nothing good would come of this conversation. They might learn the facts of what had happened when Pammy died, but she sensed lives were about to be changed—and not for the better.

Tricia swallowed before she asked her next question. "Who dumped Pammy into the garbage cart?"

"That was me," Brian admitted, turning to face them once again. "I told her to leave Eugenia alone. I only meant to scare her when I tossed her into the garbage."

"Did you know about this, Eugenia?" Joe demanded, his voice hard with anger.

"Not at first," she admitted, and turned her gaze to take in Brian. "I didn't want him to get in trouble."

"Who kept calling me, demanding the diary?" Tricia asked.

"I did it," Eugenia said. "I knew you had to have it. That stinking, evil witch stayed with you for two weeks. I figured since it wasn't in her car—"

"You broke into her car?" Ginny asked.

"We didn't have to. Brian took her keys. We drove the car over to Hanson Lane and looked through the trunk, but we didn't find anything, so we left it there. We figured Pammy would eventually find it. And then she turned up dead, and we were scared."

"What about the calls?" Tricia reminded her.

"Like I said," Eugenia continued, "we figured you had to have it, so we drove to Nashua and got one of those voice-altering things for the phone. We figured I wouldn't get in trouble if I didn't make any specific threat—and I didn't."

"It's up to the sheriff to decide if you've broken any laws." Tricia turned her attention to Brian. "And it's up to a grand jury to decide whether Pammy's death is murder or manslaughter," she said. "But either way, you're both in pretty deep trouble."

"I'm *not* going to jail," Brian said, his voice rising. "I've always liked you, Tricia, but I'm not about to let you ruin my life."

"What about *my* life?" Ginny demanded.

Tricia ignored her. "Brian, your life was ruined the moment you decided to scare Pammy Fredericks. I know you didn't mean to hurt her—but it's your fault she's dead!"

"She was a scumbag. She wanted to ruin people I care about."

"That may be true, but she didn't deserve to die."

"What about *me*?" Ginny insisted, her eyes filled with tears. "Brian, we own a house together. We're going to get *married*."

He turned his anguished gaze toward Ginny. "Babe, I'm sorry. I never thought I'd care for Eugenia the way I do. I mean, we've known each other almost our whole lives. It just . . . happened."

Just like it had happened between Joe and M.J., only Libby had never found out.

"And were you going to leave me for Eugenia?" Ginny demanded.

Brian turned away so he didn't have to look her in the eye. "I . . . thought about it." He shrugged. "Yeah, I think so."

Ginny took a few choking breaths—sounding like a fish out of water. "And what happens now that Tricia and I know you're a murderer?"

The door opened. A breathless Angelica burst in, still dressed in her fifties waitress costume, her feet encased in running shoes. Her eyes were wild with fear. "Are you okay, Trish?"

"You shouldn't have come here," Brian said coldly.

"Run!" Tricia shouted.

But Angelica just stood in the doorway, in shock.

Brian moved fast. In seconds he'd grabbed Angelica's arm and hauled her farther into the store, slamming the door before shoving her against Tricia.

"What are you doing here?" Tricia grated.

"I saw Joe shut the blinds, and I knew Captain Baker told you not to talk to him."

"So why didn't you just call nine-one-one?"

"You two shut up and let me think!" Brian ordered.

"Now what are you going to do?" Ginny demanded. "Throw all three of us into the Dumpster?"

"What's going on?" Angelica demanded.

Brian thrust his hand into his jacket and came out with a handgun, aiming it at Tricia and Angelica.

Ginny gasped. "Where on God's Earth did you get that?"

"Brian, think about what you're doing," Tricia warned. "What happened with Pammy was an accident. If you fire that gun—"

Joe stepped forward. "Nobody's firing any guns. Hand it over, kid."

Brian shook his head. "I don't want to go to jail."

"Tricia's right. You fire that gun, and that's the end of life as you know it."

"You're one to talk. Eugenia told me you shot at Tricia's windows. You shot Stuart Paige," Brian said.

Joe's head snapped as he turned toward his daughter. "That's not true! Please tell me *you* didn't do it."

"I'm sorry, Daddy," Eugenia cried. "I only meant to

scare Tricia. If Paige hadn't moved, he never would've been shot."

"You lied to me," Brian said to her, angry.

"I didn't want you to think badly of me."

Joe's face flushed, and he pursed his lips. He looked past his daughter and spoke to Brian. "You're both already in enough trouble. Enough mistakes have already been made. Don't make any more, kid."

Brian stared at the people surrounding him. The gun in his hand wavered.

"How long are we going to stand around like this?" Angelica groused. "Are you going to kill all of us? What will you do with our bodies?"

"Forensics will always nail a killer, Brian," a grim-faced Ginny piped up. "I learned that reading mysteries and thrillers."

"Shut up, Ginny! Just shut up!" Brian hollered.

Another tear slid down Ginny's cheek. "And to think I almost married you."

"We can't just stand here all night," Joe said reasonably.

Tricia swallowed. Sure they could! The best way to defuse the situation was to talk it out, not egg Brian on. But Joe took another step forward. The gun swung in his direction.

"This is insane!" Eugenia shouted. "Brian, what are you doing? Put that gun down. We'll never be together if you fire that thing."

"Quiet! Just everyone be quiet."

Joe shook his head. "I've had enough." He marched forward, his right hand reaching for the gun.

Brian shot him.

Joe staggered and fell to his knees.

Eugenia screamed and jumped forward. "Daddy!"

Mouth open in shock, Brian stared at the gun in his hand.

"Are you all right? Are you all right?" Eugenia screamed, catching her father's free arm to steady him.

Joe sat back on his heels, his face pale and sweating, his right hand clutching his left side. He took a few ragged breaths. "I think . . . I think so."

Angelica swooned, grappling for the cash desk.

As Brian turned to look, Tricia leaped forward. "Ginny, call nine-one-one!" she yelled, and lunged at Brian, knocking the gun from his hand.

It skittered across the carpet. Tricia, Ginny, and Brian all dived after it, scrambling across the floor on their hands and knees, and into the nook. Three hands snatched at it, and the gun was pushed under one of the heavy upholstered chairs.

"Get away! Get away!" Brian shouted.

"Not on your life," Tricia grated.

Their hands knocked against each other as they fumbled for the gun, but it was Tricia who came up with it. She rolled onto her backside, the gun clasped in both hands, and leveled it at Brian's chest, the way she'd seen in a hundred TV shows.

He struggled to his knees and laughed at her. "You won't shoot."

Her eyes blazed. "Wanna bet?"

"Angelica, call nine-one-one!" Ginny yelled.

The sound of a siren cut the air.

"I did that before I got here," Angelica said with a smirk.

Ginny pulled herself up with the aid of the chair's arm. "You could've said so."

"And let this bozo know it? You ought to be ashamed of yourself, Brian. Also a pretty clever ruse—me pretending to faint, huh?"

No one commented.

Brian sat in a heap, looking boneless. Joe had been right: life as Brian knew it was now over. The same could be said for Eugenia, too.

The Sheriff's Department cruiser screeched to a halt in front of Haven't Got a Clue, and Captain Baker and Deputy Placer spilled from the car. Placer kicked in the door and they sprang inside, their weapons drawn. Baker took in the scene before him: Eugenia crying, Joe bleeding, Angelica and Ginny standing guard, Tricia still flat on her butt on the floor, clutching the gun.

"What the hell?" Baker asked.

"Show's over, guys," Tricia said. "But you're more than welcome to take over."

Baker holstered his weapon while Placer kept his trained on Brian.

"What are you doing on the floor?" he asked Tricia, offering his hand.

She looked up into those mesmerizing green eyes. "Taking care of business." Her grip slackened and she handed him the gun, handle first. Then he helped her up.

She grabbed Baker's tie, pulling him close, leaned forward, and kissed him hard on the mouth, then pulled back. "You are not Christopher, and you're definitely not Russ," she declared.

Startled, Baker stared at her in incomprehension. "What?"

"I just wanted to establish that from the get-go."

"Whatever," he said, a flush coloring his cheeks, and he

removed her hand from his tie. He cleared his throat. Everyone was looking at the two of them.

It was Tricia's turn to blush.

"Now, then—what the hell has been going on?"

"I think I'll put the coffeepot back on," Ginny said wearily. "This is going to take a lot of explaining."

TWENTY-TWO

It seemed like hours later that the ambulance bearing Joe Hirt took off, heading for St. Joseph's Hospital in Milford. The EMTs didn't think he needed more than a bandage and a tetanus shot.

Eugenia had been devastated when Captain Baker slapped a pair of handcuffs on her. She cried, begging to accompany her father to the hospital, but ended up in the back of the same patrol car as Brian, on her way to the county lockup. Someone needed to call Libby and explain what had happened. Tricia didn't envy whoever ended up with that job.

Apparently Brian had learned from the mysteries Ginny had been reading that the best thing he could do was to keep his mouth shut until he could talk to a lawyer. "You're not paying for one with *my* money," Ginny declared.

Captain Baker had been all business as he rounded up the suspects, although he'd tried hard—and succeeded—not to make eye contact with Tricia.

Oh, well.

Once the cops and the rubberneckers had departed, Tricia, Angelica, and Ginny settled in the readers' nook. Tricia had scrounged a bottle of Irish whiskey, which they'd been adding to their coffee. Since it was a girls-only gathering, Miss Marple had deigned to join them, and had settled on a pile of old *Mystery Scene* magazines on the big square coffee table.

"There are no good men left on the face of the planet," Ginny complained, and swallowed another big gulp from her cup.

"Sure there are," Tricia said.

"Name one."

"Mr. Everett."

"Yeah, and he's already taken. Plus he's old enough to be *your* grandfather."

"Nevertheless, I haven't given up hope."

"Don't forget Bob," Angelica said with a wistful sigh. "He's a real gem."

If she only knew, Tricia thought.

"How can you be so optimistic?" Ginny said, squinting at Tricia. "Russ just dumped you—what a jerk!"

"Oh, Russ was just a rebound boy after Tricia's divorce," Angelica explained. "A nice little diversion, but I'll bet now she's ready for something a bit more exciting."

"We won't go into all that."

"No need to," Angelica piped up. "That was some smooch you gave Captain Baker. See, I told you you were sweet on him."

"It was a stupid, impulsive thing to do," Tricia said, embarrassed. "I was just grateful he arrived when he did. I really wasn't sure Brian would believe my bluff."

"Uh-huh," Angelica said knowingly.

"You should've shot him," Ginny growled. "Did you see the way Eugenia carried on when they hauled them both away?" She frowned. "On second thought, you should've shot her, too."

"You know that's the whiskey talking—not the way you really feel," Tricia said.

"No, I wish you'd shot him." Ginny thought about it. "Okay, maybe not to *kill*, but you should've shot him anyway." She paused. "In the butt. Twice—once in each cheek."

"I'm just glad we're all safe," Angelica said. "But there are things that need to be settled."

Yes, several big things. Like the mess that was now Ginny's life.

"That poor Libby Hirt," Angelica said with a sigh. "Her husband shot. Her daughter arrested and in love with a murderer . . ."

Ginny leaned forward and poured more whiskey into her cup. "Nah, Brian will probably only go to jail for manslaughter. The bastard!"

Tricia leaned forward and capped the bottle. "Sorry, ladies, but we've got a wedding to put on tomorrow, and this place needs a thorough cleaning."

Angelica stood. "And I've still got food to make."

None of them moved.

"I don't know if I can go to the wedding," Ginny said, her voice breaking.

"Oh, yes, you can," Tricia said.

"But my heart is broken."

"And what better way to reaffirm that you will find someone worthy of your love one day, than to attend the wedding of two people who truly love each other? They may not have much time left in their lives, but tomorrow they're going to commit to be together—for better or for worse, 'til death do them part."

Ginny sniffed. "Does it make me a terrible person because I didn't follow Brian to the jail? He betrayed me," she reminded them.

"Honey, I've been betrayed four times, and I sure haven't given up looking for someone," Angelica said.

"Does that mean you'd like to marry Bob?" Tricia asked, taken aback.

"Hell, no." Angelica thought about it for a moment. "Well, maybe. But not anytime soon. I've rushed into too many relationships. This is *my* time in life. That's why I took over the Cookery, and why I opened the café." She nodded sagely. "I've learned from my past mistakes. You ought to think about what you'd really like to do, Ginny. This could be your golden opportunity to do exactly what you want to do—maybe for the first time in your life."

Ginny blinked a few times. "I'd like to own my own business—just like you and Tricia," she blurted.

It was Tricia's turn to blink. "You would?"

Ginny nodded. "I've seen what you've done here. I know just about every aspect of the business. I could do the same thing—I know I could. I just don't have the money to get one started."

"You might if you sold your house," Angelica said.

"I'd never be able to afford the rents here in Stoneham."

Angelica's gaze rose to the ceiling. "You might if the landlord's girlfriend could persuade him to give you a break."

Ginny blinked in disbelief. "You'd do that for me?"

"Why not? Tricia says you're the best assistant in the village. Why shouldn't you try to be the best bookseller—or toy seller—or whatever you want to be?"

"That's all very good, but then *I'd* have to break in someone new," Tricia complained.

"I'm not saying any of this would happen tomorrow," Angelica muttered. "But Ginny needs a goal—one that doesn't include matrimony. What do you say, Ginny?"

For the first time in hours, a smile brightened Ginny's tear-swollen face. "I'd like that."

"And we'll help you, won't we, Trish?"

"We sure will."

"My own business," Ginny said, warming to the idea. "I like that thought. A lot."

Angelica held out her hand. "Then it's all for one."

Tricia put hers on top. "And all—"

Ginny did likewise. "For one—me!"

Their combined hands bounced once—twice—three times before springing high into the air.

TWENTY-THREE

 The bridal bouquet of white calla lilies and baby's breath looked lovely against Grace's soft pink linen suit, and the maid of honor's bouquet was made of lavender chrysanthemums, which complimented her mauve, raw silk dress. Tricia also held a wadded tissue to wipe away the tears that filled her eyes. Weddings always made her cry.

Dressed in a dark suit, crisp white shirt, and navy tie, Mr. Everett wore a solemn expression as he slipped the simple gold band onto Grace's waiting finger. "With this ring, I do thee wed."

Judge Milton smiled. "I now pronounce you husband and wife." To Mr. Everett, he said, "You may kiss your bride."

A resounding round of applause broke out among the guests as Mr. Everett landed a gentle kiss on Grace's lips—and promptly turned an attractive shade of pink.

Haven't Got a Clue had never looked as lovely. White chrysanthemums and pale pink roses decorated the counters. Ginny had arrived early that morning with a bit of a hangover and many rolls of white crepe paper, which she'd artistically draped along the bookshelves. Angelica had set up a long, linen-draped table against the wall of nonfiction titles, and lavished it with hot and cold breakfast foods. Pale pink rosettes spiraled up Nikki Brimfield's gorgeous three-tiered cake, which had taken up residence at the store's coffee station. They'd chosen their initials, G and W, in brushed silver, for their cake topper.

Half an hour before the ceremony, Russ arrived with his camera to take posed and candid shots of the bride and groom and the cake. He kept looking at Ginny, who kept her distance, and Tricia warned him that he was not to talk to her about Pammy's death, or what had occurred at the store the evening before. He frowned and instead took Tricia's picture. And he kept making excuses to be near her—asking about the food, the decorations, and any other inane thing he could think of. Tricia was civil, but soon found other places to be.

Although appointed the honorary ring bearer, Miss Marple declined to participate in the ceremony, instead watching it from her perch on the shelf behind the register, purring all the while.

While Russ snapped pictures, Tricia stepped away from the happy couple, who were receiving best wishes from their guests. Everyone from the Tuesday Night Book Club was there, including Frannie, who kept showing anyone she could corner pictures of her new cat—just like any proud parent. Nikki Brimfield looked out of place in a skirt and blouse, instead of her white baker's uniform, and Julia Overland had worn the same color as Tricia. Great minds did indeed think alike. As best man, Bob had for once for-gone his Kelly green sports coat and donned a dark suit. He looked . . . weird . . . out of his usual uniform.

Tricia traded good wishes with her lawyer, Roger Liv-ingston, and Lois Kerr from the library. Though the cer-emony was over, Stuart Paige remained seated in one of the rented chairs, looking pale, but smiling, while his flunky, Turner, stood nearby, wearing sunglasses and still trying to look like a Secret Service agent.

Angelica flitted around the room with a silver tray filled with mini quiches, offering them to one and all.

Among the missing, of course, were Libby and Joe Hirt, and Brian Comstock. No surprises there.

Distracted by the crowd, Tricia was caught off guard when Russ insinuated himself next to her once again. "I've been trying to get you on your own for the past hour. Are you avoiding me?"

"You made your feelings toward me quite clear. And after what happened at the inn on Friday, I don't think we have anything to say to one another."

"I left several messages for you to call me before then. You ignored them."

"Yes, I did."

He frowned. "Okay, I admit I made a mistake in calling off—us."

Tricia turned a level glare at him. "I take it you've had a change of plans?"

Russ frowned. "Okay, so the job in Philadelphia fell through. And I've decided not to put the paper up for sale. It looks like I won't be leaving Stoneham after all." He gave a weak laugh. "I know it's asking a lot, but I was hoping we could . . . still be friends."

Tricia said nothing.

"Actually, more than friends. Is there a chance things could go back to the way they were before I opened my big, stupid mouth?"

Tricia still said nothing.

"I'd like to think we could try."

"You *are* asking a lot."

The shop door opened, the little bell overhead ringing cheerfully. A stranger entered and paused. "I'm sorry. I thought the store was open today," he said.

Tricia strode over to the door—anything to get away from Russ. "We're opening late. As you can see, we're hosting a wedding."

Tricia did a double take. The man in front of her was Grant Baker. She hadn't recognized him out of uniform. He looked . . . nice.

He also looked uncomfortable. "I don't want to intrude," he said, already backing away.

"Don't be silly. Come on in; have some coffee and a piece of wedding cake."

He shook his head. "I only came to . . . to get a book."

"I thought you didn't read mysteries or true crime."

"Maybe I decided to broaden my horizons." He let the door close on his back and stepped closer to Tricia, lowering his voice. "Or . . . maybe I came just to see you. To see if you were free for dinner tonight."

Tricia looked to her right and left. Was he actually speaking to her?

"Um . . ." At the edge of her peripheral vision, she saw Russ nearby, eavesdropping. Tricia smiled. "I think that would be very nice."

"And I also wanted to tell you what you did for Pam Fredericks was decent and noble. Especially since you were only . . . sort of . . . friends."

Tricia's spine stiffened. She hadn't mentioned this to anyone. How had he found out? "I don't know what you mean," she bluffed.

"Claiming her body, paying to have it buried. Apparently she wasn't a very good friend to you, but you proved more than once you were probably the only true friend she ever had."

Tricia grabbed his elbow, and pulled him away from the other guests. "How did you find out?" she hissed.

"You dealt with Baker Funeral Home, right? My cousin Glenn owns it."

The breath caught in Tricia's throat. "I assumed Mr. Baker would've been more discreet."

"Don't worry; he didn't say a word. Our office was notified by the Medical Examiner when the body was released."

Okay, she could believe that.

Angelica made a pass with her tray. "Hi, Captain Baker. Try one of these delicious spinach mini quiches."

"Captain Baker?" Bob repeated, worry tingeing his voice—no doubt remembering Tricia's threat to turn him in to the law. He stepped away—fast.

"Don't mind if I do," Baker said, taking an offered napkin and two of the quiches. He bit into one, chewed, and swallowed. "Hey, these are terrific."

"Tricia helped make them," Angelica said, beaming, then moved on to another guest.

"And you can cook, too," he said, impressed.

Tricia shook her head and sighed. "My helping consisted of squeezing the water out of cold, wet spinach until it was dry. I'm not bragging when I tell you that I can barely boil water."

Baker laughed, but his expression soon became serious

again. He nodded toward Stuart Paige. "How did he get invited to this little shindig?"

"Mr. Paige and Grace—she's the bride—have been friends for years."

Baker nodded. "I understand you showed him a page from the diary."

Tricia felt a squirm crawl along her spine. "Yes. I wanted to verify my suspicions on its author."

"What have you done with the rest of your copy of the diary?"

"Copy?" she asked, in all innocence.

"Yes, all ninety-seven pages."

She sighed. "Nothing, yet. I thought I might offer it to Eugenia Hirt. It's not a very flattering portrayal of her birth mother—but it might give her an even greater appreciation for her adoptive mother. But I'll wait a while before I mention it to her. She's had enough upsets for now."

"It'll give her something to read while she awaits her trial." Baker wiped his fingers on his napkin. "I've had a chance to go through all those letters we found in the shoebox in Pam Fredericks's car. She was related to M. J. Collins, all right. The woman was Pam's aunt—her mother's sister."

Tricia sighed. "That made Eugenia and Pammy first cousins. Imagine that—she tried to blackmail her own cousin."

A burst of laughter came from the crowd around the buffet table, reminding Tricia that this was supposed to be a happy occasion. "Do we have to talk about Pammy anymore?"

"I still want to know why you did what you did—taking care of her in death," Baker pressed.

Tricia gave another long sigh. "Because . . ."

She didn't need to say anything. Officially, he needed no explanation.

Still . . .

She looked into his mesmerizing green eyes. "It was the right thing to do."

The hint of a smile touched his lips. "Yes, it was."

"Did you ever get that letter addressed to her at General Delivery?"

He nodded. "It was from her brother. It said, in no uncertain terms, that she was not to contact him or any other member of the family again. Apparently she'd taken not only the diary and the letters we found in the trunk of her car, but she'd cleaned out her mother's jewelry box and taken other valuables the last time she'd visited."

"Oh, my. Poor Pammy."

"I'd say poor Pammy's family."

The sound of a champagne cork popping was a welcome distraction. Bob Kelly held the bottle of fizz aloft. "Time for the toast!"

Angelica worked the room, tray in hand, offering glasses that were already filled. She paused in front of Tricia and Baker, gave her sister a knowing wink, and then moved off to serve the rest of the guests.

Bob filled flutes for Mr. Everett and Grace before clearing his throat. He held his glass before him. "Friends, I'm sure everyone here will join me in wishing William and Grace a long and joy-filled life together. May they always be as happy as they are at this moment."

"Hear, hear," came the chant as everyone raised his or her glass in salute.

When everyone had taken a sip, Mr. Everett offered his glass. "To my beautiful bride."

Again, those assembled raised their glasses and cheered.

Mr. Everett raised his glass once again. "And now, I'd like to say thank you to the person who made this all possible. To my employer and my friend, Ms. Tricia Miles. Thank you, Ms. Miles. You've not only made an old man feel useful again, but if it weren't for you, Grace and I would never have"—he paused, and seemed unsure of his next words—"hooked up."

Everyone laughed and then cheered.

Grant Baker turned to Tricia and lifted his glass. "Here's hoping we can"—he paused, and did *not* say "hook up"— "start out by being friends, and see where that leads."

Tricia raised her glass. "I'll drink to that." Out the corner of her eye, she saw Russ frown, but then he raised his glass, never breaking eye contact. "To us," he mouthed.

Tricia sipped her champagne and smiled. The next few days, maybe weeks, maybe months—might be very interesting indeed.

She drank to that.

ANGELICA'S RECIPES

BOB'S FAVORITE MEATLOAF

1½ pounds lean ground beef
⅔ cup seasoned breadcrumbs
1 egg, beaten
1 large onion, chopped
¼ teaspoon salt
¼ teaspoon ground pepper
¾ cup ketchup
1 tablespoon Worcestershire sauce

Combine breadcrumbs, egg, onion, salt, and pepper; mix well. Add to ground beef and mix well. Shape mixture into a loaf in a loaf pan. Mix ketchup with Worcestershire sauce and pour over the top.

Bake at 350° for 70–80 minutes (or until meat thermometer reads 160°).

Serves 4–6.

Garlic Mashed Potatoes

6 medium potatoes, peeled and quartered
4–6 garlic cloves
5–6 cups water
2 tablespoons olive oil (or softened butter)
½ teaspoon salt
Pinch of pepper

Place potatoes and garlic in a large saucepan and cover with water. Bring to a boil. Reduce heat; cover and cook for 15–20 minutes or until tender.

Drain, reserving ½ cup cooking liquid. Mash potato mixture. Add oil (or butter), salt, pepper, and reserved liquid; stir until smooth.

Serves 4–6.

Quick-and-Dirty Garlic Bread

1 baguette or small (8 ounces) loaf of French bread
¼ cup butter, softened
¼ cup Parmesan cheese
½ teaspoon garlic powder (or 2 minced garlic
  cloves)
2 tablespoons dried parsley (but fresh is always
  better)

Preheat oven to 400°.

In a small mixing bowl, combine butter with Parmesan cheese. Add other ingredients and mix well. Cut the baguette into half-inch slices—but do not cut all the way through. Spread mixture on both sides of each slice. Wrap in aluminum foil and bake for 15–20 minutes. (If you like it crispy, open the foil the last 5 minutes.) Serve hot.

Serves 4–6.

POTATO-AND-LEEK SOUP

2 tablespoons butter
2 cloves diced garlic
2 good-sized potatoes (or about 1 pound)
2 good-sized leeks (or about 1 pound)
4 cups chicken broth
¼ teaspoon salt
¼ teaspoon black pepper
1 cup milk or light cream

Clean and chop white part of the leeks. Melt the butter in a large saucepan and add the chopped leeks and garlic. Saute them over low to medium heat until the leeks are soft (about 10 minutes). Stir frequently; do not brown.

Add all the remaining ingredients to the pan except the milk/

cream. Bring the soup to a boil and then let it simmer for 15–20 minutes.

If you prefer a smooth soup, mash the potatoes in the pan, or puree them in a blender. Just before serving, pour the milk/cream into the soup; stir well, and heat through.

Serves 4.

Mini Spinach Quiches

½ cup butter or margarine, softened
1 package (3 ounces) cream cheese, softened
1 cup all-purpose flour
3 slices bacon
¼ cup chopped green onion
2 eggs
½ cup half-and-half
½ cup grated Parmesan cheese
¼ teaspoon salt
⅛ teaspoon ground nutmeg
1 (10-ounce) package frozen spinach, thawed and
    well drained (use your hands to squeeze out the
    water)

In a small mixing bowl, cream butter and cream cheese. Add flour; beat until well blended. Shape into 24 balls. Press balls into the bottom and the sides of greased mini muffin cups.

Preheat oven to 350°. In a skillet, cook the bacon until brown and very crisp; drain. Saute the onions in the same skillet with the bacon drippings for 5 minutes, or until tender, stirring constantly; drain. Place the onions in a medium bowl. Crumble the bacon into small pieces, and add to the onions. Add the eggs to the bacon and onions; beat well. Stir in the half-and-half, salt, nutmeg, and Parmesan cheese. Add the spinach; mix well to combine. Divide the mixture among crust-lined cups (do not overfill).

Bake for 25–30 minutes, or until puffed and golden brown. Cool in pan on wire rack for 5 minutes. Serve warm or cool. Store leftovers in the refrigerator.

Makes 24.

Turn the page for a preview of
the next book in the Booktown Mysteries
by Lorna Barrett . . .

CHAPTER AND HEARSE

Coming soon from Berkley Prime Crime!

The poster on the Cookery's display window had advertised the book signing for at least a month. Throngs of people were supposed to be in evidence. A temporary cook station had been assembled, with ramekins filled with diced vegetables, chopped chicken, and spices all lined up like props in a stage play.

Tricia Miles forced a smile and tried not to glance at her watch. "Everything looks perfect," she said with a cheer in her voice she didn't quite feel.

The "guest" author, her sister, Angelica, stood behind the cook station, head held high, although her eyes were watery and her mouth trembled ever so slightly. "Nobody's going to come. Not one person."

"I'm here," said Ginny Wilson, Tricia's assistant at her mystery bookstore, Haven't Got a Clue.

"And I," said elderly Mr. Everett, Tricia's other, part-time, employee.

"Don't forget me," Frannie May Armstrong said in her ever-present Texas twang. Angelica owned the Cookery, Stoneham's cookbook store, although Frannie managed it for her. Angelica also owned Booked for Lunch, a retro cafe across the street. Writing cookbooks was just another entry on her colorful résumé.

Unfortunately, the village of Stoneham, known locally as "Booktown," was more a tourist destination not far from the New Hampshire/Massachusetts state line. Not many of the locals supported the booksellers, who'd been recruited to save what had been a dying village. Shops filled with used, rare, and antiquarian books had done it, too, as evidenced by new prosperity and a much-needed influx of tax revenue.

"Wasn't a busload of gourmands supposed to arrive for the signing?" Mr. Everett whispered to Frannie.

"I got the call about an hour ago. They cancelled, but asked for a rain check. They may return some time next fall."

Tricia refrained from commenting. Thanks to the Internet, Angelica had cultivated a relationship with the "Gamboling Gourmets," who traveled New England throughout the summer, tasting the local cuisines. Tonight's signing was to be their first outing of the year, and Angelica's launch party. She'd spent days preparing a table full of desserts—all entries from her newly published book, *Easy-Does-It Cooking*, which had been officially available all of three days.

Tricia had expected at least a few more warm bodies to attend the signing. Mr. Everett's bride of eight months had come down with a cold, which explained her absence, but surely the employees at Angelica's café—Jake the cook and Darcy the waitress—might have made an effort to be there. And someone else was conspicuous by his absence.

"Anybody know where Bob is?" Frannie asked.

Bob Kelly, owner of Kelly Realty, and the president of the local Chamber of Commerce, had been Angelica's significant other for the past eighteen months—ever since she'd come to live in Stoneham.

"I'm sure he'll have a perfectly reasonable explanation for being late," Tricia lied. She and Bob weren't exactly best friends, but she tried to overlook his many shortcomings for her sister's sake.

"I saw his car parked down the street, near History Repeats Itself," Ginny volunteered. "It's been there a while."

Angelica pouted. "He said he'd be here."

"There's still time," Tricia reassured her.

Angelica nodded, resigned. "Business hasn't been good lately, and he's been preoccupied. It probably just slipped his mind."

"I'm sure you're right," Tricia said, and hoped her nose hadn't just grown an inch.

Frannie straightened the stack of unsigned books on the side table, and everyone tried not to make eye contact with Angelica as they waited in awkward silence for someone—anyone—else to arrive. Finally, Ginny suggested Angelica go ahead with her cooking demonstration.

"What's the point?" Angelica asked, defeat coloring her voice.

"Well, it's almost seven thirty, and none of us has had dinner. I can't be the only one eager to try your Hacienda Tacos."

"Good old Tex-Mex—the best food on Earth," Frannie piped up and sighed. "Next to a luau, that is." It was Frannie's dream to someday retire to the fiftieth state.

Angelica gave a careless shrug and turned on the electric skillet.

Across the street, the newly installed gas lamps glowed. The Board of Selectmen had approved the installation of the old-fashioned streetlights in an effort to capitalize on the town's history and its new lease on life. Tourists ate up that kind of stuff, and the Board of Selectmen was eager to do all it could to encourage their visits. Unfortunately, when the bookstores closed, the visitors disappeared, leaving no one to appreciate them.

Within minutes, Angelica had prepared the filling, spooned it into corn tortillas, and passed them out to her small—and hungry—audience. The desserts were then sampled, and everyone sipped complementary coffee, not making a dent in the contents of the five-gallon urn borrowed from Angelica's café.

As Angelica served Mr. Everett another portion of chocolate torte, Tricia gave Ginny a nudge. "Buy a book," she whispered.

Ginny's eyes nearly popped. "They're thirty-four dollars," she hissed. "I can't afford it."

"Use your charge card and I'll credit your account tomorrow morning. I want Ange to make at least a couple of sales tonight."

Ginny shrugged. "If you insist." She set down her cup, grabbed a copy of the coffee table–sized book filled with glossy photos, and marched up to the cash desk where Angelica stood, wringing her hands. "I don't know about the rest of you, but I'm eager to be the first to get my signed copy of *Easy-Does-It Cooking*."

Mr. Everett's nervous gaze shifted to Tricia. She mouthed the words, *Buy one—I'll pay you back*.

"Uh, uh—let me be the second," Mr. Everett said.

Luckily, Angelica hadn't noticed the exchange. She pressed a clenched hand to her lips, fighting back tears.

"You guys are just the best. Frannie, grab the camera, will you?" Angelica said. Next, she played director, carefully positioning Ginny with her back to the camera, and posed. She shook Ginny's hand. She raised a finger to make a point. She looked surprised—then serious, and, ultimately, very silly. At last, Angelica reached for her pen, wrote a few words on the flyleaf of Ginny's copy, and signed her name with such a flourish that it was completely illegible. Frannie kept snapping pictures as Angelica handed the book to Ginny.

Ginny frowned. "Live free or diet?" Was Angelica mocking the state motto?

"Yes, don't you think that's clever?" Angelica said. "I'm going to sign that in all the books."

Though Ginny forced a smile, her voice was flat. "Go for it."

As Mr. Everett stepped up to have his book signed, Tricia moved to look out the large display window that overlooked Main Street. As Ginny had said, Bob's car was parked near History Repeats Itself. Tricia's anger smoldered. How inconsiderate of Bob to ignore Angelica's very first signing. He had to know how much it meant to her.

Tricia glanced back at her sister and Mr. Everett, still posing for Frannie. In a fit of pique, Tricia decided it was time for action. She'd go find Bob and, if necessary, drag him back to the Cookery by his thinning hair.

Tricia took a Zen moment to calm herself before she spoke. "I think I'll run out and see if I can find Bob," she told Angelica. "If his car is parked down the road, he can't be very far away."

"I suppose," Angelica said. "But please hurry back to help us pack up some of these desserts." She shook her head, taking in the amount of leftover food. "I can't serve all this at the café. Would you like to take some home, Ginny?"

"Would I? Hand me the Cling Wrap, will you?"

"Be right back," Tricia called and headed out the door.

The village was practically deserted, and Bob's car was the only vehicle parked on the west side of Main Street. Tricia crossed the street and started down the sidewalk. Upon consideration, she decided she wouldn't berate Bob, at least not in front of Jim Roth, owner of History Repeats Itself. It wouldn't do to go ballistic in front of an audience. Instead, her plan was to poke her head inside the door and cheerfully ask if Bob hadn't forgotten another engagement—and probably do it through gritted teeth.

The glowing gas lamps really did lend a quaint, old-fashioned charm to the already picturesque storefronts. While an expensive indulgence, they added to the village's ambiance—especially outside of Haven't Got a Clue. It went right along with the ambiance she'd created, emulating 221B Baker Street in London.

Tricia was within two doors of History Repeats Itself when she paused to look inside Booked for Lunch. Angelica had done a wonderful job decorating the café. Heck, she'd done a terrific job managing two businesses, *and* starting a writing career. Not that Tricia had ever mentioned to Angelica how proud she was of Angelica's accomplishments. As it was, her swelled head could barely fit through a standard door.

Tricia took a step forward when she heard a *phoomph*. The Earth shook as a shower of glass exploded onto the street, and a rush of hot air enveloped her, the shock of it knocking her to the ground.

Then everything went black.

MURDER IS BINDING

FROM NATIONAL BESTSELLING AUTHOR

Lorna Barrett

The streets of Stoneham, New Hampshire, are lined with bookstores... and paved with murder.

When she moved to Stoneham, city slicker Tricia Miles was met with nothing but friendly faces. And when she opened her mystery bookstore, she was met with friendly competition. But when she finds Doris Gleason dead in her own cookbook store, killed with a kitchen knife, the atmosphere seems more cutthroat than cordial. Someone wanted to get their hands on the rare cookbook that Doris had recently purchased—and the locals think that someone is Tricia. To clear her name, Tricia will have to take a page out of one of her own mysteries—and hunt down someone who isn't killing by the book.

penguin.com

ALSO FROM NATIONAL BESTSELLING AUTHOR

Lorna Barrett

Bookmarked for Death

To celebrate her bookstore's anniversary, Tricia Miles hosts a book signing for bestselling author Zoë Carter. But the event takes a terrible turn when the author is found dead in the washroom. Before long, both police and reporters are demanding the real story. So far, the author's assistant/niece is the only suspect. And with a sheriff who provides more obstacles than answers, Tricia will have to take matters into her own hands—and read between the lines to solve this mystery . . .

penguin.com